Her gaze drifted to his mouth as he spoke, fascinated by the way the scar pulled slightly at the corner. She felt a strong urge to kiss that corner, to run her tongue along the seam and dip between his lips, along his teeth.

He turned away, and she blinked herself back to reality. She couldn't believe the thoughts that kept popping into her head when she looked at him.

And she was going to be stuck on a ship with him for almost a month.

Dressed like a boy.

Wonderful.

He set off, and she rushed after him, thankful he couldn't see the blush heating her cheeks. It was going to be a long month.

She caught up, practically jogging to keep pace with his long strides.

He looked her briefly up and down in an assessing manner that strained Alex's nerves. "You don't look like much of a sailor, and you're too young to have any skill as a carpenter."

She was surprised he hadn't already uncovered her disguise. Her instincts warned her he wouldn't be easy to fool, and she would be smart to keep her distance, even if distance was the last thing she wanted right now. Of course, it wouldn't be a problem if he decided she wasn't qualified to work on his ship.

"You're wondering what possessed him to hire me. Perhaps he took pity on me, or maybe I'm better qualified than I look," she replied haughtily, and immediately wished she could take the last part back. Now he might think she had some sailing skill.

Praise for *TIME FOR LOVE*

Winner, First Place, paranormal category
Indiana Golden Opportunity contest, 2011
~*~
Winner, Fourth Place, paranormal category
NJRW Put Your Heart in a Book contest, 2010

Time for Love

by

Emma Kaye

Time for Love

Cover Art by *Debbie Taylor*

The Wild Rose Press, Inc.
PO Box 708
Adams Basin, NY 14410-0708
Visit us at www.thewildrosepress.com

Publishing History
First English Tea Rose Edition, 2013
Print ISBN 978-1-62830-072-7
Digital ISBN 978-1-62830-073-4

Published in the United States of America

Dedication

To my husband,
who believed I could write a book before I did.
I love you.

~

To my family and friends,
whose encouragement and love
mean more than I can say.

~

To my critique partners
Ruth A. Casie, Lita Harris, and Nicole S. Patrick
whose support keeps me going.

~

And to Allison Byers
and everyone at The Wild Rose Press,
whose hard work is greatly appreciated.

Chapter One

Current Year, March 28

"Your butt's vibrating."

Alexandra Turner slapped a hand to her back pocket and felt the vibrations of her cell phone against her palm. She gaped at Cindy, the other bartender working that night, as she pulled it from her pocket. The ringtone was barely audible. "How the hell did you hear that?"

Cindy just laughed and turned away to serve a pitcher of beer to a college kid waving a twenty at her.

Alex looked down at the unfamiliar number on her display screen. Should she bother? She shrugged. It would only take a few seconds to find out. She could use a break anyway.

She signaled to Cindy she'd be right back and ducked under the bar, headed toward the stock room. She flipped the phone open on the way.

"Hello?"

The bar's music was too loud to hear a response.

"Hold on a sec, I have to get somewhere I can hear."

She pushed open the stock room door and flipped the light switch, illuminating the tightly packed room. She grimaced at the sight of the jumbled mess on the shelves. Straightening it at the end of the night would take forever.

She shoved the door shut with her elbow and leaned against a stack of crates. The relative quiet made up for the unsightly mess.

"Okay, this is better. You still there?"

"May I speak with Alexandra Turner?"

Alex could just make out the English-accented female voice over the static on the line. "Yeah, this is Alex. It's a bit hard to hear you. We've got a bad connection."

"Oh, God. I can't believe it's you! I've been trying to reach you at home, but you never seem to be there, and I just didn't feel a message was appropriate."

Alex straightened, scraping her arm on a crate in the process. *Shit.* "Who's this?"

"My name's Charlotte Evans."

A thrill jumped up Alex's spine. *Charlotte? Could it be?*

"A friend of mine happened upon your web page. She recognized me, or rather you, in the pictures. I believe I'm your twin."

Alex slumped to the floor and landed hard on her butt. Her legs wouldn't hold her up. She held the phone to her ear in a death grip. She couldn't believe this was finally happening.

"Alexandra? Are you there?"

The manic edge to Charlotte's voice broke through the haze in Alex's mind. "I'm here. I just can't believe it's you. I've been looking for you for years. I knew you were still alive. I knew it! They told me you were dead, but I didn't believe them."

Charlotte's voice faded in and out. "I...dead too."

"Charlotte! You're fading out. I can't hear you."

Alex clutched the phone desperately. She couldn't lose this call.

"…meeting with…Sawyer…Griffin… Something about…eighteen eight…call…about nine in…morning your time."

"My time? Where are you?"

"London. I'm afraid…cut out any second. …talk tomorrow and figure out details so I can come—"

A burst of static and then silence. Alex looked at the display and cursed. She'd lost her.

****

Alex paced around her small living room. She flipped her cell open to make sure it was working. Still fully charged. Ringer on max. Only two minutes since she last checked.

She picked up her uneaten lunch and brought it to her galley kitchen to wrap in plastic for later. The smell of tuna fish made her stomach growl, but she'd never get the sandwich past the lump in her throat.

"Meow!" Maximus wound around her legs, mewling his anxiety that she might actually put the tuna away without giving him his share.

She grabbed a spoon and plopped a large dollop into her cat's dish. He gulped down the treat before the dirty spoon hit the sink.

"There ya go. Happy now?" Her smile at the cat's antics quickly faded as her thoughts returned to her worry over her sister.

Why didn't Charlotte call? Or at least answer? Alex had tried the number recorded in her cell's memory at least twenty times in the past hour. She looked at the tiny battery symbol on her display. Maybe Charlotte hadn't charged her phone. That could explain

3

it.

She picked up her landline to keep her cell free and dialed 4-1-1.

"City and listing, please."

"London, England. Charlotte Evans," Alex said.

"One moment, please."

She jotted down the number then let the auto dial place her call.

A man's strained voice answered, "Hello?"

"Hi. Is Charlotte Evans at home?" Alex's voice trembled slightly as she spoke.

A tired sigh escaped through the telephone. "No, I'm sorry, she's not here. May I ask who's calling?"

"Oh. Well, do you know when she'll be back?"

"No." The strain seemed even more pronounced. "Who did you say this is?"

"My name's Alex Turner." She took a deep breath to steel her nerves and said, "Charlotte's sister."

"What! That's impossible. I'm Charlotte's brother, Steven. We don't have a sister."

"I know it sounds crazy, but I am her sister. Charlotte called me last night."

"Wait. Did you say Alex? As in, Alexandra?"

"Yes."

"Oh, my God. Charlotte told us you died shortly before she was adopted. She never said anything about searching for you."

"She wasn't. I was. I've been searching for her for years using the web, mostly. I have a few websites, and I'm all over the social networks. I tried a private eye, but I couldn't really afford him, and he never got anywhere. Charlotte said someone found one of my web pages." Alex twisted the phone cord around her hand. "So, will she be home soon?"

He hesitated a moment. "I wish I knew. I haven't spoken to her in over a week. We were supposed to meet for dinner last night, but she never showed. It's not like her, and I'm worried. I came to her flat to see if I could find something that might give me an idea where she is."

"She was supposed to call me this morning. We were going to arrange for her to visit."

"She wouldn't miss something like that. Something's definitely wrong. I'm going to contact the authorities. Give me your number, and I'll call if I have any new information. Here's mine."

Alex copied down the numbers he rattled off and gave him her contact info. They promised to call each other and hung up.

As she paced around her living room, her mind raced. What should she do now?

Had Charlotte been in trouble even as they'd spoken last night? Had she tried to give Alex some clue something was wrong?

She hadn't seemed upset, just excited. Then again, Alex didn't know how Charlotte normally sounded, and their connection had been so poor. She could have been completely freaked, and Alex never would have known.

No. She'd seemed fine when they spoke. Alex couldn't afford to second-guess herself.

So what happened between then and now?

Alex snapped her fingers and grabbed her phone once more. It was a long shot, but she quickly dialed 4-1-1 before she could talk herself out of it. "London, England. A listing for Griffin?" she asked when prompted.

Each ring grated along her nerves like nails on a chalkboard. She breathed a sigh of relief when a perky, English voice answered, "Griffin International. How may I direct your call?"

Shit. How to explain? "Um—My sister was supposed to have a meeting with someone there. I wanted to see if maybe she was still there?"

"Who was she meeting?"

"I don't know. I can't remember the name she gave me."

A short silence, then… "All right. Your sister's name?"

"Charlotte Evans."

"Oh," the receptionist's voice squeaked. "Yes. Charlotte Evans. Please hold."

Alex grimaced when an annoying musak version of some barely recognizable pop hit assaulted her ears. At least she didn't have to wait long.

"This is Mr. Sawyer. To whom am I speaking?"

Sawyer! That was it. "Alex Turner. You met with Charlotte Evans yesterday?"

"You told the receptionist you're Miss Evans's sister?" His voiced sounded skeptical, setting Alex's back up.

"Yeah, that's right." She'd spent too many years searching for a sister everyone insisted was dead to let anyone doubt she'd spoken to Charlotte.

"Where did you say you're calling from?"

"New Jersey, why?" *Shit, why'd she tell him where she was?*

Voices mumbled in the background, and there was a crackling noise as if he'd covered the phone's mouthpiece.

"We have an office in Philadelphia. I'm going to catch the red-eye. Would you be able to meet with me tomorrow afternoon?"

"What!" Alarm bells rang in her head. "What's going on? Something's happened to Charlotte, hasn't it? You wouldn't fly out here if she were fine." Alex's heart raced, and she fought to control her breathing. *Remain calm. Find out what's going on and panic later.* "Tell me now. Is she dead? Have you told her brother?" She perched on the edge of her couch and tried to prepare for the worst.

"Calm down, Miss Turner. Miss Evans is not dead."

The air left her lungs in a whoosh, and she sank back. A broken spring poked her back, but she ignored it. She closed her eyes and lay limp against the cushions. "Thank God."

"However, she is in trouble, and we think you can be of assistance. You must not discuss this with anyone, or you could put her at risk. Meet me at this address tomorrow..." He gave an address and waited while she wrote it down. "...four o'clock."

The line went dead.

****

Four o'clock the next afternoon, Alex sat in the waiting room of Griffin International's Philadelphia office fiddling with the visitor badge clipped to her favorite sweater. A grainy upside-down image of her face grimaced up at her.

Could she have taken a worse picture? It looked like she was being tortured rather than entering one of the most expensive offices she'd ever seen.

She wiggled back into the depths of the black

7

leather chair only to scoot forward again almost immediately. She couldn't get comfortable. *What's taking so long?*

She looked at the time on her cell phone—four-fifteen. Maybe he didn't realize she was waiting?

The receptionist hadn't stopped fielding calls the entire twenty minutes Alex had sat there staring blindly at the plasma TV on the opposite wall. Cable networks reported the news. Intense, young reporters spoke earnestly into their microphones as they gave their blurbs before the camera showed whatever sensational shot they'd managed to capture that made it appear as if the end of the world was imminent.

Alex couldn't care less. She just wanted to know about her sister.

Enough. She approached the busy receptionist who held up a finger to hold her off and pressed a multitude of buttons before she looked up with a smile. "Yes?"

"How much longer will Mr. Sawyer be? He told me to be here at four. I've been waiting nearly half an hour."

The receptionist's smile remained in place but dimmed somewhat as she turned to her computer and typed at a furious pace. "Mr. Sawyer is a very busy man. He knows you're here. I'm sure he'll be with you in a moment."

"Well, can you inform him again, please." Alex struggled to keep her tone civil.

The phone rang, and the receptionist turned to it, looking grateful for the interruption. "Excuse me, please." She pressed a button, and the ringing stopped. She listened for a moment, then said, "Yes, sir. Right away." She pulled off her headset and stood, motioning for Alex to follow. "Mr. Sawyer will see you now. If you'll just follow me."

She led Alex to an office at the far end of the building. A wall of windows showed off an amazing view of the city. *This Sawyer guy must be pretty high on the food chain to rate that view.*

Alex hid her surprise as a squat, balding man in a crumpled, three-piece suit stood to greet her. She hadn't noticed him sitting behind the tall stack of files in the center of an enormous L-shaped desk that dominated the room.

He was not what she'd pictured. This rumpled mess didn't match the cold, clear voice she'd heard over the phone.

She walked forward to grasp his outstretched hand. His crushing grip seemed more in line with her phone impression, and she pulled her hand quickly out of his grasp, flexing her fingers unobtrusively behind her back as she walked to the chair he indicated for her.

"Miss Turner, thank you for coming." Sawyer made a dismissive gesture, and the door closed behind Alex as the receptionist left them alone.

Alex's nerves twitched at the click of the door. All her nervousness rushed back as the quiet noise reverberated in her skull like the cocking of a gun. She cleared her throat as she took her seat. "So. What's this all about? Where's Charlotte?"

He shoved most of the files to a corner of the desk and sat back. He stared for a moment before speaking. "What did Miss Evans tell you about our meeting?"

"Nothing. We had a bad connection, the call kept fading in and out. I just heard something about a meeting with you, and that she'd call me later."

He nodded, a satisfied expression on his face.

What's he so happy about? "What's going on?"

"Miss Evans is a special client of Griffin International." He picked a file from the top of the pile and tossed it across the desk where it slid to a stop in front of her. A few pages slipped out.

Alex stuffed them back in before she flipped open the folder and sifted through photocopies of old newspaper articles. "Okay." She drew the word out, confusion showing in her voice. "So some kids disappeared about…" She looked at the date. "…two hundred years ago. So?"

Something caught her eye, and she pulled one of the articles closer to read in more detail. "Wait a second. These girls were named Alexandra and Charlotte? Now I'm even more confused."

"You and your sister were apparently named after them. They were identical twins also. That necklace you wear…" He pointed at her chest where Alex's pendant lay over her sweater. "…your sister has a similar one. Hers has an emerald dangling off the heart instead of a ruby. She told us it was a family heirloom that once belonged to the girls in the article."

Alex picked up the heart-shaped pendant in one hand and held it up to her eyes. She fingered the words on the back. *We Love You, M and F.* "I always thought my parents bought it special for me." Her chest ached, and she dropped the necklace down into the neck of her top.

Sawyer shrugged. "Well, apparently it's what got Miss Evans interested in history. She was investigating that history when there was an accident."

Alex dropped the file and slumped back in her

chair. She glared at Sawyer, unable to speak for a full second. "An accident? You said she's okay."

He nodded. "Yes. We believe she is. For the time being. But not for much longer, which is why I rushed here to meet you. We need your help to rescue her before she comes to any harm."

"Is she in a hospital or something? I'm not a doctor. What can I do if she's hurt?"

"We don't know precisely where she is, but we know where she'll be."

Alex shook her head. "You're not making any sense."

He reached across his desk and pulled a paper from the bottom of the folder Alex had dropped. "One of our researchers found this article from the London Gazette. It's vague, but we believe the woman in the article is Charlotte. According to that…" He tapped the page. "…we have only until May twenty-ninth—about two months—to save her."

She crinkled her brow, picked up the page, and forced herself to concentrate on the article. The reporter had a strange style of writing, making it difficult to read. Her horror mounted as she plowed through it. She shook her head in denial. "This can't be her. This is about a woman who was murdered. You just said we could save her. We can't save a dead woman."

"Look at the date of the article."

Her gaze traveled to the upper corner of the page. "Eighteen ei…" her voice trailed off as she stared uncomprehendingly at the year. *Couldn't be.*

"Eighteen hundred eighteen. Almost two hundred years in the past. But two months from today."

A laugh bubbled up, and she crushed the page in

her hand. "You're insane. What the hell is all this about?" She jumped up and shook the crumpled page in front of her. "I came here because I thought you might know something about my sister's disappearance, and you're playing games?"

Her chest rose and fell rapidly as she struggled for control. He was lucky he sat behind a desk. If he were any closer, she'd use that knife-hand strike on him she'd been perfecting in her karate class.

"Calm down, Miss Turner. I'm not playing games. Honest."

Alex sat back down and concentrated on smoothing out the wrinkled paper across her lap. On the off chance he actually knew something real about her sister, she had to see this through. She just hoped she could do it without punching him.

"Thank you." His chair creaked as he leaned back, apparently settling in to explain as he launched into a long winded and increasingly fantastical tale. "About thirty years ago, Griffin International was conducting an experiment when something went horribly wrong."

"What was the experiment?"

"That's neither here nor there. Suffice it to say, things did not go as planned. An explosion destroyed some very valuable equipment and killed several of our employees."

Alex raised her eyebrows. His tone of voice gave her the impression he cared more for the equipment loss than the people who died. Her impression of the man sank lower and lower the longer she was in his presence.

"We sent teams to investigate and discovered these..." He circled his hands in the air before his face.

"…swirling vortexes in place of our equipment. That was amazing enough, but we also found several bodies that didn't belong."

"What do you mean they didn't belong?"

"They weren't the bodies of our people. Not only that, but they were dressed strangely as well. During our investigations, we discovered the vortexes were portals into the past."

"Time portals?" She couldn't help glancing behind her at the door. Five steps and she'd be out of here.

Something kept her in her seat. She couldn't shake the feeling Sawyer was serious. He actually believed the crap spewing out of his mouth. He was crazy all right. But did he know anything about Charlotte? That question kept her from running out the door.

"Yes. I know it's difficult to accept, but Griffin International discovered time travel. It's amazing actually. We've opened up an entirely new division of the company to handle it and have been able to charge an exorbitant fee for its use. We naturally have to be discreet in the clients we approach, yet it's been immensely profitable."

Alex held up a hand to keep him from going on about the benefits to his company. "Assuming this is real and you're not off your rocker, what does all this have to do with Charlotte?"

"Ah, yes." He sighed. "As I mentioned earlier, Miss Evans is one of our clients. She was using a portal outside London to research the ancestors I mentioned earlier. She had just returned from a trip when a cave-in forced her back through the portal and trapped her in the past. We are working as quickly as possible to clear the portal, but it's been slow going and according to this article..." He pointed at the page spread open on Alex's lap. "...we're running out of time."

"How did you find this article? And what makes you think it's about Charlotte?"

"Immediately following the accident, I had a team of our in-house researchers scour the period newspapers for evidence of Miss Evans. They flagged this article based on the location."

"Location?"

"Yes. They discovered the body very near the entrance to the portal." Wrinkles furrowed his brow, and deep frown lines settled into what she assumed were their habitual place along his jaw. "Now, we've been able to keep it quiet so far, but word is bound to leak out sooner or later. If we're going to save our program, we can't let this happen."

"Save your program!" She stared at him in disbelief. "So the only reason you want to save my sister is so you don't risk losing your precious program?"

He at least had the grace to flinch. "Of course not. Miss Evans is a lovely woman. I don't wish to see her hurt, but our clients know the risks involved in time travel. While I sympathize with her plight, my position as president of the Griffin International time travel division makes my first and foremost responsibility to our bottom line. We are in the midst of a government evaluation. Were they to discover this problem, the government could shut us down."

"I don't even know how to respond to that," she said.

"Say you'll help us."

"First of all, I don't believe this insane story

you've been feeding me. Second, even if I did, what the hell could I do?"

"You can find your sister before anything happens to her."

"Why me? Why not send in a rescue team the minute you clear the portal?"

"We can't do that. While the government is aware of the cave-in, they're not aware anyone was using the portal at the time. And they are observing our cleanup efforts." He ran a hand through his hair, the first gesture of genuine emotion Alex had seen since she'd arrived. "They're more hindrance than help. The safety measures they insist upon are causing the process to go much slower than it should. They have no notion of the urgency of the situation."

"Then tell them about Charlotte."

"I can't."

"You won't."

He nodded. "Yes, I won't allow this situation to destroy my company."

"Bastard."

"There's no need for profanity," he said with a sneer. "I understand my decision is difficult for you to accept, but it's final."

The sneer faded, and he attempted what she guessed was supposed to be a smile, but it certainly didn't reach his eyes, and she knew he couldn't care less about her or Charlotte.

"So what are you going to do? And why am I here? You said yourself you can't just leave her there to be murdered. It wouldn't look good. So what's your plan?"

"The fewer people who know about this the better. It decreases the chance of this news leaking. As I told you, the London portal is useless. However, we do have a portal right here in Philadelphia that travels to the same time period. We can mount a rescue attempt from here."

"So the portal here comes out where Charlotte is?"

"Not where. When. The portal locations are fixed. If you go through in Philadelphia, you come out in Philadelphia. If you go now and catch the first ship traveling to London, you should have enough time to find Miss Evans before the events of this article take place. Our guess is that your sister sought the help of your ancestors." He flipped open another folder and ran a finger down the page. "The Creswells—Lord and Lady Downing. She may have even claimed to be one of their lost girls since she didn't have the resources for an extended trip. I suggest you begin by observing the Creswells' home. Maybe you'll catch sight of Miss Evans." A thoughtful look replaced his frown, and he steepled his fingers under his chin, nodding. "You could simply approach the family and claim to be their missing daughter, reunite with Miss Evans and warn her. You can't, of course, mention what you know to the family. No one can know about us."

Alex blinked and was surprised to find herself halfway to the door before she even realized she'd decided to leave. "This is insane. There's no such thing as time travel. I don't know why I wasted my time. I'm going."

"Then in two months, your sister will die."

She stopped dead in her tracks with her hand on the door handle. She twisted slowly to face Sawyer head on. "Did you just threaten her?"

He was on his feet, though thankfully he remained

a safe distance away with the desk between them.

"I merely stated a fact. You've seen the article."

The crumpled paper crackled in her hand as she tightened her fist around it. "You could have faked this."

"But why would I?"

She couldn't think of an answer.

****

Later that evening, Sawyer looked at the incoming number on his cell phone and flipped it open. "Well?" he asked.

"She met a Miss Jessica Faraday for coffee, went to the University library where she checked out a few books on history, and then went back to her apartment. Looks like she's in for the night," the member of his security team assigned to follow the girl reported. "The phone tap's done, and the transcripts will be delivered to you each morning," he said, completing his report. "Sir."

Sawyer cursed. "Who's Jessica Faraday? I want a complete background check on her. Were you able to hear their conversation?"

"No, sir. I couldn't get close enough without revealing my presence. Initial reports on Miss Faraday indicate the two are close friends. They attend a karate class together as well as get together on a regular basis. I have my men looking into it further."

"Very good." It wasn't. Could Miss Turner have ignored his edict to maintain strict silence on their mission? He cursed again. He'd deal with Miss Faraday if she became a problem. One more headache to deal with in this whole mess.

"Make sure surveillance is twenty-four seven. I

want to know if Miss Turner goes anywhere. And make sure to intercept her if she makes any attempt to contact Miss Evans's brother or Miss Faraday again. We don't want him to make a connection between us and the disappearances."

Sawyer hung up the phone.

Books on history—at least that's a good sign.

Despite all her words to the contrary, she was convinced. She'd go willingly.

Chapter Two

April 2 (57 Days to Murder)

Three days later, Alex found herself at a hotel near Griffin International Headquarters in Philadelphia, lingering in the shower. Water coursed down her body, and she hissed from the heat. Goosebumps covered her arms, and the skin of her stomach turned bright pink from the close-to-scalding water.

Of all the modern conveniences, she would miss hot and cold running water the most. Who knew how long before she'd have her next hot shower. She was determined to enjoy it, though thoughts of what she was about to do wouldn't let her relax.

At least the shower cleared the cobwebs from her head. She shut off the cooling water and stepped from the tub. She wrapped one of the cheap, thin, white towels around her body and used another to dry her hair.

A glance at the clock reassured her the marathon shower hadn't made her late, though why she should care she wasn't entirely sure. They'd wait for her. After all, she was putting her neck on the line to save their asses. The least they could do was pamper her a bit before she left. She dropped the towel on the floor and walked to the closet to dress for her adventure.

After a restless night tossing and turning, she'd

needed the extra long shower to wake her up. Now a feeling of excitement built within her. She knew it was crazy; she shouldn't believe a word Sawyer had told her, but she did. She was about to take the trip of a lifetime. Her ordinary life was taking an extraordinary turn. Frightening as hell, but a part of her couldn't wait to take that next step. In a few short hours, she'd be on her own in the nineteenth century trying to find her way to London without benefit of airplanes, on-line ticketing, credit cards, or any other modern travel convenience.

Weakness permeated her knees, and she stumbled over to the bed, sinking onto the rumpled comforter. She curled up onto her side, clutching the bedding to her stomach. *What the hell am I doing?*

She rolled onto her back, her hand pressed to her temple, trying to still the kettledrums pounding in her head. What made her think she could do this? She wasn't exactly the adventure type. Goosebumps rose on her naked skin as the air-conditioning kicked on, despite repeated attempts to turn it off. She couldn't even manage that simple task! And she thought she'd be able to travel through time, save her sister from a gruesome murder and what, save the world? She was an idiot. She should call Sawyer right now and tell him she wasn't going.

Instead, she got off the bed and pulled her clothes out of the closet. She stepped into her own bright pink striped panties, stuffed the matching bra into her overnight bag, and contemplated the clothes Sawyer had given her last night. She'd asked for boy's clothes, and he'd provided them, even after arguing with her that it was a bad idea. She'd stood her ground. She was not putting on the fancy dress and corset he'd tried to hand to her. A corset for heaven's sake!

Although what she had in front of her was pretty much the same thing, though it would have an entirely different effect. This version was supposed to downplay her assets rather than perk them up. And thankfully, it didn't have that insane rod thing going down the middle like the real corset.

She picked it up and fingered the material—basic off-white cotton, nothing special. The padding was the key. The waist had about an inch of padding all the way around but flattened out on the bottom where it hugged her hips. It made her look a little chunky but also evened out her curves so she didn't look like a woman. Alex hoped to pass for a teenage boy. She'd read enough historical novels to know women didn't travel on their own. And were fair game if they did. She didn't want to deal with that crap. She had enough on her mind.

Dozens of tiny hooks ran up the front, and it took her a full minute to fasten them all. When finished, she walked to the mirror to see the effect. And burst out laughing.

She looked ridiculous. Her breasts flattened, her waist expanded, and her bright pink underwear peeked out at the bottom. Smiling at her reflection, she considered removing the underwear but decided against it. Sawyer would have a fit if he knew, but damned if she'd show him. He'd have to take her word that she wasn't smuggling any twenty-first century items into the past.

Speaking of which, she rummaged through her overnight bag until she found the crumpled up copy of the newspaper article reporting Charlotte's murder. Confident that Sawyer didn't realize she'd kept the copy, she planned on taking it with her.

Charlotte probably wouldn't believe her when she appeared in the past with this crazy story. They might be sisters, but they didn't know each other. Without any memories of their childhood, she had no idea what Charlotte was like. But she wanted to find out. That's why she was going through with this no matter what. She'd find a way to get through it. She had to.

She smoothed out the crinkled folds of paper and folded it neatly before tucking it into a small pocket cut into the altered corset, next to a copy of the article about the fire that had killed her parents.

The hospital staff hadn't wanted to give it to her, but when she'd woken from a nearly two-year long coma with only vague memories of her family, she hadn't taken no for an answer.

For whatever reason, she couldn't bear to leave it. It would be the only connection to her own time.

She scratched at her breasts, rethinking the decision to disguise her gender. Would she really fool anyone? She'd done an internet search and discovered women had disguised themselves to take on a man's job, often remaining undiscovered until an accident revealed their gender. If they could do it, so could she. And from what she'd seen online, they weren't punished when they were caught. In the navy, they were dismissed as soon as they made port. Since that's all she wanted, what harm could it do?

She returned to the bed and picked up the linen shirt, pulling it over her head and fastening it up to her neck. The long, baggy garment dwarfed her frame, but when Sawyer had explained everything, he'd reassured her it was supposed to be that way. Convenient, since it would be easier to hide her figure that way. She was supposed to tuck the shirt around her in lieu of underwear. Yuck. She'd keep her own.

Pants next. These were baggy, too. A panel flapped open where the zipper would be, so she fastened the buttons on either side. She scratched at the itchy fabric. She'd better get used to it quick since she'd be wearing them all the time.

Sawyer had given her only one other set of clothes. Apparently, people didn't have lots of extra clothing back in the day. She'd even have to sleep in them. Who knew if she'd need that extra set? Life on a nineteenth century ship didn't afford a girl much privacy. With so few clothes and no shower, being around her would be less than pleasant.

Although, if she wanted to put a positive spin on it, lack of showering would probably discourage anyone from getting close enough to see past her disguise. She laughed wryly at herself and tugged on her boots.

Dressed in the unfamiliar clothes, she went through her gear for the hundredth time as she waited 'til it was time to meet up with Sawyer. She had insisted on keeping the bag with her once Sawyer had gone through everything last night.

She hadn't wanted to give him the opportunity to screw with her supplies behind her back. Not that she had any reason to suspect he would, but trust didn't come easy. Living on the streets as a teen had seen to that.

She had a warm wool coat, blanket, comb, soap, toothbrush and paste, and a small jar of suntan lotion.

She'd insisted on the lotion even though it wasn't historically accurate. Sawyer had had a fit before finding a jar she could put it in. But she'd be burnt to a crisp if she set sail without it, so she'd insisted.

She had enough food to last a few days. Nothing perishable and all of it wrapped in cloth rather than plastic or even paper bags. Something as simple as packing a lunch was complicated without all the small modern conveniences.

She filled a flask with bottled water from the mini bar and tucked it into her pack. She bent forward to fiddle with the knife tucked into her boot. Not particularly comfortable, but she'd have to get used to it. She'd questioned the need for it, but Sawyer told her it might come in useful. She didn't want to think why.

She put two long gold chains around her neck with her family pendant, careful to make sure they weren't visible beneath her shirt. She tucked some rings into an inside pocket of her pants. She'd cashed out her savings account to buy things she'd be able to trade for money in the past. Luckily, she hadn't paid next semester's tuition yet, or she'd have had nothing. Sawyer had given her a few coins, but she wasn't going to rely on what he supplied.

Getting a fair price for the jewelry would be her first obstacle. Not being familiar with what they would be worth at the time, she would have a hard time negotiating.

She separated her heart from the rest and ran her fingers lightly over the inscription on the back. *We Love You, M and F.*

She'd been tempted to sell it once or twice over the years when times had been particularly tough and she'd no idea how she would pay for her next meal. She'd even had it appraised once and learned it was worth quite a bit of money. The appraiser had declared the ruby flawless and had made an offer to purchase it.

She'd never been able to do it. She couldn't part with it.

The front had her name and on the back was the message from her parents. Except it wasn't from her parents was it? Not really.

A perfect, tear-shaped ruby dangled from the bottom. Its deep red color and myriad facets reflected the light in a fascinating way that had gotten Alex through many a boring math lecture.

She'd always thought her parents had selected it personally for her because red was her favorite color. She'd cherished the thought.

The pendant felt cold as she dropped it back down under her shirt.

She jumped at the screeching of the alarm clock. Time to get up. And she'd worried she would oversleep.

Alex walked into the bathroom and flipped the switch. Her scissors lay where she'd left them by the sink last night. She couldn't bring herself to cut her hair then, but she was out of time. She grabbed the scissors with one hand and grabbed hold of her hair with the other. With a deep breath, she focused on the ends of her hair and made the first cut. A huge hunk of brown hair fluttered into the sink. She cut off at least six inches. The ragged ends tickled her chin, and she forced herself to continue cutting. Soon, her hair covered the sink, and what was left on her head stuck out at odd angles like a fluffy pincushion.

It felt strange and light. She ruffled the base of her neck and turned her head from side to side trying to see if the ends were even. Not great, but if she continued she'd end up with a crew cut, and she didn't need to go that short. It would have to do. She could still tie it back with a short length of leather. Tied back, no one would be able to see how uneven it was. They shouldn't care anyway. The haphazard style would probably add to the impression she was a boy who wouldn't care about such things.

She took one last look at herself in the mirror and put her hand to her hair. She missed the feel of long, flowing hair cascading down her back, but it was too much of a giveaway for her current disguise. This cut gave her a slightly unkempt look. She shrugged and, with a final scowl at the young man looking back at her, headed down to breakfast.

****

After breakfast and much too quickly for Alex's peace of mind, they arrived at the portal. It wasn't much. She could see how someone might walk right into it without noticing. There was simply a distortion in the air, similar to heat waves shimmering off a highway on a scorching-hot July afternoon.

"That's it? You described it as a vortex or black hole. I was expecting more," Alex whispered. Despite its inconsequential appearance, its presence reverberated deep in her bones, and she stared at it in awe.

"They were much more obvious the first few years. Since then, they've settled down like this." Sawyer waved toward the distortion, obviously not as awestruck as she was. His voice rang out loud and clear in the small space, rattling her nerves.

She took a deep breath, almost time. "So, how does this work exactly?"

"You just walk right through. You'll be a bit disoriented when you get there, so take time to sit and rest before you head out. Better to get settled a bit where no one can happen by. You'll need this." He handed her a lantern. "It's pitch black on the other side, no lights." He waved vaguely at the fluorescents above them.

"Once you feel ready, follow the tunnel to the surface, and walk down to the wharf. You remember the path we described?" After Alex nodded, he continued, "It will take you a few hours to walk it. Once there, you should book your passage right away, in case a ship is ready to depart. Ship captains or their business agents will probably be at one of the local taverns if they're looking for passengers or workers. Many tend to do business that way. Ask at the docks for ships headed to London, and someone will direct you to a likely captain. You need to get to London ASAP if you're to find Miss Evans in time, so don't delay."

"Right." Alex took a deep breath. With a tight grip on her canvas bag and the lantern, she walked through the portal.

Chapter Three

Philadelphia
April 2, 1818 (57 Days Remaining)

Alex doubled over, clutching her stomach. She tried to suck in her breath but couldn't. Fire ripped down her limbs. She refused to look at her hands; afraid her nails had peeled back.

The damp ground pressed against her forehead, and she could breathe again. She scraped her cheek trying to reassure herself her skin hadn't been stripped from her body and found she lay on the cave floor—skin and nails intact.

Only it wasn't the same cave.

She could distinguish her immediate surroundings from the weak light of her lantern. She was damn lucky it hadn't gone out. As it was, it lay against a boulder in danger of tipping over. Hand trembling, she reached out and set it right. The last thing she needed was to stumble around in a pitch-black cave.

The slight shimmer of the portal got her moving forward to put some distance between them. *How would she ever have the nerve to go back through that thing?*

Sawyer was gone, and she used every curse she could think of as she stood and dusted herself off. *A little disorienting, huh!* Even though the pain was gone, the thought of it made her sick. She kept herself from retching by sheer force of will.

Alex closed her eyes and took a deep breath, bursting into a fit of coughing when she sucked in a lungful of dust. When her coughing stilled, she took another cautious breath and counted to ten, then one hundred. She held the lantern aloft and looked around, stifling the feeling of being entombed within the cold, damp earth. She wrinkled her nose to suppress the sneeze building from the combined smell of dust and mildew.

Obviously, Griffin, International had done a bit of work to make it a more suitable atmosphere for their experiment. The cave in the future had an even floor and steel beams reinforcing a ceiling covered with fluorescent lights. This rough, small cave had an uneven floor that tilted and curved in all directions. Rocks jutted out from the wall, and water dripped along a jagged seam at the top of the passage. An ice-cold drop plopped onto her cheek and she shivered, hunching her shoulders under the coarse fabric of her coat.

She wiped her hands over her legs to remove the tiny pebbles lodged in her palms, then sucked on a knuckle scraped raw in the fall. She held the lantern high and looked for the way out. One path led away from the portal, so she made sure she had everything and headed out.

About half an hour passed before she made her way to the surface. The climb wasn't that steep, and she managed with little difficulty, though it was slow going. With such weak light, she inched along to avoid tripping over the rocks that jutted into her path or bashing her head against the stalactites that dropped out of nowhere in her way.

At long last, a hint of light filtered through a large bush covering most of the entrance. A few minutes later, she found a space to crawl through, but it wasn't easy. Her clothes and hair snagged on branches, and she had to be careful not to rip anything. She used her knife to cut through the worst of the branches, but it took her almost as long to work through the mess as it had to get there.

She finally forced her way through and reached for her water, taking a long fortifying gulp before taking stock. A quick glance down revealed her clothing didn't appear to be much better off than her hands. Dirt covered every inch she could see. She untangled some of the snags in her hair as she pulled out bits of leaf and twigs.

So much for first impressions. She would have to find a place to wash before she met with any of the ship captains. She was to follow a stream to the town. She would try to clean herself up a bit when she found it.

If she found it.

****

That night, Alex stood outside *The Troubled Tavern* for a long while, listening to the familiar sounds of a bar at happy hour and working up the courage to enter.

Inside, the first mate of a ship named *The Reliant* was hiring sailors for their trip to London leaving the next day. They didn't take passengers, but she was determined to sail on that boat. Another wouldn't leave for London for a few weeks, and she didn't have that much time. She'd read the trip took about a month,

30

more for bad weather, and the article was dated less than two months from now. She might not arrive in time if she waited.

A scuffling sound came from a dark alley that ran along the side of the building. *Rats?* From this angle, she could only see a few feet in, though the smell seemed to have no trouble making its way to the street. She suppressed her gag at the stench, but the thought of what scurried around in the dark made her shudder. A flash of movement too high to have been anything creepy crawly and a quickly muffled woman's scream had her moving toward the sound before she had time to think better of what she was about to do.

"Hey!" Alex shouted as she rushed to the mouth of the alley.

Three figures struggled in the dark but came to a surprised halt at her shout. A skinny, rugged-looking man grasped a woman from behind with one arm about her throat and one hand covering her mouth, cutting off her screams. A shaft of light fell across their faces as they stared at her. Terror shined through the woman's huge eyes. She resumed her struggles to break free of the man's grasp, and he gave a grunt of effort.

A second man dropped his hold on the girl's long skirts and turned to face Alex. A knife glittered in his hand, and Alex swallowed down her fear to face him. "Let her go."

He didn't respond, simply gestured with his knife for Alex to come to him.

She looked toward the pub door, but the revelry from within was too loud. No one inside would hear a scream for help. She wiped sweaty palms against her pant legs and stepped forward, making sure to stay within sight of the pub's entrance. Surely someone would come out soon. Stalling was her best option. Even her black belt in karate wasn't enough to take on two armed men. She needed help.

"I believe the lad told you to unhand the woman."

Alex jumped and whirled toward the deep voice behind her. Relief warred with disconcertion that she hadn't heard the man's approach.

Despite the danger of her situation, she couldn't help but stare at his powerfully-built broad shoulders, muscular chest, and strong limbs. She guessed him to be about six foot two, and he didn't look to have an ounce of fat on him. His loose white shirt was open at the neck with a scarf of some kind crumpled to each side as if just recently untied from around his neck. Wavy, jet-black hair tangled about his shoulders. A breeze blew the long strands across his face, and he pushed them back.

She bit back a gasp as he lowered his hands, revealing a face that sent a jolt through her and set her heart racing. Half his face lay in shadow, and the dark hid the color of his eyes, but she was left with an impression of strength. A square jaw, slightly crooked nose, and high cheekbones fit together so well she had the insane desire to run her fingers along his jaw and cover his firm, sensual lips with hers. A vaguely triangular, jagged scar ran from his temple to the corner of his mouth and down to his jaw. The skin inside the triangle was rough and reddened.

The way his mouth tilted up slightly, as if in amusement, amplified the fierceness of his face. Not the emotion she would expect given the seriousness of the situation. She thought to see tension in his face, but he appeared completely relaxed, even pleased. A sense of anticipation hung in the air, and she got the impression he relished the idea of a fight. He brought his hands to his hips, resting one on the hilt of a wicked looking knife tucked at his waist. The threat couldn't have been more clear.

Alex tore her fascinated gaze away to look back down the alley at the girl who continued to struggle against her captors. Both men appeared to have dismissed her completely from their thoughts and focused on what was clearly the bigger threat to their fun.

The knife had disappeared, and the creep held his hands out in a placating gesture. "This ain't your fight. We're just havin' ourselves a little fun."

The savior nodded toward the struggling woman. "She does not appear to be having fun, and I have decided to make this my fight. Unhand her." He strolled forward, past Alex and into the alley. As he drew closer to the two men, he towered over them, forcing them to tilt their heads back to keep his face in view. They looked at each other and, as if of one mind, turned and fled down the alley, pushing the girl into her savior's arms, effectively preventing him from giving chase.

Alex rushed forward and helped the girl stand on her own, disentangling the two strangers. "Are you hurt?" she asked once the girl seemed steady.

The girl pressed one hand to her forehead, the other to her heart and closed her eyes. "I shall be fine. I simply need a moment to recover my breath."

"Right." Alex turned away to give the girl a chance to recover without being stared at. "Thanks," she said to the man. "I can't tell you how glad I am you came along. I was about to get my a—" She had to watch her mouth, or she'd get herself in a load of trouble. "Ah, I was about to be beaten rather soundly. I don't think I could have handled both of them."

He raised his brows and stared down at her, a strange smile twisting his mouth. "Yet you would have attempted to 'handle them' regardless?"

Alex shrugged, trying to sound nonchalant. "Well, I was hoping to stall them. I figured someone would come out of the pub sooner or later. Anyway. Thanks." She held out her hand. "I'm Alex. Alex Turner."

Her hand looked tiny engulfed in his firm, yet gentle, grip. He didn't try to crush her hand as so many men did who felt a handshake was a test of power. The calluses that lined his palm were enough to tell her he was a man of strength, though that was obvious enough just by looking at him, which she had to stop soon or risk unmasking herself. Acting like a boy was new to her, but she was pretty sure they didn't drool over handsome men.

His touch somehow calmed her, and the fear that had threatened to choke her only moments ago began to recede. She tried not to think about the impression she was giving him with her sweaty grip, while his was, or had been, perfectly dry.

"It is a pleasure to make your acquaintance, Mr. Turner." He bowed slightly and released her hand. "I am," he hesitated slightly, "Nicholas Somerville."

She felt the loss of warmth all along her body and stuffed her hands in her pockets. She rocked back on her heels, uncertain what to say next. What do you say to a man who just chased off two would-be rapists? She cleared her throat and turned back to check on the girl, and tensed up immediately when she got a good look at her face.

Her eyes were huge in her pale, thin face as she stared beyond Alex. The terror she'd attempted to stifle had returned, and she backed up against the wall.

"What?" Alex whipped around to check the alley and was surprised to find it empty. From the look on the girl's face, she'd assumed her attackers were sneaking up behind them. She turned back to the cowering girl, wrinkling her brow in confusion.

"I believe her relief at being rescued was short-lived," Nicholas said contemptuously. His lips tightened, and Alex could practically hear his teeth grinding. Alex's confusion must have shown because Nicholas flicked his fingers to indicate the scar on his face. "I apparently do not meet the requirements of an appropriately dashing hero."

"Seriously?" Alex exclaimed to the stupid girl. "He just saved you, and you're afraid of him?"

The girl turned her frightened gaze on Alex. "I beg your pardon, sir?"

Alex jerked in surprise at being addressed as a man, disconcerted that she'd forgotten her disguise for even a moment. She couldn't afford to be careless.

"I did not mean any disrespect to the..." She hesitated slightly before continuing, "...gentleman." She bobbed a curtsey and looked steadfastly at the ground.

"What, precisely, are you doing in this alley at this time of night?" Nicholas asked.

The girl kept her eyes downcast as she answered, "I was separated from my escort and seem to have lost my way."

Nicholas raised his brows. "You certainly have." He sighed. "I suppose there is no help for it. Wait here, and I will summon a hack to carry you home." He turned to Alex. "Will you remain with her a moment until I return? She should not be left alone in this part of the city. I shall not be far and will return in an instant if I hear your call."

Alex nodded, and Nicholas strode off into the night. She watched him leave, wishing his coat were a little shorter so she could get a good look at his ass. She blushed and cursed to herself when she realized what she was doing. She really had to be more careful, or she'd blow her disguise before she'd even been here a full day.

She turned back to the girl, who also stared after Nicholas, though Alex suspected their thoughts were nothing alike.

The poor thing was a mess, fidgeting with her clothing, trying to get herself back together. Half her hair hung in a mess of curls with hairpins clinging in random spots while the other half pulled back in what had probably been a rather intricate chignon earlier in the day. Dirt smattered the hem of her delicate blue and green flowered gown.

Alex felt a spurt of rage at the way the fabric was a wrinkled mess where one of the men had gathered it in his hand to pull the skirt up to the girl's waist. If Nicholas hadn't come along when he did! She didn't want to think of it.

She bent to pick up a dainty, jeweled comb from the ground at her feet and brushed dirt from its teeth. "Are you good?" She stopped fiddling with the comb and concentrated on the girl.

"I do not know." When she turned to face Alex, tears glittered in her eyes. "It will be terribly difficult to arrive home in a hired carriage without notice. I do not have sufficient funds to pay and shall be required to request the money from my parents. They will be cross with me for leaving the house at this hour." Her high-pitched voice and fast rate of speech made it difficult to follow her. She reclaimed her comb and began pulling pins from her hair. "Oh dear. I must look dreadful. I cannot allow myself to be seen in such a state. My parents shall think the worst."

"So you snuck out? Well, your parents will probably be upset about that, but when you tell them what happened, they'll be happy you weren't hurt."

The girl clutched Alex's arm with surprising strength. "I cannot possibly tell them what almost happened. They would be furious! Please, you musn't say anything to them!"

Alex brushed off the girl's clinging grip. "Fine. Fine. How could I say anything? I'm not taking you home."

The girl dropped her arm. "You are not going to accompany me?"

"'Course not. Why would I do that?"

"I believe she prefers you as a companion to me," Nicholas said.

Alex jumped as his large hand engulfed her shoulder. "I didn't hear you approach. Damn, for such a big fellow, you're really quiet."

His frown turned to a grin, and her heart skipped a beat. If she'd thought he looked sexy when he was all fierce and scowling, it was nothing compared to his smile. She turned away as the clip-clop of horses' hooves echoed down the alley, and a carriage came to a stop a few feet away.

"If you'll allow me?" Nicholas held out his arm to the girl, and she placed her trembling hand on it.

Unsure whether he intended to escort the girl home or to the carriage waiting only a few feet away, Alex turned back toward the pub entrance. Nicholas could return any moment, and it was probably wiser not to be alone with him. He was bound to notice her interest in him without the distraction of a cowering girl nearby. She couldn't afford to let that happen.

She ignored a pang of regret and pulled open the door.

****

A wall of smoke and the reek of dozens of unwashed men hit her like a roundhouse kick to the face. She blinked watery eyes as she made her way to the bar. She tried to keep her expression neutral, it wouldn't be wise to look as disgusted as she felt.

The barman was serving a round at the far end of the bar, so she took a few minutes to look around. She needed the time to steady her nerves.

Men crowded around the tables, laughing and downing drink after drink in an all too familiar frat-boy style. Alex grimaced when one of the men reached out and grabbed the waitress around the waist, bringing her in close and spilling a drink down his shirt. The waitress smacked him in the head, and his friends all laughed.

Exactly like the bars she'd worked in.

Except, in the far corner, sitting alone with his back to the wall was the most gorgeous man she had ever seen. His short, blond hair was slightly tousled but looked perfect on him. She had the impression he had carefully arranged it that way. She couldn't help comparing him to Nicholas and found him lacking, despite his flawless appearance. He didn't seem real, where Nicholas felt entirely too real.

She seriously needed to get her mind off that man.

She watched with amusement as all the waitresses found reasons to walk past or stop at his table so they could swing their hips or show off their cleavage. He appeared to enjoy the show but made no move to leave his solitary table.

Two men took the empty chairs across from the Adonis, blocking her view. But not for long. They left after only a short while and didn't appear too happy.

"Watcha need?"

Alex jumped and turned her attention back toward the barman, who had come over while she watched the stranger.

"I'm looking for the first mate of *The Reliant*. I heard he would be here tonight."

The barman pointed to the handsome stranger. "That's him." He looked Alex up and down with a derogatory sneer. "You don't look like no sailor."

Alex smiled tightly. "Not yet. Anyway, can I have two of whatever he's drinking, please?"

The barman looked slightly mollified now he saw she was to be a paying customer and brought her the drinks. Her money disappeared into his pocket, and he said, "Ain't gonna be easy signing up with that lot. They don't hire just anyone on *The Reliant*. Most of the crew's been with them for years."

He picked up a glass and started drying it with a dirty rag he un-tucked from the front of his pants. Alex repressed her shudder and decided not to look at her glass too closely.

"Only seen the captain once m'self. Keeps away from most folk around here, don't want to be seen much. Lets Mr. Grayson over there act for him." He looked like he was waiting for her to show some interest so he could share the latest gossip with a newcomer.

She was only too happy to oblige. She leaned forward and gave him an encouraging smile. "Why's that?"

"Scary devil, he is. Only got the one glimpse of him m'self, but heard tell one whole side of his body ain't nothin' but scars. He were caught in some ship explosion in their war with France a few years back. Saved a dozen men, but got caught in the explosion. Most o' his crew were those ones he saved. I heard tell he has a hard time getting new crew members because they're too afraid to work for him."

"Really? How sad." Alex couldn't help but think of Nicholas. Was it a coincidence she'd met a man that fit that description? She could see him as a hero. After all, he'd just saved her ass.

"Sad? I don't know 'bout that, but we won't have to worry 'bout him much longer. This is his last trip."

"Oh? Why?"

"I hear as how he's some type o' titled English lord, probably came into some money and figures he don't have to work no more." Someone called for his attention from the other side of the bar. "Good luck," he said before turning away.

Alex picked up the drinks and walked to the first mate's table. He was talking loudly to some sailors at the next table, so she waited for him to finish his conversation.

Luckily, he was busy—she needed a moment to stare. Despite all the smoke clouding her vision, she stood almost awestruck at blue eyes so clear and bright she would have sworn they were contacts if she hadn't known that was impossible.

She blinked a few times before surreptitiously observing the rest of him. Now that she had the chance to get a better look, she thought he was a bit too pretty for her tastes. Men should be more rugged looking. Like Nicholas. A woman shouldn't feel like she was competing to see who was prettiest.

When he stopped talking and his gaze raked her from top to bottom, she gave him a friendly smile, holding out one of the drinks.

"Care for a drink?"

He smiled back and gestured to an empty chair as he took the offered drink. "Don't mind if I do. Jonathan Grayson, First Mate of *The Reliant*. I don't believe we've met?" He took a healthy drink from the glass and sighed appreciatively.

She took a gulp from her own glass for courage and gasped as fire raced to her stomach and pungent whisky fumes seared her nose hairs.

Working at the bar, she had preferred to keep her wits about her and had never developed a head for strong drink. Besides which, beer and tequila shots were more in the college style than whisky.

She coughed to cover her reaction, but he laughed, obviously not fooled for a minute. He seemed remarkably alert given how much of the vile stuff she'd seen him down from her post at the bar. Had she been bartending, she would have had some serious qualms about continuing to serve him, even though the whisky could have been tap water for all the effect it seemed to have on him.

"My name's Alex Turner. I'm interested in booking passage on your ship. I need to get to London quickly, and the next ship doesn't leave for a few weeks."

"We don't take passengers. No space for them. Crew and cargo only. Sorry." He gestured to a pretty waitress walking by, and she changed direction immediately.

She exaggerated the swing of her hips as she hurried toward them, flipping her hair out of her face and smiling suggestively.

Before he could say anything, Alex handed her their empty glasses. "Two more, please." Looking disappointed that drinks were the only thing ordered, the waitress nodded and walked away.

The Adonis turned back to Alex after watching the waitress sashay out of sight. "I'll take the whisky, and you're welcome to stay and keep me company, but I'm afraid our business is done."

"I heard you're hiring. Anything entry level available?"

He looked confused for a second, but realizing she was asking for work said, "We only need two more people, so unless you're a carpenter or a sailor, I can't help you."

"Please, I'm desperate. I don't know anything about sailing, but I work hard and I learn quickly." He still looked unconvinced so she burst out, "I'll work for free." She held her breath and waited.

He stared at her a moment, tapping a finger on his chin. "It must be a pretty important reason, so I'll give you the chance." His face hardened, and his look sent a chill of fear down her spine. "I better not have any reason to regret my generosity, or you won't make it all the way."

****

The next morning, Alex left the hotel just as the sun peeked above the horizon. She wasn't taking any chances on screwing this up. She'd bought some extra food the night before and figured she'd just hang out on the dock and eat her breakfast while she waited for the crew of *The Reliant* to wake up. Before she even reached the end of the street, she knew she'd made a huge mistake.

The peaceful, pre-dawn she'd expected was punctuated with the shouts of men calling out orders in some kind of sailor speak she didn't understand, while others waved goodbye to families lined up along the dock.

Her stomach churned with anxiety as she watched a ship getting smaller and smaller in the distance.

She'd missed it.

Women with small children in tow slowly turned and made their way away from the docks, chatting with each other as they walked. Alex stood still and ignored their curious gazes as they walked around her.

She couldn't take her eyes off the tiny, white sails that seemed to her a sign of defeat. She'd failed already. She couldn't even manage to get on a freakin' ship that was supposedly expecting her. Why had she ever thought she could do this?

A woman with a kind face, a baby cuddled in her

arms and two toddlers clutching her skirts, approached. "Don't worry child, it's a short trip they're taking. Is it your father or brother on *The Lamprey*?"

Alex tore her gaze away from those mocking sails. "Excuse me?"

The two little ones peeked at her from behind either side of their mother's skirt, their nearly identical faces reminding Alex of Charlotte. The knot in her stomach spread upwards and wrapped around her heart. She pressed the heel of her hand against her sternum and tried to concentrate on the mother's voice.

"Is it your father or brother that sails on board *The Lamprey?* Is this their first time? You'll miss them terribly, but you'll get used to it. My Louis is gone more often than not—"

"*The Lamprey?* You mean that wasn't *The Reliant?*" Alex's heart leapt with excitement. *Please say no!*

The woman shook her head, and Alex felt like hugging her. "Thank you! Thank you! I thought I was so screwed." She ignored the woman's look of surprise and rushed away. The relief was immense, but she wouldn't be able to relax until she found the right ship.

The sky had lightened considerably by the time she found someone to point her in the right direction.

The Reliant, eerily quiet next to the commotion of the ship in the next berth over, floated safely in the harbor. She muttered a brief thanks under her breath at the sight and hurried down the dock toward it.

She didn't see any means of boarding the ship, so she walked to a barrel and sat to eat her breakfast while she waited for someone to show up.

She wondered whether she should try calling out to

the ship when a deep voice with an incredibly sexy English accent reached her ears, sending a shiver up her spine. She hadn't thought to hear that voice again and tried to ignore the rush of pleasure it gave her.

"He's not back yet? Does anyone know where he spent the night?" Alex didn't hear the response, but a minute later a gangplank was lowered, and Nicholas appeared at the top. He made his way down to the dock with the easy stride of a man well used to the sea.

She knew the moment he spotted her. Their gazes connected, and she was caught like a deer in headlights as he walked straight to her. Her mind went blank. The man was going to think she was an idiot. Somehow, she lost the power of speech whenever she laid eyes on him.

His eyes did it this time. She'd always been a sucker for hazel eyes. She could get lost in the complex mix of green, brown, and gold. And those lashes. Women would kill for lashes like that. It must be a sin for a man to be blessed with them. She hadn't been able to see them last night in the darkness of that alley. Alex's body heated, and she just managed to speak before making a complete fool of herself.

"Oh, you must be the captain. Do you remember me? I'm Alex Turner. We met last night." He looked annoyed, but she couldn't figure out why, so she kept talking. *Yeah, he's definitely going to question whether there's something wrong with me.* "Mr. Grayson hired me for your trip to London." She was pleased her voice was only slightly breathless and didn't quaver even as her insides melted.

His expression cleared somewhat, though she sensed he was still annoyed for some reason. "So that's where you went last night. I returned, and you were gone."

He was annoyed she'd left last night?

"Come with me. I am off to fetch Mr. Grayson. It may be useful to have some assistance."

Her gaze drifted to his mouth as he spoke, fascinated by the way the scar pulled slightly at the corner. She felt a strong urge to kiss that corner, to run her tongue along the seam and dip between his lips, along his teeth.

He turned away, and she blinked herself back to reality. She couldn't believe the thoughts that kept popping into her head when she looked at him.

And she was going to be stuck on a ship with him for almost a month.

Dressed like a boy.

Wonderful.

He set off, and she rushed after him, thankful he couldn't see the blush heating her cheeks. It was going to be a long month.

She caught up, practically jogging to keep pace with his long strides.

He looked her briefly up and down in an assessing manner that strained Alex's nerves. "You don't look like much of a sailor, and you're too young to have any skill as a carpenter."

She was surprised he hadn't already uncovered her disguise. Her instincts warned her he wouldn't be easy to fool, and she would be smart to keep her distance, even if distance was the last thing she wanted right now. Of course, it wouldn't be a problem if he decided she wasn't qualified to work on his ship.

"You're wondering what possessed him to hire me.

Perhaps he took pity on me, or maybe I'm better qualified than I look," she replied haughtily, and immediately wished she could take the last part back. Now he might think she had some sailing skill.

He snorted, and she got the feeling amusement had replaced his annoyance, though his expression hadn't changed.

"My guess would be pity. He sometimes has more heart than sense." He sighed. "Despite some of his more—emotional—decisions, he's a good first mate and has served me well. We'll have to see how you fare." He gave her a slightly puzzled look. "There's something about you though. I can't quite put my finger on it."

Alex breathed a sigh of relief when they arrived at the tavern where she'd met the Adonis the night before. This time of the morning everything was quiet, and they had to wait a few moments before anyone came to see what they wanted.

A sour-faced woman entered the room, muttering about the hour and cursing under her breath. But after a quick glance at Nicholas's face, she quieted and listened to his request. She told them which room the first mate was in then quickly disappeared through the door by which she had entered.

"Follow me." Nicholas climbed the stairs and knocked loudly on the appropriate door. He didn't wait for an answer before pushing it open.

The Adonis slept soundly in the middle of the large bed that dominated the room. A blanket draped around his hips didn't disguise the fact he was naked.

Alex had a difficult time deciding where to look. On his left, the pretty waitress from the night before was hastily pulling the covers up to her chin, while another woman on his right merely reached over to try to waken her bed partner, as though the appearance of two people at the door was hardly cause to cover up.

"I can see why he didn't show," Alex muttered under her breath. She hadn't meant to be heard, but apparently Nicholas had good hearing and laughed.

"Quite understandable," he said, still chuckling.

Meanwhile, the first mate opened his eyes and looked up at the captain. "Bloody hell. Am I late?"

****

They waited downstairs next to the bar while the Adonis got dressed. He came down a scant five minutes later apologizing profusely. He stopped suddenly when he caught sight of Alex. "Who are you?" He frowned.

Her eyes widened. She had realized he was a bit drunk last night, but it hadn't occurred to her he wouldn't even remember her. *What am I going to do now?* The beginnings of panic started in her chest. But before she could say anything, a look of recognition dawned on his face, and he smiled.

"Oh, now I remember. You're the lad who works for free."

Nicholas interrupted, "Free, hmmm? So, it wasn't pity or extraordinary talent that got the job, you were merely a bargain."

A blush started in her cheeks, and a knot grew in her belly. She couldn't afford for him to decide not to hire her.

"I need to get to London as quickly as possible, and your ship is my best option. I promise I'm a fast learner, and I'll work real hard. You won't be disappointed." She spoke quickly and hoped she sounded more confident than she felt.

"See that I am not. I don't take disappointment well. Now, we must get back to *The Reliant*. We have much to do before we set sail, and we are already behind schedule."

Chapter Four

April 9 (50 Days Remaining)

Alex grasped the rail as a course correction caught her off guard. She'd heard the call to make a starboard turn, but she'd forgotten which direction that was and hadn't adjusted her weight properly.

She didn't know her left from her right anymore. Left was larboard and right was starboard, but only when facing the bow, which she had to keep reminding herself, was the front of the ship.

They spoke English, but she'd be damned if she knew what they were saying half the time. At least she'd gotten used to being called *boy*. All it had taken was a good smack upside her head to ensure she wouldn't forget that one again. Apparently, ignoring a crewmate wasn't a good idea, even if she didn't realize he was talking to her.

Overall, the first few days had gone remarkably well. Most of the crew was friendly and willing to help her learn the ropes. She thanked her lucky stars she appeared so young. They didn't expect quite so much from her that way.

She waited for the ship to straighten course before continuing to the galley. Time to get the captain's dinner ready, and she had been made the unofficial cook's assistant. Oh, if Jessie could see her now! Her friend used to tease Alex unmercifully about her lack of skill in the kitchen.

As she entered the galley, she smiled at Bartholomew Adolphus VanWiesel, known to all as Cook for obvious reasons. He looked a bit like a weasel with his wiry frame and beard that seemed to take over his entire face, but he was a sweetheart, and she enjoyed helping him.

"Ah, good." He tossed her a potato and pointed to a huge pile next to him. "Get those ready while I start the sauce."

He cast an encouraging grin, barely noticeable through his hair, and turned his attention to a bowl so large he could practically curl up in it.

As he chatted about this and that, Alex recalled him telling her the circumstances that brought him on board *The Reliant* when he had no real love for the sea.

He had signed on after a disastrous *affair of the heart* had left him unemployed and without references. Having little chance of securing another position in a respectable establishment, he had been drowning his sorrows in drink when he met the captain.

"It were years ago, right after the captain had left the Royal Navy and bought *The Reliant* with money his mother had given him. He had a foul temper in those days, nearly scared me out of me wits when he sat down at the table next to mine.

"He were a sight to see with the scar on his face still fresh and bloodied, part of his hair shaved away from another wound at the back of his skull. Then Mr. Grayson comes in, and the barmaids start preening and smiling to get his attention, fighting over who would serve him." Cook winked at Alex, before adding, "All the wenches act that way around him. And I've watched our first mate in too many tavern brawls to mention when the other men get jealous. But that's another story.

"So then he strolls over and sits down with the captain, and I laughed out loud at the looks of dismay on all the women's faces. None of them relished the thought of coming closer to the captain, even for the chance to bed our handsome Mr. Grayson.

"Well, that laugh caught the captain's attention, and he turned those piercing eyes of his to me. Shocked me to the core when I realized he was also amused by their reaction.

"Turns out they were discussing the crew they had been taking on for *The Reliant*, and I heard them say they was still needin' a cook.

"Now, I thought to myself, he might be a right scary lookin' devil, but if he could laugh at his own self, then he couldn't be that bad. Better than starving anyway, so I popped over and presented me credentials.

"They had heard the details of my situation, everyone had! Rumor flies faster than the wind in the houses of the *ton*, but he didn't mind and here I am. And now that he's a marquess, he's taking me with him, and I'll be able to get away from the sea and have a proper kitchen again."

She had been dying to ask Cook about his *affair of the heart* but hadn't wanted to be rude. In any event, he had switched to another topic, and the moment had passed.

Her ears perked up as she heard Cook mention the captain. "What was that?"

"Oh, I was just saying as how the captain's going

to miss the sea when he returns home."

"It's true, then? This is his last trip?"

Cook nodded. "Yes. He'll be much too busy now he's to be Lord Oakleigh. Mr. Grayson will take over as captain. The first mate's learned well. He'll make a right fine job of it."

She nodded; the crew had almost as much respect for the Adonis as they did for the captain. He'd do well. She wished him luck of it.

The watch called out the hour, and she threw her last potato into a dish. "Gotta go. My turn in the rigging. I'll come back after and help you serve dinner." She returned his absentminded wave goodbye and rushed out.

She'd only taken one watch so far but couldn't wait to do it again. It was amazing and she loved it. Sitting up in the rigging with the ship and the sea laid out below her, she felt as though she were flying. Just climbing up there was an adventure, with the ship pitching and heaving under her. The motion of the ship was exaggerated at such a great height, but it made it all the more exciting.

Coming down after her hour-long watch was more of a letdown than she'd counted on. She spotted the ship's carpenter, Mr. Duff, below and worried the voyage might not continue to go as smoothly as it had so far.

The previous carpenter had elected to stay behind in America since this was the captain's last trip. Mr. Duff didn't fit in well with the crew and was universally disliked. But they had been hard pressed to find a man with the special skills needed, and Mr. Grayson had reluctantly hired him the same night as

Alex.

Like a typical bully, he picked on anyone smaller or weaker than he was, and was smart enough to do it out of sight or earshot of anyone who might come to their aid. Alex believed Nicholas and Mr. Grayson were largely unaware of the problem as it was not in the nature of most of the sailors to complain.

And, just as she'd feared, since she appeared to be so young and slight, she was a prime target. He knocked her down the last few feet with a five foot length of wood intended for a minor decking repair. She landed hard on her backside with a startled, "Oof."

"Clumsy little fellow, ain't you." He laughed as she picked herself up. "You best watch you self, or you might get hurt."

Alex suppressed her wince of pain and gave Mr. Duff a smile. A few members of the crew were around. She didn't want to appear weak in front of them.

"Don't worry about me. I can handle myself." She looked him up and down. "Did *you* need some help? You seem to be having a bit of trouble carrying that heavy board."

She kept an all-too-innocent expression on her face as she said it, but she could have bit her tongue the moment the words were out of her mouth. The result was satisfying, but she had a feeling she'd pay for it later.

Mr. Duff's pockmarked visage turned purple with rage. She was saved from his response as Nicholas and Mr. Grayson appeared from below deck at that moment.

"Is everything all right here?" Nicholas asked, a slight frown upon his face.

She smiled. "Everything's fine sir. I was heading to

the galley to help Cook serve dinner." She nodded to Mr. Duff and left, but not before noting the scowl on his face.

Next time, she'd have to keep her big mouth shut. And there would be a next time, she had no doubt. She couldn't afford to get into it with the carpenter. She'd avoid him whenever possible and keep her head down when it wasn't. She knew it wasn't over.

****

The next night, another encounter made Alex desert all hope for a peaceful journey. The night shift was on duty with the majority of the crew asleep. Alex was returning from the galley after helping Cook clean up from Nicholas's weekly dinner party for his senior staff. The time was much later than usual, and when she walked around a corner, she almost collided with a young girl coming out of the cargo hold.

The girl stopped dead in her tracks, and her eyes widened in terror. It took Alex a second to overcome her surprise and realize the girl must be a stowaway who was probably terrified at being discovered. Alex gave her what she hoped was a reassuring smile and held one finger to her lips as she motioned with her other hand for the girl to precede her back down to the cargo hold.

Alex used her lantern's meager light to find the girl in the dark after closing the hatch. The girl cowered on the far side of the hold, half hidden behind some large crates piled high to the ceiling. She looked to be about fifteen, with long, brown hair pulled back into a single braid and dirt smudged along her cheekbones. She was a tiny thing, maybe five feet at most. Alex's heart went out to her.

Alex was unsure of the punishment for a stowaway, but it wouldn't be pleasant. She remembered reading that throughout history punishments for stealing were very harsh. *Cutting off a hand or something?* Alex couldn't remember exactly, but she shuddered at the thought. Not only did a stowaway steal passage, but to survive she must be stealing food and water as well. "Don't worry, I won't give you away," Alex whispered as she moved closer.

The girl's jaw dropped, but she quickly clicked it shut and looked wildly around for a way to escape since Alex blocked the hatch. Alex's brow furrowed as the girl seemed ready to panic.

The girl gave up her search and raised her chin in a defiant manner. "I know what you want, but I won't do it. I'll scream if I have to."

Alex gaped at her and then realization came. The girl thought she was about to be raped.

Alex hurried to reassure her, "No, no. I don't want anything, I promise. I won't hurt you. Let's sit, and you can tell me how you came to be here." Alex approached the girl, squeezed into a tight spot next to a water barrel and sat, her knees tucked practically to her chin. She patted the floor of the narrow aisle by her side. "Have a seat. My name's Alex. What's yours?"

After a few moments of shifting from foot to foot, the girl sat. "Evelyn Burges." Her eyes narrowed, and she tilted her head to the side as she peered at Alex. "You won't reveal my presence? Why?"

"Well, I'm not sure what the punishment is for stowaways, but I suspect it's not good, and I wouldn't want anything to happen to you." She shrugged. "You seem harmless, and we have plenty of supplies, so I don't think anyone needs to know."

Evelyn peered closely at her face and suddenly gasped. "You're a woman!"

Alex flinched. She tasted salt as drops of sweat met her tongue when she bit her upper lip.

Evelyn just smiled and said, "Don't worry, I won't tell anyone either."

"How did you know? Is it so obvious?"

"Not obvious, no. There are subtle signs, the gentleness of your eyes, the way you hold yourself… Things a man would never notice. They would never believe a woman capable of passing herself as a man, so it wouldn't occur to them to question. They're so convinced of their superiority and that women are weak and stupid." She sounded bitter and much older than she appeared.

Alex didn't want to know all the girl must have gone through in her short life. "Well, now that we've agreed to keep our secrets. Tell me how you got here."

Evelyn shrugged. "I came to America with my employer. She died shortly after."

Alex waited for her to continue. When it appeared she wasn't going to, Alex prompted, "And…?"

"And her new husband had no use for a lady's maid. Particularly one who did not wish to return his affections. He turned me out without a reference. As my family resides in England, I wished to return." She looked around the cramped space. "This seemed my only option."

"So he just threw you out with nowhere to go?" Alex fisted her hand and slowly released it. "The bastard." She ignored Evelyn's gasp and peered closely at the girl's face. "How old are you?"

"I've seen fourteen years."

"Fourteen! Aren't you a bit young to take a job so far away from your family?"

"Mrs. Ashton lives, lived, in Cambridgeshire, not far from the Thorpe country estate. My mum is an abigail to Lady Thorpe," she explained. "This visit was to last a few months. I was hired when her previous maid could not accompany her on the journey." She wiped a tear from her eye. "Mrs. Ashton became ill on the passage and never recovered."

They talked for a few hours, until Alex realized how late it must be and said goodnight. She promised to return as often as she could with food and water so Evelyn would not have to risk leaving the hold.

As Alex drifted off to sleep, she thought about her plan to spend the voyage relaxing and making plans to find Charlotte. She had barely given her sister a second thought since stepping on board. Oh well, she thought, still plenty of time.

Although, if things continued as they were, she would be lucky to survive the trip.

Chapter Five

April 12 (47 Days Remaining)

Two days after finding Evelyn, Alex slumped against the rail and watched the sun dip into the sea. She tried to dig out some of the dirt from beneath her fingernails, but it was a lost cause. She was going to have to get a bigger hot water heater when she got home. She could probably spend a week showering and still not get clean.

There were compensations. The view, for one. She'd never been on a cruise—who could afford it—but now she got the appeal. The sunset was absolutely breathtaking. The riotous display of color and the way the fading light glistened off the ocean as far as the eye could see was incomparable. Exhausted as she was, the sight still managed to fill her with awe.

The deck shivered as heavy footsteps approached. It was *him*. She knew it. Damn, she should have known better than to relax at the rail during sunset. The captain and his first mate were almost always hanging about at this time of day.

"I was beginning to believe you avoided me." Nicholas leaned an elbow next to hers. "But I could not fathom any reason why you should."

She *had* been avoiding the rail the past few days. The view wasn't quite as relaxing with the two of them around. They would politely include her in their conversation, but they made her so nervous she could only mumble vague replies.

It didn't help that they seemed intent on finding out more about her. A topic about which she was fluent, but couldn't exactly share.

"Of course not, sir." A big fat lie. Alex hoped he couldn't hear the loud and rapid beating of her heart, thundering in her ears. She inched to her left to put space between them. He stood to her right, his scar prominently displayed when she glanced at his handsome profile before staring back out at the horizon.

He tended to flaunt the scars, practically daring people to stare. Of the few new members of the crew on board for this trip, she was the only one he hadn't lambasted with some scathing remark about their rudeness when they did. The old crew took it in stride.

"The correct form of address is my lord or captain." His lofty tone was belied by the twinkle in his eye, giving the impression he teased.

"Of course—Captain." She couldn't bring herself to call him my lord. It just didn't feel natural.

He chuckled. "I prefer that one myself, and yet, I don't seem to have much choice in the matter." He sighed and leaned against the rail while he stared out over the water. "I was never supposed to have the title. My brother was raised for it, I never was. If only Lucius had had a son—but alas, he had four daughters. How he must have hated the thought I would inherit the title."

Alex wasn't sure what to say but felt some type of response was necessary. "I was sorry to hear about your brother."

He shrugged. "We did not get along well. And we

were only half-brothers. Our father married my mother shortly following Lucius's mother's death. I don't think Lucius ever forgave him, and he certainly never forgave my sister and me."

"That's terrible—to have family and not appreciate it. I would have given anything to have a brother or sister as I grew up."

"I thought your business in London had to do with a sister." His brow furrowed as he turned slightly to look at her.

"We weren't raised together. I was told she died in the fire that killed our parents, though I didn't believe it. We'd just found each other again when she disappeared. So I need to get to London as soon as I can. I'm hoping it won't be too difficult to find her once I get there."

"You don't know where she is?"

"No." Alex cringed inwardly at how she must sound—running off to find her sister with no clue how to do it. He probably thought she was an idiot. "But she was raised in England, and we apparently have some distant family connections in London she may have asked for help."

He nodded. "I see. Was it your family that alerted you to your sister's disappearance?"

Alex shook her head. "No. I have no idea if she ever got in touch with them." She shrugged. "I guess I'll find out when I get there."

"Perhaps I can help you."

"That's very kind of you, but I wouldn't want to impose. I'm sure I'll be fine on my own." She didn't plan on staying around any longer than necessary once they arrived in London.

"I insist. My mother knows virtually everyone in London society. I feel sure she can help you. Besides, you are a member of my crew, and I feel compelled to help." Fine lines crinkled the corners of his eyes as he smiled, his face softened by the pleasant tilt of his lips.

Her heart did a little flip, and she tried to ignore the uncomfortable feeling he was being so generous while she was deceiving him. Her disguise was definitely beginning to lose its charm.

She nodded. "Thanks," she said, not knowing how to get out of it gracefully and fully intending to leave before it became an issue. She liked the captain far too much already. Any extra time in his company would make it harder to leave. A complication she didn't need.

A faint pang in the vicinity of her heart made her wonder if it was too late.

****

Nicholas stayed at the rail for a while after Turner left. What had caused him to speak of Lucius? He didn't discuss his brother with anyone, yet tonight he had revealed more to a stranger than he ever had, even to his closest friend.

Somehow, the boy didn't feel like a stranger. From almost the instant they met, Nicholas had felt comfortable in his presence. There had been a brief moment, when he thought Turner was like everyone else who saw his scarred face for the first time, transfixed by the sight and unable to look beyond to the man beneath. The familiar leap of anger died quickly as the moment passed, and the boy seemed to take no further notice of his scars.

Turner's determination to become a valuable member of the crew certainly impressed him. After

Grayson had explained his reasons for hiring the lad, they had agreed he would most likely be of no real use during the journey. Instead, he had proved to be as hard a worker as he claimed. No matter how menial the task, he had done it without complaint and done it well.

Nicholas had surprised himself again with his offer to help the lad find his sister. An offer he suspected Turner had no intention of accepting. Why would he? He obviously had money since he had planned to travel to London as a passenger, so he probably had his own resources to use in his search. Yet he had accepted the change in his plan without complaint and set right to work, not the usual reaction of a person accustomed to wealth and leisure.

He had even earned the respect of the crew without appearing to try, by simply keeping his head down and working hard. As though the respect of the crew was nice to have, but not something he strived to get.

Turner had lost some of that respect by not standing up for himself against the new carpenter, Duff. Nicholas sensed it wasn't fear that kept him from fighting back. He found Turner to be a courageous young man, and his reluctance to face Duff seemed at odds to his personality.

No matter his reasons, Nicholas worried if Turner didn't do something soon, it was going to get worse. Not only would he have to worry about the carpenter, but the rest of the crew as well. The men wouldn't care to have a coward in their midst.

Nicholas was fully aware of Duff's actions. He knew everything that occurred on *The Reliant*. All the incidences had been minor, and since they needed the carpenter, Nicholas had yet to intervene with any punishment. He had surreptitiously requested Grayson switch duty shifts around so the people Duff bullied were generally kept out of his way. He hoped this would be sufficient, but he had some doubts, especially since Duff seemed to make more of an effort to torment Turner than anyone else.

Perhaps it was time for Grayson to have a word with the boy.

****

As Alex was finishing her breakfast rations the next morning, she was surprised to have the Adonis plunk down next to her.

"When you have finished, I would like a word with you, Mr. Turner." Deep lines marred his forehead, and his perfect lips turned down in an uncustomary frown.

Wondering what she possibly could have done wrong, she swallowed the last of her hard tack, which settled like a lump in her stomach. "Yes, sir." She wiped her mouth and stood, waiting nervously for the first mate to rise.

He led her down several corridors until they came to a stop next to the hatch leading into the hold. She tensed. *Oh no. They can't have found Evelyn, can they?*

He turned to her and said, "We can talk here."

"Yes, sir," she said, hiding her trembling hands behind her back. In a small voice, she asked, "Is something wrong?" Best to get it out in the open as soon as possible. She might die from nerves before he got around to it. It could take hours to figure out what he wanted while he danced around a subject.

He looked slightly taken aback at her bluntness but seemed to shrug it off before saying, "As you wish, I will get right to the issue at hand. I am—concerned—

about you."

"Concerned? Why?" she asked in surprise.

"My concern is not entirely for your welfare, to be honest." He smiled slightly. "More about the potential for disruption you may cause among the crew."

"I don't know what you mean," she said, although the little knot in her stomach whispered that she knew all too well, better than he did she hoped, trying not to glance at the hold door.

"Do you know anything of the history of this crew?" he asked.

"Uh, a little."

"We fought in the war together and know each other well. We can count on one another in battle and handle whatever the situation demands. Other than Mr. Duff and a few sailors we hired for this final trip, the captain handpicked each member of this crew. They have all proven themselves under the most difficult of circumstances. This ship runs as smoothly as it does because we know each other so well."

"I had wondered whether it was common, the way everyone works so well together," she interjected. "I mean there are minor fights here and there, but I would have expected more when you coop up such a large group of men together for such a long time."

"Actually it's particularly uncommon. The captain pulled us out of the alleys and slums of London when he bought *The Reliant*. Most of us were left to starve after the war was over, and we were no longer needed to serve in His Majesty's Royal Navy." He gave a harsh laugh. "Deserted by the very people for whom we risked our lives. They had no more care for us than a cavalry cares for its horses, probably less so. For saving us from the slow starvation of our families and ourselves, we would each gladly give our lives for the captain, yet he has done even more for us. Not many captains treat their crew so well." He paused for a moment, as if considering his next words. "Before the captain's mother discovered where he had gone and managed to secure his lieutenant's commission, he served a few years as a common sailor and never forgot the experience. Life on board a navy vessel is extremely harsh. He vowed it would be different when he had a ship of his own."

"I don't understand, what do you mean, secure his commission?"

His eyebrows lifted. "You really know nothing about sailing or the navy, do you?"

"I didn't grow up near the water, so it never came up."

In a voice that sounded like he was teaching the alphabet to a two year old, he explained, "Despite his humble beginning in the Royal Navy, the captain worked his way up to midshipman, and after the required time, he passed his lieutenant's exam with ease. However, he did not have sufficient funds to pay for the confirmation paperwork, nor did he have anyone of influence to secure a position for him. It would have taken many years before one became available to someone without connections. However, his mother contacted a few of his late father's friends and made it all possible."

"What do you mean when his mother found out where he was?" she asked. "Did he run away from home or something?"

Looking like he was beginning to regret saying

anything at all, he said, "The captain does not discuss this. You will have to ask him if you want to know details. Suffice it to say, his experience in the navy is why this ship is run as it is."

"So what does this have to do with me?" she asked.

"As I have said, we know each other well. We do not know you."

"Well, they haven't exactly made an effort to get to know me. So there's not much I can do about that," she said. "Why are you telling me this?" She fought back a giggle at the way he sucked in a deep breath and let it out slowly, as if counting to ten. Perhaps she was a little too direct. The poor man always looked nonplussed when forced to talk to her.

"The crew wonders whether you would be any assistance in battle or if you would turn tail and hide."

"Are we going into battle?" she asked, startled. Until his meaning became clear and the heat rushed to her face as anger spurted suddenly to life. It was too much. "I've done everything I've been asked no matter how awful, and I haven't complained once. How do they know what I would do? They've made a point of keeping their distance. So I don't give a shi—I don't care what they think." She was shouting by the end and glared at a sailor stumbling past the other end of the corridor because he was paying more attention to her than where he was going.

"Please lower your voice to a civilized level."

She bit her tongue to hold back a sharp reply.

"It is not a matter of whether you shoulder your share of the workload. The captain and I have been pleasantly surprised in that regard. We did not set our hopes too high."

"I'm overwhelmed by your praise," she stated wryly, still smarting from the thought that the entire crew apparently thought she was a coward.

"You should be. However, we were discussing the situation with the carpenter."

"We were?"

"Yes."

"What about him? He's my problem, why should it matter to anyone else how I handle it?" she asked in confusion.

"You're not dealing with him. You have let his taunts continue unchallenged. You have, in fact, been a coward."

"That's crazy! Just because I don't want to fight doesn't make me a coward."

"It's not a question of what you want. You have little choice. It is simply a matter of standing up for yourself rather than letting the situation worsen. To the crew, you appear to have no concern for your honor. The only answer is that you must be afraid."

"Humph." She looked him in the eye. "And what do you think?"

"I must agree with the captain on this one. I think you have reasons for ignoring Mr. Duff, and though I cannot imagine what they may be, I do not believe it is cowardice."

"The captain thinks the same?" A surge of warmth entered her chest. She didn't want to admit how important it was that Nicholas think well of her.

"Yes. He convinced me of it." He looked searchingly at her. "Do you care to tell me what those reasons are?"

Not sure how to respond, she thought for a moment

before speaking. "Well, I wasn't sure what the rules are about fighting. You and the captain helped me when I really needed it. I didn't want to repay your generosity by causing trouble. Besides, I believe that fighting should be a last resort. Sticks and stones and all that," she quipped, waving her hand airily in front of her face. How shocked would he be at the real answer? *I'm afraid that if I fight the bully my disguise will somehow slip, and you'll find out I'm really a girl.* She would love to see his face though, she thought, stifling another giggle.

"Consider yourself warned. Either you prove to the crew you are not a coward, or life is going to get much more difficult for you." He crossed his arms and looked down his nose at her. Deep furrows etched his brow as he frowned.

"I understand you don't want the crew annoyed, or distracted or whatever…" She shrugged. "…but I don't care what everyone thinks. Why do I need to prove anything?"

"If you think Mr. Duff's taunts are unpleasant to deal with, just wait until the entire crew is on his side."

****

Alex thought about her conversation with the first mate as she continued to have problems with Mr. Duff. He pushed or tripped her when the opportunity arose. If he couldn't abuse her physically, he made cutting remarks at her expense to the rest of the crew.

Now that she had a bit more insight into the crew's thoughts, she could feel the time was coming when she would have to defend herself more definitively. The crew would demand it. They were becoming less friendly with every run-in she had with Mr. Duff. The crew's respect continued to slip away, but she didn't know what to do. She thought she was dealing very well with the taunts and torments, but it was obvious the crew didn't.

Men are strange creatures. They would prefer she fight and risk getting seriously hurt instead of being sensible and ignoring the taunts. And she was under no illusion that anyone thought she could win. Mr. Duff was a big man. No one who looked at the two of them would pick Alex to be the winner in a fight. They took her inaction for cowardice, and this was apparently a horrible sin for a man.

The funny thing was she felt pretty confident she could beat Mr. Duff in a fair fight. He was a brute, but he didn't have any particular fighting skills. She had a black belt in karate. He wouldn't know what hit him. But despite her concern about being unmasked, she did believe that fighting should only be a last resort. That concept had been instilled in her for as long as she'd studied martial arts.

Then one day, Mr. Duff pushed her too far.

Chapter Six

April 18 (41 Days Remaining)

Alex watched the sun begin to set while listening to the pleasant sound of Nicholas's voice as he and Mr. Grayson discussed the progress they'd made that day. They'd only spent a few minutes with her at the rail when a woman's piercing scream ripped through the air.

Alex whipped around and ran for the cargo hold, ignoring Nicholas and Mr. Grayson's startled exclamations. Fear froze the blood in her veins as she ran. Someone had found Evelyn. An ominous silence followed the initial scream, heightening Alex's fear rather than soothing it.

The situation was worse than she'd feared when she reached the hold and looked down through the open door. Evelyn struggled on the ground with a man lying on top of her, his one hand covered her mouth while the other groped at her skirts as she kicked and thrashed about wildly.

As Alex rushed down the ladder, the man reached back and struck Evelyn hard in the face and the young girl went still.

Fury burst through every pore of Alex's body as she kicked him in the ass, sending him flying over to the other side of the now still girl. The man looked up in surprise, his hand moving quickly to something at his waist. Alex recognized Mr. Duff with the glint of steel in his hand, and her brain registered the fact he was holding a knife, though she didn't take her eyes off his.

He looked at her and sneered, "You! Bugger off, I'm busy. If you're lucky I won't tell the captain you're the one been keeping this little bit o' fluff down here." His lip curled in a nasty version of a grin as he stood and tucked the knife back into his belt. "That's right. I saw you sneaking around here earlier and came to find out what you were up to. Figured I'd have me a bit o' fun 'fore I go to the captain." He stretched his arms behind his back, hitting up against the bulkhead, apparently confident Alex wasn't a threat.

When Alex spoke, it was in a voice so cold and calm she surprised even herself. "Step away from her, now."

The smile on Mr. Duff's face flickered briefly, and she caught a glimpse of uncertainty in their depths before he recovered. "I ain't done yet."

Before he could turn back toward Evelyn, Alex struck. She punched him hard in the gut. He doubled over, and she grabbed his arm, pulling him forward and using his own momentum to push him toward the ladder. He landed sprawled on his hands and knees, right at the feet of Nicholas and Mr. Grayson.

Nicholas took in the scene at a glance, and to her surprise he nodded, acknowledging the look in her eyes and her silent plea to deal with Mr. Duff herself.

"Both of you, topside. You can fight this out above deck. Mr. Grayson, take this girl to my cabin and see to her welfare. Join us when you are through." Nicholas preceded them out of the hold.

Mr. Duff staggered up from his position on the floor and followed him. "Captain, he been hidin' her in here the whole time. Stealin' food and water from the crew. I was jus' about to go an' get you when he attacked me fer no good reason."

Nicholas turned and even Alex quailed at the look in his eyes, glad it wasn't directed at her. "I saw exactly what you were about to do, and it did not involve fetching me. You are lucky I do not just slit your throat right now. Instead, I shall allow the two of you to provide some entertainment for the crew before I settle on punishments for your crimes." He ascended the ladder without another backward glance.

Seeing he couldn't expect any help from that quarter, Mr. Duff silently followed. Alex close behind. As she emerged from below, her eyes not yet adjusted to the relatively bright light above deck, he aimed a vicious kick at her head.

She had expected a dirty trick and managed to grab his foot and send him sprawling onto his backside, giving her the chance to reach the deck unharmed.

Evelyn's scream had caught the crew's attention, and the majority stood around watching. They gasped and muttered angrily at Mr. Duff's underhanded tactics. His face flushed as he looked around at the large audience.

Alex yanked off her shoes and socks, and then circled Mr. Duff as he struggled to his feet. The shaking of her limbs stilled, and ice water ran through her veins. She flexed her fingers and cleared her mind. Focus was the key. She thought of all she had learned in karate class. She could win this fight but would have to be very careful. Mr. Duff was no match for her skills, but he was stronger and larger. If he landed one solid punch, she'd be finished.

No one made any sound as Mr. Duff mirrored Alex's movements. They circled each other in silence until it became too much for Mr. Duff and his taunts began.

Alex struggled to keep the rage from her face and making any rash moves as his words penetrated the preternatural calm that had descended upon her.

"Worried your little whore wouldn't want you anymore after she had a real man?" He laughed and seemed to regain his confidence with each word he uttered. "She sure was eager to try. You must notta been doin' right by her. Shoulda slapped her round some. Bit of a hellcat that one. Wanted it rough, and I was willin' to give it a go."

The thought of what he would have done to that poor child if Alex hadn't been there drove every other thought out of her head. She attacked.

She sensed rather than heard the indrawn breaths of the crew but gave them no thought as she reached her target. It should have been over quickly, but there's no telling what will happen in situations like this.

****

Nicholas watched the two men circle each other. He wasn't sure it was the wisest course of action, but he had read the look in young Turner's eyes and recognized his need to deal with this himself.

He watched them closely. Duff had the advantage in height and weight—probably why he had selected the boy to bully in the first place. He appeared to pose no threat. But Nicholas had seen the way Turner handled himself in the hold. He was small but seemed to have some fighting skills. Nicholas hoped it would be enough to keep him from sustaining any real injury.

Grayson appeared above deck, the girl beside him. She looked pale and weak but had a determined look on her face.

"I believe I told you to bring her to my cabin, Mr. Grayson. This is no place for a woman."

"I tried, but as soon as she came to, she insisted on coming straight to you. She claims Mr. Turner did not assist her on board and only recently found her."

The girl lifted her chin and looked up at Nicholas. "I alone am to blame. Mr. Turner had nothing to do with…" Her words trailed off as she caught sight of the two men facing each other and realized what was happening.

Nicholas was surprised to see a look of panic enter her eyes.

"Stop this. You can't let them fight!"

She obviously felt something for Turner and worried for his safety, so he used a gentle voice to reassure her. "He will be all right. The worst he shall receive is a few bruises, maybe a broken nose or rib. I will not allow it go too far."

"But that man has a knife! He'll kill her!" She clapped her hands over her mouth, stifling a gasp.

It took a moment for her words to sink in. Nicholas looked at the girl in amazement. "Her?"

"I—I meant him. He'll kill him." But it was too late.

With understanding came a rush of anxiety. Even as Nicholas turned to the two combatants, he realized he couldn't stop the fight. A flash of steel at Duff's waist drew his gaze and the words "willin' to give it a go." reached his ears a fraction of a second before Turner, *Miss* Turner, attacked.

The muscles all along his neck and back stiffened. His mouth fell open as he watched along with the rest of the crew as she launched herself at the man who topped her by at least a foot and landed a punishing blow before he'd even had a chance to bring his fists up. The look on Duff's face was almost comical as he realized his would-be victim wasn't such an easy target.

The sunset they'd been admiring moments before created shadows across the deck and the combatants, making the fight all the more dangerous. The crew brought out lanterns and held them high to light the scene.

It soon became clear Turner would be victorious, and the crew rowdily cheered her on. They did not view Duff with fondness.

Nicholas worried that any interference on his part would distract Turner and in that moment provide an opening for Duff's knife. Though he had yet to draw the weapon, Nicholas was sure he would. A man like Duff would not think twice about killing to save his own skin.

Nicholas knew Turner also carried a knife, but he didn't think she would use it. No, if this fight turned deadly, it would be at Duff's insistence.

Yet, even as he looked for an opening to put an end to it, he found himself enjoying the spectacle. Were she a man, he would have relaxed and cheered them on with the rest of the crew. He had never seen this type of fighting and marveled that a woman displayed this type of skill. He would never have believed it possible were he not seeing it for himself.

A fierce desire to see Alex—he could no longer think of her as Turner, Turner was a young boy, Alex was a fully grown woman—naked came unbidden to his mind as he watched her bend in ways he'd never thought possible. His body tightened as her movements gave evidence to the lithe body hidden beneath her disguise. His imagination filled in what her clothing concealed, and he marveled that he had not realized her true nature from the start.

He had assumed from her delicate frame she was younger than she claimed, but now he felt like an idiot for not realizing only a woman could have such purity of features. He longed to see her in appropriate clothing. He imagined she would be quite beautiful.

She moved gracefully around the deck, her whole body involved in the fight. For not only did she punch with her hands, she kicked with her feet and contorted her body in a variety of ways to evade Duff's attempts to reach her. With each strike, she cried, "Key-Yah!" in a loud voice that carried across the deck and emphasized each blow Duff received.

Fear mixed with pride as Nicholas watched her block a blow with her arm while simultaneously stepping away, causing Duff to stumble forward right into the foot she'd brought up to kick him in the sternum, sending him flying once more onto his arse.

He slid several feet across the deck, before coming to a stop against the mainmast. A snarl curled his lips, and he wiped spittle from his chin as he pushed up, bracing himself against the mast. He staggered forward, seemingly having difficulty keeping to his feet. Until he got within striking distance.

Nicholas's thoughts abruptly returned to the

present as the crew gasped as one. He took an involuntary step forward, then came to an abrupt halt in surprise.

With a flurry of movement the crew would no doubt recount for many years to come, the fight came to an abrupt end.

Duff let fly a punch that seemed sure to connect with Alex's head when suddenly, her head was out of range. Her body inverted. Her hair trailed along the wood planking. One hand touched the deck, and her upper body seemed impossibly close to her left leg. With a loud shout and grunt of effort, her right foot connected with Duff's chin, knocking him to the ground. She leapt onto the prone man, landing another blow to his face.

Nicholas watched for movement, but she appeared to have knocked Duff unconscious. She stood and stepped back, only just then realizing they had drawn a crowd. A becoming blush spread across her cheeks as her gaze found his, and their eyes connected. A bolt of heat shot straight to his lungs and restricted his breathing until a movement behind her drew his attention.

Duff rose behind her, the knife in his hand aimed at her unsuspecting back. Even as he ran to intervene, he knew he would be too late.

Chapter Seven

April 18 (41 Days Remaining)

Alex gasped in great lungfuls of air as she stood over Mr. Duff's prostrate form. She hadn't realized how nervous she'd been until this moment. The tide of rage and adrenaline that had kept her going slowly ebbed away, leaving her shaking and weak.

The sound of cheering brought her back to reality with a crash. She looked up to see the entire crew applauding as they made their way toward her from the various vantage points from which they had watched.

Heat spread across her cheeks as she looked around shyly, eager to know what Nicholas thought of her skills. She searched for some sign he was impressed.

Their gazes connected for a brief moment. She wasn't sure whether she imagined the heat blazing from the depths of his gorgeous hazel eyes before his gaze drifted past her. As he started toward her, his look became one of mingled fury and fear, which warned her of the danger she suddenly sensed from behind.

She jumped to the side, simultaneously turning toward the threat. She was quick, but not quick enough, and the blade sliced through the thick padding of her disguise to the flesh of her stomach.

She stood in shock as Nicholas appeared at her side, having managed to knock Mr. Duff unconscious with a single blow. How could such a large man move so fast? She pressed a hand to her wound and swayed.

Nicholas held out a hand to steady her. "Are you injured?"

She gathered herself enough to form a reply. She wanted nothing more than to fall into Nicholas's strong arms, but it wasn't going to happen. No room existed for a show of weakness given her current deception. She put on a brave face and managed a weak smile.

"I'm fine. Just a scratch." She could see the concerned and skeptical look in his eyes. She wasn't fooling anyone. She looked around to give herself time to think and spotted Evelyn standing anxiously a few feet away. "I suppose I should clean it up a bit though. If you don't mind, perhaps I should go below and have Evelyn take a look at it?"

She bit her lip as she waited for his reply. If he allowed it, she had some hope that punishment for their crime wouldn't be too severe. If he was angry, he wouldn't give them time together. Besides, he had allowed her to fight Mr. Duff. He'd looked almost as sickened as she'd felt about what could have happened to the poor girl.

Her side stung where she pressed her shirt against it. Nausea threatened. She couldn't stand here much longer. Plus, she needed a moment alone with Evelyn to find out whether Nicholas or Mr. Grayson had given any indication of the punishment they planned. Flogging was a common punishment for more serious crimes aboard ships of this day, but Nicholas was not the kind of man who would inflict such punishment on a woman. If worse came to worse, she would reveal her deception. Besides the fact she didn't think she would be able to handle being flogged, she certainly didn't want her secret revealed in such a way before the crew.

"Good idea. Mr. Grayson, help Mr. Turner to my cabin. I'll help the young woman gather what supplies she requires and bring her down shortly." Nicholas scrutinized the crowd, many of whom jostled each other to get a closer view. "Show's over. Everyone return to your duties."

He motioned to two burly sailors standing next to the still unconscious Mr. Duff. "See that he is locked up. I will deal with him later. Unfortunately, we need him. For now."

The two men nodded before they picked up Mr. Duff, none too gently, and carried him off.

Alex clutched at the hand Mr. Grayson held out. He winced as she squeezed with all her strength. She needed to take her mind off the pain.

"For now?" she gasped out.

Mr. Grayson nodded, and they made their way, slowly, to the captain's cabin.

"Yes," he said. "Were a carpenter not a necessity on a journey such as this, it's doubtful Mr. Duff would survive much longer. As it is, we may have need of his skills, and the captain is making sure the crew knows a more fitting punishment will come, even if it must be delayed for the duration."

"They'd kill him?" she asked. "How'd they know so quickly?"

He frowned and scratched at the five o'clock shadow covering his jaw. "They watched. The captain himself couldn't have torn them away from the spectacle."

She shook her head. "No. I mean, Evelyn." The

effort of talking drained her energy. She leaned more heavily on Mr. Grayson's arm. "Who told?"

He braced himself against her weight and snorted. "No one. They are as yet unaware of what occurred in the hold. They merely think you decided to defend yourself. His despicable show of cowardice during the fight is what has earned their wrath."

"Oh." *Men are strange creatures.*

****

Mr. Grayson left Alex alone the second he saw her safely ensconced in a chair. To distract herself from the pain, she inspected Nicholas's cabin as she waited for Evelyn. Since her serving duties ended with carrying dinner to the door, she'd never made it all the way inside.

The comfort level was not what she would have expected. *The Reliant* was a merchant ship. The design screamed it in the details. While everything was clean and in immaculate condition, it was also simple with little ornamentation. This room looked nothing like the rest of the ship.

The room, larger than she had imagined, had been the setting for a few of her tamer fantasies concerning the gorgeous captain. Most of them involved the captain being so overcome with desire for her they never make it to his bed.

The massive bed in question stood off to the left, covered in a beige and brown comforter, with a pile of pillows that made Alex groan with longing. She'd been sleeping in a hammock slung up in the crew quarters and missed the comfort of a real bed.

A large screen protruded from the wall—no, from the *bulkhead*—to the side of the bed. It would block the bed from the rest of the room when open, but it was folded back at the moment, so she had a clear view.

The comforter was flipped back as if waiting for Nicholas to slip naked between the sheets, stretching his large, well-muscled form luxuriously against the soft fabric and…

And she put that train of thought firmly from her mind before she made a fool of herself flinging into Nicholas's arms the moment he walked in the door.

She rose from her chair and stepped closer to a curving wall of windows that dominated the opposite side of the room. The glow of the moon and stars reflected off the water, creating a dazzling light show that took her breath away. The sun had finished its descent during the fight, and the stars had come out to take its place. She hadn't realized the fight had taken quite so long. No wonder she was exhausted.

Catching her reflection in the windows, she grimaced. Her hair hung in lank strips around a pale face. Streaks of filth and a touch of blood accented the gauntness of her cheeks. Her hand clutched her side. She released the pressure slightly, pleased to see the bleeding had stopped.

It still hurt.

Her clothing was ruined. Blood drenched the side of her shirt around a hole torn in the fabric. She could see the binding, which was holding together better than her shirt due to all the padding that disguised her slim waist. Her clothing hung loosely. She'd added additional holes to her belt loop to keep her pants up. The change in diet from her normal frozen dinners and fast food to the very simply cooked ship's fare combined with the change in daily activity had caused her to lose weight.

Blood and dirt covered her pants. She didn't think she would be able to salvage any of it, and her other clothing wasn't in the best shape either. With so few items of clothing to wear, they had all taken a beating. She'd ditched her neon pink panties when she'd narrowly escaped being caught with them while she attempted to get them clean. The only positive thing was her appearance fit with the rest of the crew. All the dirt and grime helped to hide her feminine features.

Good thing she didn't have a mirror. She hadn't felt self-conscious about her appearance until now. It dashed her erotic visions of Nicholas being overwhelmed by her beauty. All she'd attract like this were bloodhounds. What dog could resist her stench?

Turning away from the windows, she almost knocked into an enormous desk. A few heavy objects clustered in the corner, but it was mostly cleaned off at the moment. She imagined Nicholas used the knick-knacks to weigh down the charts stored in a handsome storage cabinet to one side of the windows.

The desk did double duty as a dining table. The captain took his meals in his cabin with the first mate and often some of the other higher ranked members of the crew. Several chairs were pushed to the side near the cabinet, in addition to the one behind the desk.

She selected one to sit on and hissed at the renewed stinging in her side. What was keeping Evelyn with the bandages? Surely she should have been here by now!

If she weren't so exhausted, she could pass the time with one of the books jam-packed on the shelves that covered the bulkheads. She'd always thought literacy wasn't exactly widespread in this time. Instead, she'd found Nicholas's books were a kind of library for the crew's use. She'd been tempted to borrow one but hadn't had enough free time to bother.

The books contributed to the masculine feel of the room. Most had fancy dark leather binding with gold lettering on the spines, but those that weren't seemed to be covered in cardboard or something, she couldn't really tell without looking closer. And she wasn't sure she could manage to get up, let alone stand around examining the bookshelf.

The books were intimidating, actually. She would need to have her PhD just to peruse the titles. She certainly couldn't picture throwing any of them in her bag and heading to the beach. On the other hand, they gave off a sense of peace and tranquility that made the room comfortable and welcoming. The garish coloring and sensational covers of modern paperbacks would have ruined the effect.

Alex twisted in her chair to see more but gasped as her clothes rubbed against her cut. She wanted to remove her clothes so she could get a sense of the damage but was afraid Nicholas would return with Evelyn at any moment. She couldn't be half-dressed when he came in. Instead, she faced forward and wondered what kept them.

****

Nicholas led Evelyn to the cargo hold. He wanted to speak to her privately without a chance someone might overhear. She followed him without question, only the stiff set of her shoulders indicating her nervousness.

As he closed the door behind them and turned to face her, a wave of irritation washed over him. She stood huddled against the far bulkhead, looking at him with eyes opened wide with fear and a hint of resignation.

His anger left him as he realized her fear would be justified. He did not intend to punish her, but how could she know that? Most captains would be certain to bring some punishment to bear in such a situation. His shoulders twitched in memory, and he could practically feel the lash of the starters across his shoulder blades. The bosun's mate on his first ship had been fond of prodding everyone with those short ropes, whether they were working diligently or not.

He sighed. "I mean you no harm. I simply wish to speak with you without chance of being overheard."

She nodded, obviously not believing a word he said, her hands gripped together so tightly her knuckles turned white. "Yes, my lord."

He folded his arms across his chest and leaned back against the bulkhead. "I don't wish for you to tell Miss Turner…Is that her real name?"

"Yes, my lord. Her given name is Alexandra."

The headache plaguing him eased slightly. Knowing Alex had not lied about her name relieved his mind somewhat. "I would prefer you not mention to her that I know her secret."

Evelyn's mouth gaped open. Whatever she had been expecting, it hadn't been that. "Whyever not?"

"It would be extremely unsettling to the crew. If I must acknowledge she is a woman, then we cannot go on as we have done. It would be necessary to remove her from her duties and provide suitable quarters. Any number of accommodations would be required. I would rather avoid the disruption."

Evelyn furrowed her brows. "I don't understand. She would not demand any such changes. She may be a lady by birth, but I do not believe she expects to be treated as such."

"Lady?"

"Yes, I'm sure of it." She edged closer to the exit, while trying to stay out of Nicholas's reach. "Should not we return to her? I should see to her injury."

She held something back, but he was willing to let the subject drop. He did not wish the girl to know how deep his interest in her *lady* ran. "As soon as you give me your word you won't tell her what I know."

"I will not betray her trust." The chit raised her chin stubbornly.

Nicholas admired her loyalty.

"Will you keep silent to protect her then? I am unsure how the crew would react to the news the young boy they welcomed into their midst has been lying to them. They may require she pay for her crimes." He held up his fingers one-by-one. "Failing to disclose your presence, stealing food, misleading myself and my crew—she faces the lash." Nicholas kept his face perfectly blank. *Would she call his bluff?*

The blood drained from Evelyn's face. "You wouldn't lash a woman!"

"No." He couldn't bring himself to lie about such a thing convincingly. "But there are other punishments..." He let the words trail off to let her imagination supply the rest. "I will waive all punishment in return for your silence."

"You'll give me your word as a gentleman that she will not be punished?"

"Yes."

"Agreed."

****

Alex gripped her head to keep it from exploding. The bang of the opening door made her wince. She'd been waiting so long, she'd wondered if they'd forgotten about her. They had probably only been a few minutes behind her, but it felt as though an hour had gone by.

Evelyn rushed to her side the moment she entered the room, Alex's small bag of belongings swinging from her hand.

Nicholas stayed at the door and said, "Let me know if you need anything, miss." He pulled the door shut behind him when he left.

"Can you lock the door?" Alex asked Evelyn.

Evelyn examined the door. "There's no key." She looked back at Alex. "I don't think he'll come in; it should be safe."

"Take a chair and lodge it against the door. I don't want to take any chances."

Evelyn shrugged and followed her instructions while Alex started to undress. She couldn't, however, manage very far. Her hands shook, and she couldn't steady them long enough to undo the buttons on her shirt.

"Here, I'll do that." Evelyn brushed her hands aside and with the practiced confidence of a lady's maid proceeded to undress her, slowing only to carefully pull the bindings away, which had become stuck to the wound from all the blood.

Alex looked down at herself and cursed, nauseated by the sight. She quickly looked away.

Evelyn peered closely at the razor-thin, five-inch

gash and seemed encouraged at the sight.

"It bled quite profusely but doesn't look serious. Hold still while I clean it." Evelyn quietly set to work, a frown creasing her brow as she bent to her task, avoiding Alex's eye.

Alex watched her in silence, wincing now and then, but feeling much better now she could see it wasn't too serious. Evelyn's attitude was bothering her more than the wound. She looked like she was biting her tongue, itching to make some comment, but too unsure of herself and their friendship to risk crossing the line.

When the bandaging was complete and Evelyn had helped Alex dress, she bustled around cleaning up, maintaining that same irritating and uncharacteristic silence. After enduring this silent treatment for several minutes, Alex had had enough. "Go ahead. Say whatever's on your mind."

Evelyn looked up, her lips compressed into a thin line, clamped so tight they turned white. She let out a gusty breath, and the words finally burst forth, seemingly against her will. "Why did you interfere? You were hurt. It could have been much worse!" Tears slid slowly down her cheeks. Guilt made Alex flinch as she realized how much Evelyn had worried. "You may be dressed like a man, but you're not. You should have let it alone."

Alex started to protest, appalled at the idea of standing by and letting that man rape a child.

Evelyn brought her hand up in a silencing motion and continued her tirade, "How do you think I would have felt had you been seriously hurt or died defending my honor? After all you've done for me, I couldn't bear it." She was sobbing so hard by this time, she barely got the words out.

"What was I supposed to do? Let the bastard rape you?" Alex asked incredulously.

"Better my virtue than your life!"

They stared at each other in silence for several seconds. Alex didn't know what to say. How could she convince Evelyn she had no choice? That she wouldn't have been able to live with herself had she done nothing.

Alex looked away first, too tired to continue. "I'm sorry I worried you, but it wasn't your fault. No, no, listen to me," she said as Evelyn looked ready to protest. "Mr. Duff's been after me since we set sail. I've been trying to avoid a confrontation, and the situation's been getting worse daily. At least with the way it happened today, I was prepared. If he had forced the issue, he would have done it when I was at a much greater disadvantage." She leaned back in the chair and let her eyes drift shut. "Besides, it's over now, and no one found out about me."

Chapter Eight

April 19 (40 Days Remaining)

Alex woke the next morning floating on a cloud. But the scent was wrong. A cloud might smell like the sea and salt breezes but wouldn't have that indescribable scent that made her nipples tighten and her stomach tingle. She frowned and stretched sore muscles, stopping suddenly as the pain in her side recalled her to reality. Her eyes flew open.

Sunlight flooded the room and ricocheted off a beautiful crystal paperweight on one of the shelves, causing an eye-catching array of rainbows to chase across the ceiling.

She turned her head ever so slowly to the side and released the breath she hadn't realized she held when she saw the empty space beside her. She couldn't remember getting into Nicholas's bed. The last thing she remembered was talking to Evelyn and resting her eyes.

She glanced furtively around the room. She clutched at the sheet tucked up beneath her chin. The whisper soft cotton brushed against her naked breasts. Where were her clothes? How the hell was she going to get out of here?

The door banged open, and Evelyn walked through carrying a tray. She kicked the door shut behind her with a loud thump.

Alex let the sheet she had instinctively clutched to her chin drop an inch, and her stomach growled at the delicious smells wafting from the tray.

Evelyn flashed a cheery smile. "Cook fixed you something special for breakfast. Seems you're a real hero now. Defending the innocent…" Pointing to herself, she lowered her head modestly, peering up coquettishly through her rapidly fluttering eyelashes. "…defeating the monster, and providing quite a show for the crew at the same time. They can't stop talking about the fight." She placed the tray on the bed and gestured for Alex to help herself.

Alex dug into the food, ravenously hungry after the exertions of the previous night. She slowed down when she noticed Evelyn's disapproving look, which changed to a smile when Alex selected a dainty piece of egg with her fork. Evelyn pulled up a chair next to the bed and sat, immediately setting to work deftly applying needle and thread to Alex's damp, yet blood-free bindings.

"What happened last night?" Alex asked between small forkfuls. "I don't remember anything past you bandaging me up."

"You fell asleep in the chair, and when the captain came to see how you were, he said you could use his room for the night."

"How did I end up in the bed?"

Apparently consumed with completing a particularly difficult stitch, Evelyn mumbled a reply about Alex waking enough to stumble over.

Alex wondered if she had given Evelyn a rough time but decided not to ask. "Well, whatever. Tell me about the captain. Has he said what he plans to do about us?"

Evelyn looked up and seemed to consider the question carefully. "I don't think you'll be punished. Like I said, you're a bit of a hero to the crew; it might be hard to punish you without causing trouble."

She looked back at her sewing. "As for me, he hasn't said anything, but I don't think it will be too bad. Everyone's been very nice, much nicer than I deserve. I haven't been treated like a criminal at all. If I'm lucky, he'll hire me as a scullery maid and garner my wages until I've paid him back. It will take many years, but he seems like a kind man, and I could do worse than being maid to a Marquess."

"And if you're not lucky?" Alex didn't like the sound of Evelyn's best-case scenario—indentured servitude had never been described as a pleasant situation in any history book she had ever read. If Evelyn considered that the best case, how bad would the worst case be?

"If luck is not with me, he'll consign me to debtor's prison."

She shrugged as if it was no big deal, but her hands trembled, and the moisture in her eyes collected as she tried to hold back tears.

Alex wrapped the sheet around herself and got up to put an arm around Evelyn's shoulders. "Don't worry. It'll be all right."

Evelyn turned in her arms, and Alex held her tight as she wept, a few silent tears sliding down her own cheeks to fall unheeded on Evelyn's head.

Surely, Nicholas wasn't the kind of man to do such a thing? But then again, how well did she really know him or his views? From what she'd read, and granted most of her knowledge was from historical fiction and romances, but still, the aristocracy wasn't known for its concern for the serving class. Nicholas might have no idea what would happen if he handed Evelyn over to the authorities thinking he had no other choice.

Whatever the case, Alex couldn't bear the thought of anything more happening to Evelyn. She had to help the girl, no matter the cost. She began to form a plan as she patted Evelyn on the back, waiting for the tears to subside.

****

A short while later, wearing her second best set of clothes with the newly repaired binding clinging damp and clammy to her skin but still disguising her figure, Alex went up on deck to confront Nicholas.

At this time of day, he would be on the quarterdeck with Mr. Grayson, overseeing activity on board and issuing orders. Unlike many merchant captains, Nicholas didn't spend a great amount of time in his cabin. He preferred to be above deck when possible.

She didn't get past a few steps before the crew besieged her to shake her hand and discuss the fight.

She paused to bask in the crew's newfound admiration and let them bolster her spirits before the task ahead of her. She hadn't realized how much it had bothered her being alienated from the crew as she'd been. She'd told herself it didn't matter what they thought of her, avoiding a fight had been the wisest course of action. Knowing she was right hadn't made her feel any better.

But now she was welcome into the fold with open arms. She had never felt quite so accepted before in her life. To these men, she had shown her courage, and that was all they needed.

With promises of an exhibition of her skills once she felt completely healed, she was allowed to make her way to the quarterdeck.

She paused when he came into view. He laughed at something said behind him, his face turned to the side. The wind plastered his shirt tight to his body, exhibiting an impressive display of muscular chest and arms. His hair whipped around his head, tugged loose from the little strip of leather he usually wore.

Thank goodness he didn't follow the common practice among sailors of using tar to keep their hair under control. She loved the way his hair looked flying this way and that. She could imagine what it would be like to bury her hands in it.

He belonged on the cover of a men's magazine with a caption, "Ideal Body in 15 Minutes a Day—See Page 95 for our exclusive new workout." Or maybe the cover of one of her favorite romance novels, all that was missing was a beautiful heroine glued to his side, looking breathlessly into his face, waiting to be kissed.

Alex blinked and shook herself when she realized she pictured herself as the heroine. The image sent a thrill all the way to her toes.

He turned then and saw her. She forced herself to focus and move toward him, outwardly calm. She hoped he would attribute her flushed cheeks to the exertion of being up and about so soon.

"Feeling better?" he asked, as she came up alongside him.

"Yes. Thank you," she replied. "I appreciate you letting me use your cabin. I hope you weren't too uncomfortable last night?" *Jeez, what am I doing? Get to the point already!*

"Not at all. I bunked with Mr. Grayson. I had worse quarters in the Navy. It was no problem for one night."

She glanced at Mr. Grayson, but he made a great show of examining a length of rope and seemed disinclined to join their conversation. His attitude toward her had changed, but she put that thought to the back of her mind so she could concentrate on the task at hand.

She took a deep breath and looked Nicholas straight in the eye as she asked, "So what do you plan to do about Evelyn?"

"Shouldn't you be worried about what I plan to do with you?"

A cry rose in her throat, but she swallowed it down. Reassured by Evelyn's confidence she wouldn't be punished, she had convinced herself she was safe. With his words her fear returned, but she squared her shoulders and replied, "Obviously that's a concern, too, but I'm more worried about Evelyn."

"I see." He looked away from her and appeared lost in thought as he watched the crew going about their work, an occasional laugh or muffled curse reaching their ears from time to time.

She kept her silence and watched with him as she waited.

After a while, he returned his gaze to her and said, "I have yet to decide what is best. I am within my rights to throw her back into the cargo hold for the duration of the trip and turn her over to the authorities when we get home. Most other captains I know would do so, or worse."

He paused and Alex held her breath.

"She owes me for her passage, and she has caused quite a disruption. I am not particularly fond of Mr. Duff, but I would not be facing such problems if she were not on board."

Alex gritted her teeth to keep from saying anything. She had a strong urge to throttle him for implying it was Evelyn's fault Mr. Duff had tried to rape her, but killing the captain wouldn't exactly help her cause, so she resisted the enormous temptation.

Her thoughts must have shown on her face, however, because Nicholas said, "I am not saying it was her fault. We both know Mr. Duff is a..." He rubbed the back of his neck and gave a slight cough before continuing. "I believe you know what he is. However, you must admit, he could not have tried to abuse her if she were not on board in the first place."

Alex saw his logic and allowed herself to relax the tiniest bit. "I see your point." She waited for him to continue, but he remained silent, and she couldn't wait any longer. "I may have a solution for you, if you want to hear it."

"Please do."

"I could pay her passage."

He gave her an odd look. "Why?"

"What do you mean, why? Why does it matter?"

"I am merely curious. You barely know her, and yet you have risked your job, your life, and now your money for her. Why?"

Alex shrugged, but before she even realized she planned to answer, the words burst bitterly from her mouth, "Because she's just a child! She should be at home worrying about what to wear or whether some boy likes her. She shouldn't be on her own trying to figure out where her next meal will come from."

"You sound as if you are speaking from experience."

"I am. I left…I set out on my own when I was a little older than she is. I remember those days living hand to mouth, always worrying where to go, how to eat." Alex turned away and watched the light dance on the water as she struggled to keep back the tears.

When she had herself under control, she continued, "I just don't want to see anything happen to her. She has family in London. She can return to them and go on with her life. She won't be able to do that if she's under an obligation to you."

His voice was quiet when he spoke, and Alex thought she detected traces of sympathy and understanding in his tone, "Fair enough."

"Thank you." Alex reached up around her neck and pulled out one of the gold necklaces she kept hidden there. She had pulled out the wrong one and went to tuck it back in, but he was too quick for her.

He ran his hand along the chain at her neck, moving slowly down and letting the pendant rest against his finger. Alex let her hand drop to her side. Even that brief touch of his fingers against her neck sent a shiver down her spine.

"This will do," he said, and made to lift the chain over her head.

"Not that one." She grasped the ruby dangling from the bottom of the heart pendant. Her fingers grazed his, and the contact sent a frisson of sensation along her skin, increasing the turmoil in her mind as she tried to come up with a suitable excuse for keeping the necklace. "That one...um...was my mother's. I was named after her." She stammered, and heat crept up her neck and along her cheeks.

She wasn't a very good liar. But she relaxed when he didn't question her. However, he didn't let the necklace go either and proceeded to lift it over her head, his expression blank and unreadable.

"You want to pay for Evelyn? This is what I want. I have a lady friend that would like this." He put the necklace in his pocket and looked at her, one eyebrow raised in question.

Alex felt sick to her stomach at the loss of the necklace, one of the few links to her family. She watched it disappear into his pocket and regretted its loss but knew it had bought Evelyn's freedom, and that was more important. Besides, if all went well, she would find her sister and have a chance at a real family, the necklace didn't matter. She would have to keep telling herself that.

"Fine." She turned and left without a backward glance.

****

Nicholas watched her walk away, admiring the strength of character it had taken for her to approach him, as well as the firm backside he could see due to the trousers she wore. His flesh rose at the sight, and he wondered how he had ever mistaken her for a man.

He took her necklace out of his pocket. He wasn't sure why he had insisted on that particular payment when he could see it meant a great deal to her. Or why he made up the ridiculous story about giving it to a mistress. He would enjoy placing it around Alex's neck once more when his plan came to fruition. She would not be without it for long.

The beautiful piece was obviously very expensive. The flawless ruby was of good size, and the craftsmanship was superb. He could well imagine his mother having such a piece made for herself when his father had been alive to pamper her every whim. Alex could have easily used it to purchase passage to London, yet she obviously wasn't aware of that. Strange to carry your wealth in jewels rather than coin, yet not know their value.

If not for the engraving of her name, he might have thought it stolen. That would explain her hurry to leave America though not her limited knowledge of the value of what she carried.

No. He could not picture her as a thief. He was an excellent judge of character, and the thief theory did not feel correct. Although, she had managed to fool him into thinking she was a man, so maybe he wasn't as perceptive as he thought.

Grayson came up beside him. Nicholas tucked the necklace back in his pocket before turning to greet him.

His friend's discomfort was palpable. Knowing his first mate as he did, he suspected Grayson was about to broach a subject he worried would be ill received by his captain and friend.

"What's on your mind, Grayson?"

He cleared his throat. "It's the girl—Miss Turner. What are we to do about her?"

"In what way?"

"In what way!" he squawked like a parrot. "I know you don't wish to let anyone know about her." He squinted at Nicholas and crossed his arms over his chest. "Although I don't believe the crew would react as badly as you seem to think. But the issue is how we are going to keep her from working without letting on we know her secret."

"Why would we keep her from working?"

"Why?" He spluttered. "Because she's a woman! We can't have her working! She should be knitting or..." He seemed to be casting about for other suitable woman's work, but was at a loss as to what women actually did with their time. "She shouldn't be swabbing decks or repairing sails. A woman can't handle the work we need done."

"She has done well. All reports say she is quite competent once a job has been explained. She seems capable of much I never would have thought possible for a woman. Fighting Duff for instance. I have never seen anything like it."

"Well, yes, she does seem a bit out of the ordinary." Grayson shook himself. "But she's scheduled for the watch day after tomorrow. Are you seriously going to allow a woman up the rigging? I can understand letting her continue with her less arduous duties, but I can't in good conscience set a woman to such a dangerous task."

Nicholas frowned. The idea of Alex in danger made his blood run cold. "I'll think of something to keep her from anything dangerous, maybe some new assignments..." his voice trailed off. This had some potential, something to keep her from danger and at the same time throw them together more often.

He hadn't explained to Grayson the real reasons he wished to keep Alex's gender a secret. He'd said she had earned the right to secrecy, and they should respect her wishes. He also said he wanted to avoid any more unpleasantness with the crew. They might make life very difficult for her if they knew the truth. Grayson had argued, but in the end agreed.

If his first mate had known Nicholas's plan to get to know Alex better, without her being suspicious of his motives, he might not have given in so easily.

Chapter Nine

April 20 (39 Days Remaining)

Alex woke after a solid night's sleep and threw off the covers, determined not to spend another day holed up inside. She needed the sun on her face and the wind at her back. The thought of lying around doing nothing made her skin crawl. She'd come back to this cabin immediately after securing Evelyn's freedom and hadn't left since.

Evelyn had insisted. She wouldn't let Alex return to duty right away, even though the cut on her side had scabbed over nicely and only smarted a bit when she moved suddenly or tried to reach too far. She'd found that out the hard way when she reached for a book high up on the shelves.

Inspecting Nicholas's room had lost its appeal in short order. She kept expecting him to walk in and catch her rooting through his things. She jumped a foot every time someone walked by the door. The stress wasn't helping her heal any faster.

Browsing his books had seemed innocent enough. Who cared if he caught her in the act of reading? But she'd stopped when she realized going through his shelves, seeing his keeper books, and the knick-knacks he cherished, gave her a sense of him that disturbed her thoughts. Mostly because she liked it too much.

Evelyn tried to get her to return to bed but Alex refused, insisting instead she needed to leave Nicholas's cabin before he kicked her out.

While Evelyn grumbled she should still be resting, they cleaned the cabin of all traces of her stay, and Alex gathered her meager pile of belongings to return to her own hammock with the crew.

Emerging from the cabin, she headed to the bow where she slung her hammock and ran into the Adonis. He jumped back as if stung. His gaze darted up and down the corridor, anywhere but at her. He mumbled something incoherent and moved to pass her. His gaze fell on the bag hanging from her shoulder, and he stopped. "What do you think you are doing?"

Startled at his belligerent tone, Alex clutched her belongings and answered warily, "Moving back to the crew quarters."

"You can't do that!" He swung his arms wide and blocked her way. His eyes bulged and she had to repress a giggle at his shocked expression. "It's indecent!"

"Indecent? What do—" That's why he had been acting so strange lately. She looked up and down the corridor before grabbing his arm and pulling him into Nicholas's cabin, shutting the door quietly behind them. No one would disturb them since she had elected to move her things when the captain would be busy on other parts of the ship.

She spun around and glared at him. The strap of her bag caught on her shoulder as she planted her hands on her hips. The meager weight of her belongings settled with a soft thud against her lower back. "How did you find out?"

His face changed from ghost white to beet red in seconds. His head swiveled side to side as his gaze darted around the cabin.

She widened her stance before the door. No way was he getting out of here before she had a full confession.

He cast her one more glance before he dropped his chin and began a thorough inspection of his shoes, as if they were the most fascinating things he had ever seen. "Find out what?" He snuck a peek at her through lowered lashes.

Amusing really to watch this gorgeous ladies' man act like a child caught with his hand in the cookie jar, thinking of a way to avoid punishment. She sighed, walked up to him and took one of his hands.

He flinched but didn't move away. They stood like that until he slowly brought his eyes up to hers.

"I thought we were friends," she said. "We've spent some time talking on this trip, and I have valued those conversations. I didn't tell you the truth about who I am, but you must believe it was necessary. I never meant to hurt anyone." Now that he was looking at her, she squeezed his fingers before letting go and stepping back a few paces.

"It's difficult to come to terms with knowing you are a woman. And now that I know, I can't allow our routine to go back as it was, but those are my orders."

"Orders! So the captain knows?" She pressed her fingers to her temples. This was getting out of hand. "Since when?" Nicholas hadn't acted any differently. Could he have known all along?

"Since the fight. Evelyn told us." Her face must have shown how betrayed she felt because he hurried to add, "Don't be upset with her. She's a wonderful girl and very loyal to you. She was so alarmed when she saw you fighting Mr. Duff that the truth slipped. She tried to recover, but it was too late."

"Of course, it was too much to ask of a young girl, particularly after what happened to her." She lost her train of thought momentarily while a vivid picture of Mr. Duff striking Evelyn flitted through her memory.

Alex looked up when Mr. Grayson shifted and reached to take her bag out of her arms.

"What are you doing?"

"You won't need to move." He held up the bag and tossed it onto a chair. "Since the secret is out, you can stay here. Evelyn can stay with you while the captain takes over the cabin we gave to her. We'll think of something to tell the crew." He waved his arms in a vague sort of way. "Maybe we'll say your wound was worse than it is. You should probably stay in here as much as possible. Evelyn can keep you company." He smiled at her for the first time since the fight. "I'm glad that's settled." He started toward the door, mumbling something about delivering her meals, when she stopped him.

"I have absolutely no intention of staying locked up in this cabin or quitting."

His mouth dropped open. He snapped it shut and rubbed his hand along his jaw. "Pardon?"

Her nails dug into her palms. She forced her hands open and flexed her fingers, fighting to control the urge to hit something. The nerve of that man! What was Nicholas trying to pull? Acting like nothing had changed, when, if she looked at things from his point of view, everything had.

She couldn't help the twinge of disappointment that Nicholas hadn't pulled her into his arms and kissed her senseless when he realized the truth. To be honest, a part of her had hoped for such a reaction. Her frustration fueled her anger, causing a buzzing in her head, like a swarm of bees defending their hive. Concentrating on her problem proved difficult.

She took a few deep breaths. Despite what was going on, she wasn't spending the rest of the trip hiding in this cabin. A glance at that heavenly bed caused a small part of her to cry out—why not! Take advantage, live a life of luxury for once.

No. She firmed her resolve. Nicholas was up to something, and she wasn't going to figure it out cooped up in here.

She stalked over to Mr. Grayson and grinned at his nervous start. "Don't worry. Here's what we're gonna do."

****

Tired but triumphant, Alex left Mr. Grayson an hour later. Convincing him to listen had taken some time. Persuading him not to tell everything to Nicholas took even longer. Suspicions of his friend's motives finally turned him, rather than any of her arguments, which were rather weak, even to her ears. An amazingly loyal friend, he would never have let her see any hint he might doubt Nicholas's character, but he obviously didn't agree with the reasons Nicholas had given him and thought there might be a less honorable motive behind it.

The only way to find out what Nicholas was up to was to let the game continue uninterrupted and let him play out his hand. She wouldn't let on she was aware

Nicholas knew her secret and see what happened.

Convincing Mr. Grayson had been her only real obstacle, and was easily overcome, once he listened to her.

He, of course, wanted to go straight to Nicholas and confess. She had resorted to standing in front of the door and refusing to move until he listened. Reluctant to use force to move her, he had succumbed to her demands.

She found his behavior toward her baffling, unlike anything she was used to. She couldn't decide whether to smack some sense into him or give in.

He acted as if she was a porcelain doll that might break at the slightest provocation and deserved to be waited on and cosseted. Swear words should never be uttered in her presence, let alone come out of her mouth. He was appalled she had been living among the crew, not only for her sake but for theirs as well. She did feel a twinge of guilt about that. She hadn't considered how the men might feel about having a woman in their midst.

During all their previous conversations, he had never doubted her intelligence, yet he suddenly acted as if she were incapable of understanding the most basic of topics. Getting him to listen to her and pay attention felt like pulling teeth. It was infuriating.

But on the other side of it, a little voice inside her head kept saying, isn't it nice that someone actually wants to take care of her for a change?

In the end, he agreed not to tell Nicholas on the condition she not return to her old hammock. He suggested she take the extra bunk in Evelyn's cabin but didn't care where she slept, provided it wasn't with the crew. His sense of propriety just couldn't handle it.

She refrained from laughing when he said she should worry about her reputation if anyone ever found out. People would think she was... Well, she wasn't about to find out what people might think of her because he turned bright red and cut himself off. Apparently, this was another subject not suitable for her delicate ears.

The comment about her reputation made her think he worried Nicholas's motives might not be so pure. Had Nicholas made some sort of sexual comment about her? The thought that sex might be the underlying motive seemed ludicrous given the situation. After all, how would Nicholas expect to seduce her if he had to treat her like a man?

No, she didn't think that could be the motive, even if the thought did send a little thrill of anticipation running through her veins. It didn't matter. As long as Mr. Grayson did what she wanted, who cared why?

****

Alex decided to sleep in the hold where Evelyn had hidden. She took her things, as well as a spare hammock, and made a spot for herself. The privacy would be nice, even if the hold was dark and hot with a smell strong enough to knock her out.

After setting up her new space, she went to talk to Evelyn. She wanted to know why she hadn't told her about Nicholas and Mr. Grayson. She felt betrayed. After all she had done to protect her, she would have thought Evelyn would feel some loyalty toward her.

Evelyn wasn't in her room or the galley, and Alex finally found her up on deck enjoying the fresh air. She stood with her hands clutching the rail, her face tilted and eyes closed in the breeze that brushed stray hairs off her forehead.

Sailors cast quick glances of interest as the breeze lifted her skirts to flutter around her calves, pressing against her legs and showing off her delicate ankles and feet. No one stared, however, and the glances, while interested, were not threatening. Alex was pleased to realize there would be no trouble along those lines.

She hadn't expected this protective attitude toward women that most of the men had. She had thought men from this time treated women with disdain—that women suffered nothing but abuse and threats unless protected by the male members of their families.

It wasn't that way at all. They treated Evelyn like a precious and rare flower they were thrilled to have found blossoming in their midst. Obviously, there were exceptions, like Mr. Duff, but that would always be true in any society at any time. But in general they held women up on a pedestal—the higher the woman's social class, the higher the pedestal.

She had first noticed it when the men's talk would turn to women, as it often did late at night when they would gather to share stories and enjoy a little leisure time.

Sailors were a romantic group. Probably because they spent so much time at sea, away from their wives and girlfriends. They tended to endow women with almost fairylike qualities.

Evelyn seemed firmly placed on a pedestal, and Alex was glad of it. With the danger of Mr. Duff out of the way and Alex's deal with Nicholas, Evelyn should be safe until she could return to her family.

Evelyn must have heard her approach because she

turned to greet her with a smile of welcome on her pretty face. "Did you see, aren't they beautiful?" She gestured over the side of the ship, and Alex moved to the rail for a better look.

A pod of dolphins raced through the water next to the ship. Every few moments one would jump across the bow, as if on a dare from its friends. Alex smiled and watched as the dolphins played.

After a while, Alex looked around, and when she saw no one within earshot, she turned to Evelyn. "I spoke with Mr. Grayson today. I found out why he's been acting so strange around me." Evelyn tensed and Alex tried to keep the hurt from her voice. "Why didn't you tell me they knew?"

Evelyn looked like she was about to cry as she stammered an apology. "I am so deeply sorry. It was entirely my fault... And I was just trying to help... And it seemed the only way... And I didn't know what to do... And..."

She was upset and babbling. Alex could only make out about one word in five.

"Slow down, slow down." She patted Evelyn's hand where it rested on the rail. Picking up on the few words she had grasped from Evelyn's tumbling explanation she asked, "What was the only way?" More was going on than she'd thought.

Evelyn took a few calming breaths and was able to get a little control over herself. "I made a deal with the captain," she mumbled, her eyes downcast and speaking so softly Alex had to lean closer to hear.

"What kind of deal?"

"I agreed not to say anything if he promised you wouldn't be punished for hiding me. I know I betrayed your trust in me by not telling you the truth." She took a deep breath and looked up, her chin tilted and a hint of defiance in her eyes. "I would do it again."

Alex stared at her, dumbfounded. What courage this little girl had! Nicholas was a very imposing figure. For Evelyn to stand up to him and fight to protect her was overwhelming. She fought back the tears of gratitude that threatened to choke her.

"I could hug you right now if I thought it would go unnoticed, but I wouldn't want to ruin your reputation. They seem so very important to everyone around here. Thank you."

She could practically see the tension flow from Evelyn's shoulders, and her grip on the rail loosened. "You're not angry with me?"

"No, of course not. You were looking out for me, and I'm grateful."

Then another thought struck her, and her face warmed with fury. "That bastard!" she exclaimed, and—ignoring Evelyn's shocked gasp—hit the rail with the flat of her palm. Then shook her hand to lessen the sting.

In answer to Evelyn's silent question, she said, "I just realized, when I spoke with him he had no intention of punishing me. He deliberately brought it up and made me worry. What is he up to?"

"I'm sure I don't know, but if I were you, I would try to stay as far away from him as possible."

Alex agreed. But exactly how far could she get from the captain of a ship in the middle of the Atlantic Ocean?

Chapter Ten

April 21 (38 Days Remaining)

The next day, Alex headed to take over the watch at her scheduled time, looking forward to the solitude. Unable or unwilling to stay cooped up in either the captain's cabin or the hold, she had spent the majority of her time on deck. The crew sought her out constantly, pressing her for a karate demonstration. She put them off for the time being but would have to give in sooner or later. She planned to think over what she could do while on watch.

However, when she arrived to relieve the previous watch, he informed her of a change in the schedule. She had to report to the captain's cabin for a new assignment. As she turned to make her way, she thought she caught Mr. Grayson's eye on her, though when she turned to see, he was looking the other way.

She approached Nicholas's cabin cautiously and knocked lightly at the door, pushing it open slowly at his, "Enter." She tried to compose her face to hide her nervousness at the idea of being alone with him but wasn't sure if she was successful.

He stood behind his desk, leaning over some papers and didn't look up immediately at her entrance. She was very glad for that brief moment to tamp down the raging desire that rushed through her at his appearance.

He must have just finished a bath. She could see the tub over to the side of the room out of the corner of her eye. She had no attention to spare; it was consumed by the trails of water running from his wet hair down over his broad shoulders and onto his wide, naked chest.

One hand slowly wiped away the moisture with a small towel draped casually over his left shoulder. The slow, sensual movement of the towel mesmerized her as she followed its progress back and forth over his chest and down across the hard, flat expanse of his stomach. Her gaze drifted from the wandering towel to the line where his pants barely clung to his hips, half the buttons undone as though he'd donned them in haste, and he'd yet to secure the rest.

She had to stop gawking before she succeeded in picturing him without even that loose and inadequate covering. She looked up to find his heated gaze on her. Heat scorched her cheeks, and she forced herself to stare beyond him out the window.

"You wanted me?" she asked, surprised at how calm her voice sounded, until her face practically burst into flames when she recognized her inadvertent double entendre.

She risked a quick peek to see if he'd caught her Freudian slip. He dropped quickly into the chair behind his desk, though not quickly enough to hide the increasing bulge in his pants that showed he had, indeed, caught on.

So that was it. She wouldn't have thought it, but the evidence was quite clear. He wanted her.

She ignored the thrill the thought gave her.

Instead she concentrated on his deception and how exactly he expected to seduce her if he had to act like he thought she was a man. Was he hoping she would be so overcome with lust at the sight of his half naked, wet, hard body she would forget herself and jump him? She snorted quietly to herself, not very likely! But as she looked at him, she conceded that his vanity wasn't all that misplaced.

"Ah, Turner. Yes. I have decided to assign you a new duty to take advantage of your unique talents."

Alex almost jumped when he spoke; her mind had drifted so far. His warm, husky voice floated across her skin like a caress. She could listen to that accent of his all day.

She snapped back to attention, baffled. "My what?" Her voice squeaked slightly. That couldn't mean what it sounded like, could it? Did he really think all he had to do was order it, and she'd act the whore for him?

"Your fighting skill of course. I have never seen its equal. You will teach me."

His face was a mask of innocence, though she sensed he knew what she'd been thinking. She felt the color blossom in her cheeks. It seemed red was her new color. At least, whenever Nicholas was around.

"I—oh." She really had to stop making assumptions. "I'm not a master. I'm not qualified to teach. I still have more to learn myself."

"Is that so? However, you know more than I, so we'll give it a try, shall we." It was not a question. "We can start tomorrow. See Mr. Grayson for your new schedule." He got up from the desk and walked toward her.

She watched him approach, her heart beat

increasing in tempo until he stood in front of her, and her breath caught in her throat. He smelled delicious. What a treat to her senses being so near a freshly washed man. Especially this one.

Her eyes widened to take in all the glorious skin that lay bare before her. His left shoulder, upper arm, and side of his neck appeared rough and discolored— she assumed from the same battle that had left the scar on his face. Further evidence of his heroics. The pain he must have suffered to protect his crew was unimaginable. She wished she could have been there to help him through it.

A trickle of water slid down his muscular bicep, and she followed its path with her eyes. Her hands clenched into fists in an effort to keep her hands off him. She should move away, but her body refused. She couldn't think with him so near.

She stood immobile, waiting for him to touch her.

Her eyes drifted closed as he leaned toward her and snapped open again when he reached past her.

He grabbed a shirt off a peg behind her head and started to shrug into it as he watched her, a look on his face as if he wondered why she was still there. "That will be all."

Her cheeks blazed as she let out her breath in a gasp. She mumbled an apology, then turned abruptly and practically ran from the room.

****

Nicholas laughed softly to himself as the door slammed shut behind Alex. He was quite pleased with her. She was doing her best to hide it, but she was obviously as attracted to him as he was to her. His scars didn't seem to scare her as they did so many others. She had been devouring him with her eyes, not staring with the fascinated horror his scars provoked in others.

He'd known a moment's hesitation in flaunting his scars to such a degree, but she'd passed his test with flying colors. For some reason it was important she know the full extent of his injuries. He kept his shirt on in even the most intimate of situations, yet that was not in his plans for Alex. He suspected he could truly be himself with her, and so far he had not been disappointed.

Alex had noticed the scars, he was sure, but hadn't been put off by them. None of his mistresses had ever managed to hide their revulsion successfully. It had become a fact of his life. A fact he hated, but had no power to change.

He grinned to himself. He was looking forward to this seduction. She was different from any woman he had ever met and was driving him wild with the need to possess her completely. But he was a man who enjoyed the thrill of the hunt as much as the satisfaction of success. He wanted to prolong the game for a time, see where it would lead, before drawing it to its inevitable conclusion.

He had no doubts about that conclusion. She would be his. It might take some time, more time than he'd ever taken to acquire a mistress in the past. But he would not buy her affection as he had essentially purchased his mistresses.

Alex could not be bought. He was sure of it. However, once she accepted their mutual attraction, he felt confident she would give herself to him freely. She was not one to stand upon the proprieties.

The only uncertainties were how long he would be

able to keep himself from her and what would happen when they arrived in London.

Perhaps he would set her up in London as his mistress. Once he had her in his bed, he would not want to let her out of it for some time. Too little time remained before they reached London, and he would never tire of her so quickly.

He sat back at his desk and picked up a paperweight. A gift from his mother. She, no doubt, would be displeased at the notion of him setting up a mistress so soon upon his arrival in London. She likely had his future mapped out for him by now. He'd be forced to face introduction upon introduction of marriageable young ladies when he returned.

He would indulge her to a degree, but he was not yet ready for marriage and would see she knew it. While he cared little for the views of strangers, he had no wish to cause his mother or sister any undue anxiety or scandal. He would, therefore, be discreet with his plans for Alex.

Alex's distant family connection could pose a problem. If they proved to be a respectable family of the *ton*, they might object to his taking her as his mistress.

He brushed the notion aside. They would have no say in the matter. He would help Alex find her sister because it was important to her, but he would not allow anyone to come between them.

****

Alex rushed back on deck. The wind felt good on her flushed skin and lifting her face into the wind, she breathed deeply. Her racing pulse gradually quieted, and she mentally reviewed her meeting with Nicholas and her reaction to seeing him half-naked.

Immediately the image of him rose up in her mind to tease her with a dozen minor details she hadn't even realized she noticed but now seemed burned into her mind's eye.

The varying colors of his skin. The red, puckered skin of his scars. The deep golden bronze of his face, neck, and forearms that faded to the lighter copper glow of his chest and stomach. The glimpse of pure white where his trousers hung lower than normal and barely covered that area never exposed to the rays of the sun.

The way the light reflected off water droplets on his skin, causing him to sparkle and dazzle her eyes with his slightest movement.

When he'd moved toward her, his heady male scent had made her want to step closer and breathe in the intoxicating mix. The ever-present salty brine of the sea and an herbal scent from whatever soap he used for bathing. She had noticed before that he bathed much more frequently than was common among the men of his crew, and she envied that luxury. Her scent was quite strong, having had little chance for the privacy needed to get completely clean.

A fantasy of sharing a bath with Nicholas came to her mind. She pulled her thoughts abruptly back as she realized she was rubbing her thumb back and forth over her lips as she imagined the warmth of his mouth pressed to hers, their soap-slicked bodies rubbing against one another. The way these thoughts kept coming unbidden to her mind confused her. She should know better than to think such things were possible outside of the movies.

But that was what he was after, wasn't it. A real

life porno. The girl comes in, takes one look at the man, and suddenly they're on top of each other. So why was he pretending not to know about her?

Was it a game to him, a challenge to while away the hours at sea and relieve the boredom? The thought got her pulse racing again, this time with anger rather than lust. She'd teach him a lesson.

She paced, the need to do something physical while she thought made it impossible to stand still. Her steps became increasingly difficult as the boat rocked up and down on waves that rose higher and higher as she fought for balance. Her stomach lurched, and she grabbed hold of the rail as a particularly forceful wave broke against the hull.

She gasped at the dark clouds rolling in on the starboard side. She hadn't even noticed them until now. Her experience was limited, but even she could recognize a major storm approaching.

She hurried to the galley and heard the storm break overhead just as she entered the room. Cook looked green in the dim light. As he struggled around his normally cheerful domain, he clutched his stomach and gave intermittent moans as the ship rocked around them. She rushed to help as he hastily secured everything not already bolted down.

The pitch of the boat got stronger and stronger until she could barely stand. To steady herself, she wedged one foot against the bottom of the cabinet and another against the sturdy chopping table bolted to the floor in the center of the room. She sighed in relief as they stowed the last of the gear safely away.

Her relief was short-lived. The force of the next wave threw them both off their feet. She landed with an "oomph" and then struggled to her knees.

Above the howling of the wind and the lash of the rain on the deck above, she heard a terrified scream and a call that froze the blood in her veins.

"Man overboard!"

Chapter Eleven

April 21 (38 Days Remaining)

Alex and Cook stared at each other in horror before they both struggled back onto their feet. She chewed at her lower lip, thinking. She was supposed to stay below deck, out of the way during a storm. She wasn't skilled enough to be of much use and would probably be more of a hazard than a help if she were to go above.

The dim light filtering into the galley was fast disappearing. Lanterns couldn't be lit; fire was an even bigger hazard on a wooden ship than the storm. The thought of waiting it out in the dark, with no notion of what was going on above was too terrible to bear.

"I'm going to see what I can do." She may not be able to help run the ship, but maybe she could help with any rescue efforts. She needed to keep busy.

She made her way topside, ignoring Cook's repeated calls, "Come back, ya fool. Don't be an idiot."

She was almost too late. She reached the ladder just as they struggled to batten down the hatch after a sailor who had gone below to fetch more rope.

"Hurry!" the sailor yelled. "We need to seal this hatch."

Walking under a waterfall would have been gentler on her body. The rain hit her head with enough force to knock her back down the ladder a few rungs. It took a huge effort just to pull herself up and help re-cover the hatch.

Visibility wasn't much better above, but Alex caught the sound of men struggling with something toward the stern. She made her way back, clinging desperately to the lifelines rigged along the way.

At last, she found several of the crew, all pulling a rope the far end of which was lost to sight over the side. A large section of rail was missing, obviously washed away along with whoever had gone overboard.

She made out Mr. Grayson at the front of the rope, coordinating their efforts, shouting, "heave" and straining with all his might along with the others. She wouldn't be a great help, but she got to the end of the line, grabbed a section of rope, and lent her own meager strength to their efforts. The man before her glanced her way briefly before returning his full attention ahead with only a weak grunt of acknowledgment of her presence.

She assumed the man they were trying to save must have grabbed hold of the rope before a wave swept him over. She couldn't imagine it would have been possible to get a rope to him after the fact in these swelling seas. He was lucky he had been able to hold on.

Time passed slowly as they all held desperately to the rope. Long periods passed where they simply strove not to lose any ground, followed by brief but furious hauling to take up the slack as a wave brought their quarry closer.

When at last a cheer went up, starting at the front of the line closest to the rail, Alex barely had the strength left to see whom they had saved.

When she finally looked up, two men lay sprawled

on the deck, chests heaving and coughing up great spouts of seawater. Her heart leapt into her throat when she recognized Nicholas. A rope pulled tight under his arms, and in between coughs and ragged breaths, he worked furiously to loosen its hold.

Mr. Grayson came to his aid, pulling his knife free of his boot and slicing the rope. Nicholas gasped, and Alex felt air rush into her lungs as she too began to breathe once more. She watched him expand his massive chest with great gulps of precious air.

The men cheered and patted Nicholas on the back before returning to the duties they'd ignored in their efforts to save their friends. Two helped the other half-drowned man below, while Mr. Grayson stayed next to Nicholas.

Alex sat, gathering her strength to return below. Nicholas glanced her way, and their gazes locked. He abruptly cut off his conversation, and Mr. Grayson half-dragged, half-carried him across the deck to drop him at her feet.

Nicholas glared at her. "You shouldn't be up here," he shouted.

"Help him below," Mr. Grayson yelled before turning and stalking off, leaving her alone with Nicholas.

It took her a moment to get to her feet and find some sense of balance on the slippery and heaving deck, but she managed. She could feel the weight of Nicholas's stare though she was too busy watching her footing to check. She sensed him shifting and realized he had positioned himself so she was more or less pinned against the bulkhead. There was no way around him. *Did he think she'd leave him there?*

She wasn't sure how she was going to get him to his cabin if he wasn't able to stand and walk at least partially under his own steam. He offered no suggestions while she looked down at him, just continued to watch her in silence. She knelt next to him and grabbing his arm wrapped it over her shoulder. She stumbled slightly, and he steadied her with a grip that was much stronger than expected.

She braced herself. "On three. One. Two. Three." A bit awkwardly but easier than anticipated, they got to their feet and stumbled their way to the hatch where another crewmember waited to let them go below deck.

Nicholas's gaze remained locked on her, and embarrassed, she looked away, aware of the way his body pressed along the length of hers. "Can you make it down the ladder? I don't think I can help."

He nodded and climbed down on his own, moving slowly and coughing slightly as he went. At the bottom, he leaned against the wall as if too exhausted to move any further, and she self-consciously realized he was watching her.

He flung his arm back over her shoulder as someone sealed the hatch. They staggered down the pitch-black corridor, Alex aware of every brush of Nicholas's well-muscled leg against hers. She kept her right hand pressed to the wall. His cabin would be the first opening on that side.

She got him through the open door with little difficulty, but just as they made their way into his cabin, the ship rolled violently and flung them across the room. Right onto his bed.

Alex struggled wildly to release herself from the fluffy mass of comforter, pillows, and the contrasting hardness of Nicholas's body pressed tightly against hers. He suddenly seemed a dead weight trapping her beneath him where moments before he'd barely needed her help to walk.

Finally managing to sit at the edge of the bed, Alex took a moment to get her bearings before looking to see whether Nicholas needed her. She sucked in her breath and had to remind herself to let it out again. With her eyes adjusted to the darkness, enough light filtered through the wall of windows to allow her to see him quite clearly. And to notice she wasn't the only one affected by those moments spent rubbing up against each other.

He lay on his back with his arm over his eyes. His wet shirt clung to his chest, one side pulled up around his ribcage, leaving a taught expanse of stomach visible and leaving the rather large bulge in his pants exposed to her view.

She scurried off the bed before he could see her reaction and moved toward the trunks where he kept clean linens. Occasional coughs came from the bed, but otherwise he remained still and silent while she gathered towels, dry clothes, and ointment to treat the rope burns.

He didn't look up until she stood over him and offered the towel and clothes. He appeared to have mastered the urges of his body and seemed too tired to do much more than struggle to an upright position.

Taking pity on him, she said, "I'll help you with your shirt and see to your rope burns, but I'm afraid you'll have to deal with the rest yourself." She unbuttoned his shirt in a businesslike manner, dried his upper half as best she could, and left the towel over his hair for him to continue.

When she reached for the ointment, he grabbed it from her and said in a raspy voice, "I can handle the rest on my own. Thank you."

She nodded and headed to the door but paused when she heard the ointment slip from his fingers and saw his head drooping on his shoulders. At the sight, her reticence vanished, and she returned to help before he toppled out of bed.

He was sound asleep the moment his head hit the pillow. What should she do? She didn't want to leave him in his wet pants but all the men would be busy fighting the storm and wouldn't be able to help him for quite some time.

After a few minutes of tugging and cursing, she managed to strip him down and anoint his cuts and abrasions. Then she rolled him more toward the center of the bed and flipped the comforter over him to keep his now naked form from getting cold.

She should have left immediately, but she couldn't resist looking at him resting so peacefully. He looked younger and carefree with his face relaxed in sleep. She sat next to him and tenderly brushed a lock of hair out of his face.

Or, at least, that was what she meant to do, but the ship hit another massive wave, and she lost her balance, pitching forward to land straddled across his body, her face inches from his. She watched his face breathlessly before trying to wiggle off him when he didn't open his eyes.

As she started to move, a small smile spread across his sleeping face. He shifted slightly so she lay more comfortably across him, reaching up a hand at the same time to grasp the back of her neck. Then he slowly brought her lips to his as she froze in panic and perhaps a twinge of anticipation.

His hand on the nape of her neck was cool, and while he exerted enough pressure to move her forward, it felt more like a caress than force. In contrast to his hand, his mouth blazed with heat. She tasted the salt of the sea on his rough, chapped lips and practically melted into him.

The kiss started slow and slightly hesitant, as if he were unsure whether it would be welcome. When she yielded and her mouth opened with a sigh of pleasure, he deepened the kiss. The touch of his tongue, first against her lips and then upon her tongue, stoked the fire within her.

He started to roll over, but the comforter caught between them, preventing the movement. As he tried to free himself, his lips slid off hers, and Alex, coming to her senses, leapt from the bed, narrowly avoiding the arms that reached for her a second too late.

Amazingly, he still didn't wake up but continued to roll over onto his stomach and lay still, his breathing deep and even. Alex watched him for a full minute in disbelief, before tiptoeing to the door and out into the hall.

Rain continued to pound hard against the hull, but the pitch and roll of the ship felt as though the storm was starting to break up. Before, the sounds of the crew hard at work had been drowned out by the ferocity of the wind, but were now faintly audible.

She breathed a sigh of relief once she'd fumbled her way back to her lonely hammock in the hold. She could hardly believe she had been tempted to give herself to a man who wasn't even awake!

It took a long time for sleep to claim her, what with the storm surrounding the ship and the even more ferocious storm within her traitorous body. Gradually her pulse slowed, and she was able to rein in her thoughts and return them to her earlier contemplation of how to make Nicholas regret his decision to play with her.

Slowly a plan formed, but when she finally dozed off, her dreams were not of the lesson she would teach Nicholas but of the kiss they had shared.

****

Nicholas opened his eyes slowly when the door banged shut. He let out a frustrated sigh. If he weren't so exhausted, he might not have bungled things so badly.

At least he hadn't completely lost all sense of reality and had managed to feign sleep when she slipped from his grasp. He had used all his willpower to stay still when he desperately wanted to go after her. Finding her on top of him had nearly been his undoing, and even though he was in no shape to take full advantage of the fact, at least one part of his body had been willing to try.

The feel of her had been intoxicating. He could have made it to his cabin on his own, but the chance to touch her without suspicion had been too much to resist. She was tall and strong for a woman, her body fit perfectly to his, though had he been asked previously, he would have stated he liked small, delicate women.

He tried to imagine the figure she disguised. Padding surrounded her waist, and he was in an agony to know how she would feel stark naked against him.

Was her waist as narrow as he envisioned? Her breasts as full?

Had he not just nearly drowned and been on the brink of exhaustion from saving his crewman, he would have been able to take better advantage of the opportunity of having Alex in his bed. Though his appearance may have displeased his mistresses, his prowess in the bedroom had not. At the very least, he wouldn't have scared her off by being such a clumsy oaf and tangling himself in the bedding.

What had come over him? No woman had ever made him lose control over himself like that. He was in no condition to make love to her, so why had he risked scaring her off for a simple kiss?

Nicholas groaned and rolled onto his back. That kiss was definitely not simple. The blood in his veins sang with the memory. He ached to find her and continue what they had started.

But no. He wanted to prolong the masquerade, it had so much potential. Tipping his hand too early could ruin everything.

She believed he had kissed her in his sleep and was unaware of what he was doing, and to whom he was doing it. On the morrow, he would act normal and proceed as planned.

Exhausted as he was, it took a long time to fall asleep and when he did, his dreams were consumed with images of bright green eyes and a treasure hidden beneath men's clothes.

Chapter Twelve

April 22 (37 Days Remaining)

The next day dawned bright and clear. Everyone set about the tasks of cleanup and repairs.

Alex meant to avoid Nicholas as much as possible. If he remembered their kiss at all, he would probably think it had been a dream. Why she was so nervous to be around him, she wasn't sure.

As she joined in the cleanup, she realized she had a legitimate reason not to want to be near him. He was all over the ship, overseeing everything personally, and nothing pleased him. He barked orders at everyone, and the atmosphere on the ship degenerated. The crew was tense and grumbling whenever he was out of earshot, anxious and silent when he was near.

Never having experienced a storm at sea, she feared the damage to the ship must be extensive—his mood reflective of his worry over getting them to London safely. Cook quickly relieved her of this worry.

"Is it that bad?" She kept one eye on the door in case Nicholas decided he'd had enough topside. She could hear him stomping around as she and Cook put the galley back together.

She heard a muffled, "What?" coming from the vicinity of her feet and looked down to see Cook rummaging through a number of bags on the floor.

She squatted beside him, arms resting on her knees. "The storm. How bad's the damage? Will we make it to London?" She linked and unlinked her hands waiting for his answer. She hadn't been this nervous during the storm.

"Nah, that storm weren't nothing," Cook said. "Been through worse. Though it's a good thing the captain didn't pitch Mr. Duff over the side after all. We'll need him to fix that rail and a few other items what were damaged."

"So Mr. Duff's been set free?" she asked, one worry gone but another stacked firmly in its place.

"He'll be allowed out to make repairs but locked up any time he's not working. Don't worry none. He'll be on his best behavior, hoping to be set free when we reach London."

"Go free! That bastard should be locked up for a long time." She huffed.

"Well, I said that's what he'd be hoping, not what the captain were likely to do." He went back to work.

After she finished in the galley, she went to find Evelyn, who hadn't endured the storm very well. Being confined in a small dark room while the ship rocked violently around her had left her bruised and exhausted.

Alex sympathized with her misery. After all, hadn't she gone on deck in the middle of a violent storm just to avoid what Evelyn had gone through?

Alex had visited her immediately after the worst was over and, against Evelyn's feeble protests, had cleaned up the corner of the room where the poor girl had been sick the night before. Alex had left her tucked in bed before setting to work and hadn't had much chance to look in on her since.

She peeked into the room, and sure enough, Evelyn slept soundly. She eased the door closed and almost ran into the Adonis.

"The captain is ready to start those lessons you discussed. He'll expect you in his cabin in half an hour." He rubbed the back of his neck, head tilted down. Someone called his name, but he made no move to leave.

"Is there anything else?" she asked, when he didn't say anything immediately.

He continued to stare at his feet, avoiding eye contact. "I love Nicholas like a brother. He saved my life and the lives of many others on this ship. He is an honorable man, and I have never questioned his motives before..." He stopped suddenly.

"But?" she prompted.

"He's not himself where you're concerned. I think he...desires you." He blushed and shifted his weight from one leg to another.

"He said that?" She hid her amusement at his obvious discomfort at discussing such a topic with her. *He's such a prude.*

"No. He hasn't said anything, which is why I am nervous about his intentions. His behavior in regards to you is unusual. I'm unsure what it means."

"Well, thanks for the warning. But I can take care of myself." She smiled at him, touched by his concern. How sweet of him to worry and warn her when it was obviously so hard for him.

If only Nicholas showed even a fraction of that concern.

****

Alex made her way slowly to Nicholas's cabin. His

foul mood made her nervous. What could he want from her? Just a simple karate lesson?

Did he realize they had kissed, or perhaps remember it as though in a dream? Could their kiss be the source of his bad mood? She got the feeling he wasn't a man much used to suffering from unfulfilled desire. If he wanted something or someone, he would get it. She doubted he would have much trouble with women. He could certainly pour on the charm when it suited him. She couldn't begin to guess why he was going through such trouble with her. It would have been much simpler for him to expose her disguise and then try to charm her.

He must be one of those men who simply enjoyed the hunt. Having to treat her like a man made it more of a challenge. At the very least, she doubted she'd be bored. This could get interesting.

She wanted to deliberately entice him, make him desperate to have her, and then leave him cold. A karate lesson could be a good place to start. It would give her the opportunity to be subtle and keep him from catching on to what she was doing.

She could find plenty of excuses to flaunt her body and innocently touch him while showing him the various stretches and movements he wanted to learn. A simple stretching demonstration would show off the curves of her body and her flexibility, while she would need to touch him here or there to correct his own position. It should be simple.

Or maybe not. She tried scratching an itch on her stomach and met the thick padding of her disguise. Shit. Her figure wasn't exactly enticing, hidden as it was.

Doubts crept in. What made her think she'd be able

to turn him on? She looked like a chunky boy. She sniffed the air, her nose wrinkling. A smelly, chunky little boy. Not exactly playmate of the year material.

And did she really want to mess with him when he was in such a crappy mood? She was a bit afraid of facing him after how he'd been ranting and raving all morning.

No, if she were honest with herself, that wasn't the real problem. She was more afraid of her attraction to him. For a moment during that amazing kiss, she had lost all sense other than the feel of him. If he hadn't broken off the kiss when he had, how far would she have let things go? All the way?

She was worried about herself, not him. He wasn't the kind of man who would resort to rape. He seemed too honorable. He'd been genuinely enraged at Mr. Duff's attempt with Evelyn. No, she was more afraid he would so befuddle her senses that she would forget to say no until it was too late. And she knew from experience what that was like. She wasn't keen to go through it again.

****

Lost in thought as she was, Alex reached Nicholas's door before she'd had the chance to work out what she planned on doing. She knocked quickly and firmly before she could lose her nerve. She didn't want him to find her out in the hall, afraid to knock. Could she go through with her plan? Could she even face him?

He pulled the door open a scant second or two after her knock and stepped aside to let her in. He wore the same scowl that had been on his face all day, and she quailed slightly. She didn't have much choice though,

135

so she walked past him into the room.

She kept her face averted from the bed, which seemed to occupy a much greater space in the room than she had thought previously. To avoid facing him any sooner than absolutely necessary, she looked around and assessed the rest of the space to see where they should set up.

"I think we can begin with a few stretches, but we may want to move up on deck before I try to show you anything more. We don't really have enough room in here." She looked back at Nicholas who still stood next to the door.

"And good afternoon to you, as well," he said sarcastically as he shut the door, a slight twitch at the corner of his mouth.

"Oh. Sorry," she mumbled, embarrassed already.

The scowl on his face relaxed into a rueful grin. "You needn't worry; I don't bite." He gestured to the chairs situated in the center of the room and moved to the one on the far left, closest to the bed. "Please, be seated."

She walked to the chair furthest from him, wondering why he didn't sit. She repressed a grin when the reason became clear. To hide her amusement, she looked down. He may be pretending she was a man, but apparently, certain social niceties were so ingrained he couldn't sit while a woman remained standing. As soon as she was ensconced in her comfy armchair, he lowered himself to his.

"Tell me how you learned to fight."

Her tension eased a little. She had worried over nothing. He didn't act as if he remembered their kiss. "I started when I was a gir—a child. When a dojo opened up nearby, the director at our orphanage arranged lessons for us. She thought the exercise and discipline would do us some good."

"What is a dojo?"

"It means 'sacred hall of learning.' It's a school to teach karate."

"They have schools in America for this?" he asked.

His tone of voice warned her she might be straying into the dangerous territory of historical accuracy, but it was too late to take it back, so she plunged ahead. "It was a small place, closed up a few years later." She rushed on, "But it got me started, and I found new instructors once I was on my own and had enough money for lessons."

He made no remark, so she continued, "I'm not going to get into all the history and the proper words for everything. We don't have enough time left, and I'm not qualified. I'll just try to teach you some of the basic moves. It takes years to learn, and we don't have that kind of time."

He seemed a bit disgruntled by this last, and she wondered if he had thought she could teach him everything in only a few lessons. Of course, maybe he wasn't interested in learning at all, and this was just an excuse to spend time with her. The thought gave her a brief rush of pleasure.

"If nothing else, I can show you a few of the more basic moves. It's great exercise and a good way to relieve stress."

"Show me," he demanded.

She stood and began to move. Her movements were a bit stiff at first, but as she focused on her form, she relaxed and devoted her attention to perfecting each movement as she'd been taught. As she lost herself in the movements and her body flowed gracefully from one position to the next, she forgot to worry about enticing Nicholas. Without looking, she asked him to stand next to her and follow her movements.

She went through some of the first positions she had ever learned with exaggerated slowness, aware of his attempts to imitate. His coordination was extraordinary. It had taken her years to do as well as he did right off the bat. He would learn quickly.

"Good. Stop now and get into the starting position." She demonstrated one more time. "Not bad, just a minor shift here..." She placed her hands on his hips to shift him slightly. His swiftly indrawn breath brought her attention to his face, and before she was aware of him moving, he had her locked in a heated embrace.

Mind-blowing sensation quickly followed a brief moment of shock. Her arms seemed to move of their own accord to wrap around his waist, and her head tilted slightly to encourage him to deepen the kiss.

With a groan, he pulled her tighter to him with one hand and cradled her head with the other. The feel of his hard body pressed so closely to hers brought a rush of heat to her core, and her stomach clenched in anticipation. Anticipation of what, she wasn't quite sure, and her anxiety came swiftly back to the surface. She tore her mouth away from his and leaned against him, her head resting on his chest as she tried to steady her shaking limbs. She breathed deeply, and his scent filled her awareness.

He rested his chin on top of her head, cleared his throat and whispered huskily, "That was unplanned. I hope I did not frighten you. Are you all right?"

"What did you plan?"

"I'm not exactly sure," he said, laughing roughly at himself. "But I just couldn't seem to help myself. And now..."

She stiffened in his arms. She was sure he was going to tell her he regretted it because she was such a bad kisser.

"...that I have you in my arms, I don't think I can possibly let you go."

She looked up at him in surprise. "You're not disappointed?"

"Disappointed?" His eyebrows twitched upward, and he leaned back to look her in the eye.

She blushed and tried to pull out of his arms. "Nothing," she mumbled.

He wouldn't let her go but cupped her face with his hands, forcing her to look at him. "Why would you think I would be disappointed?"

She closed her eyes and tried to keep the tears she could feel building up from falling and humiliating herself further. "It's nothing, don't worry about it. I should go."

"I don't think so." He gathered her close and pulled her onto his lap as he sat in the nearest chair. He gently brought her head to rest on his chest and said simply, "Tell me."

She wiped a tear surreptitiously from the corner of her eye and said, "I'm not very good at this."

"Good at what?"

"You're not going to make this easy by just letting me go and forgetting about this, are you?"

"Certainly not."

"Fine," she retorted. "This." She waved her hand back and forth between them. "You and me. Kissing. Making love. All of it. Are you happy now? I'm not good at the whole intimacy thing. You should just forget about me because you'll only be disappointed." She struggled to get up but stopped when she realized he was shaking with laughter. She was so astonished she sat still and watched him until he quieted down. "I'm serious, and I don't think it's funny."

"I know you are and I'm sorry, but that is the most ridiculous statement I have ever heard." He shook his head, a wide smile lighting his face. The grin slipped as he ran a gentle finger along her jaw, wiping away the tear that had slipped down her cheek. "Where did you ever get such an insane idea?"

"I thought I was in love once. I would have done anything for him," she said quietly and shrugged. "He wanted to, so I said yes. It was not good. He tired of me real quick after that. A few weeks later, he told me how bad I was, and then walked out of my life."

"How old were you?" He frowned.

She couldn't look at him and wondered what he was thinking. The warmth had left his voice, and it occurred to her that virginity was a much more valuable commodity in these times than it was in the future. "We were fifteen."

"Fifteen! You weren't even out yet. Who was this boy that your guardians would allow you to be alone together?"

She looked at him in surprise. "It's not like that where I'm from. Girls weren't kept separate from boys. We never had a problem finding places to be alone."

"Where exactly are you from that they have such

strange ideas?"

"It's not important." She brushed his question aside. This conversation had been bad enough. She certainly wasn't going there. "Will you let me up now?" She tried to push up using the arms of the chair.

"No." He held her until she stopped struggling. Then he took hold of her chin and forced her to look into his eyes. "I think this boy was a bloody idiot, and so were you for believing such nonsense."

"I'm not an idiot just because I can accept that I'm not a passionate person and don't enjoy making love," she grumbled.

He looked deep into her eyes and lowered his lips to hers. His mouth teased hers until she relaxed in his arms and gave herself up to the intoxication of his kiss. With one arm trapped between them, her free hand stole up to his head and tangled in the hair at the base of his neck. Her clothing chafed against her suddenly sensitive skin, and the thin barrier of his shirt seemed a cruel device meant to torture her as she longed to feel his naked skin next to hers.

He released her mouth with a gasp and leaned his forehead against hers as she let out a small moan of protest. "Not passionate? Bloody hell. Any more passionate and *The Reliant* would go up in flames. I think someone needs to explain the meaning of the word to you." A wicked grin spread across his face. "And I think I'm the man to do it."

The next few hours were devoted to her education.

Chapter Thirteen

April 23 (36 Days Remaining)

Nicholas lay awake watching Alex sleep beside him. An odd impulse, and one he had never before experienced. He wondered at it.

He never lingered after making love to a woman once their needs were met. There was no reason to stay. Not that he was a selfish lover. No. He always made sure he left his women as satisfied as he was. He found it deeply gratifying to be able to please a woman in bed and took great pride in doing so. He was just never under the illusion their brief liaisons were anything more than a mutual fulfillment of desire. He took great pains not to get involved with any women who could possibly expect, or want, more. Since the war—since his scars—none had.

The feeling was new to him, this desire to memorize the curve of her shoulder and the color of her lips. Was it her inexperience that moved him? He had never been with a woman of so little experience before. She wasn't a virgin, but she had learned nothing but pain and humiliation from the loss of her innocence. She had been completely unaware of the pleasure to be found in the act of making love. Her response had been extraordinarily special.

Perhaps he should have taken a slower approach in

introducing her to the pleasures of the flesh. Her tentative, yet passionate, response to his kiss had been his undoing. He'd barely maintained enough control to bring about her release before succumbing to his own. Their first time together should have been a much more leisurely affair, but his body had had other ideas.

He had been selfish in not resisting the lure she held over him. It amazed him to find he could not seem to get enough of her. He had come to her repeatedly during the day and into the night. Her poor body was not accustomed to such use, and yet she had continued to respond with marvelous ardor until she at last fell into an exhausted slumber near dawn. Even now, he felt his flesh rising at the thought of the pleasure she had brought him.

She rolled over in her sleep, and the covers fell aside to reveal her firm backside. He admired the womanly curves of her body. The padding she had worn had disguised these traits extremely well.

As he watched her sleep, Nicholas wondered why he hadn't realized the truth immediately. She appealed to him in a way that made perfect sense now he knew the truth. He must have known on some level. But for whatever reason, his mind had been unable to accept what his body recognized.

Her hand fell open on the pillow beside her head.

That should have been a dead giveaway. He reached out and stroked a finger along a small scar on the back of her right hand, causing her fingers to twitch slightly. Though roughened by hard work and exposure to the sea air, the bones were delicately shaped and elegant, more suited to painting landscapes than hauling cargo and scrubbing floors.

He turned her hand over gently and examined her palm. Calluses indicated she was used to working with her hands. If she had been unused to manual labor, her palms would have been blistered and red but still soft underneath, not tough like they were. He suspected life to this point had not been easy for her.

A sudden fierce rush of protectiveness made him wish to erase all the unpleasantness she had ever faced. He knew what it was like to make his own way in the world. That kind of life was hard enough for a man. He couldn't imagine how rough it must be on a woman.

I can do nothing to erase the past, but I can certainly provide for a more pleasant future. I know just where to start.

****

Alex woke slowly to the sound of voices. She pulled the cover over herself in alarm but quickly realized the open screen hid the bed from view of the rest of the cabin. She waited for the men to leave and listened for the sound of the door closing before cautiously peeking out into the room. What she saw took a moment to register, but when it did, "Oh my!"

Nicholas looked at her with a pleased smile on his face. "Impressed?"

She got up and hurried to stand next to him. In her excitement, she forgot she was completely naked. Heat warmed her cheeks when his grin widened and she realized the cause, but made no move to cover herself. After last night, modesty seemed a bit absurd, even if some habits were hard to break. Besides, she wouldn't need clothes for what he obviously had in mind.

The glow in his eye as he ran his gaze up and down her body reassured her she had nothing to worry about, and she pushed away her lingering modesty. Right now, she had eyes for one thing only.

"For me?"

At his nod, she grasped his hand. She sighed with bliss as he helped lower her until she lay immersed in a glorious hot bath.

"Oh." She groaned. "This is heaven. I haven't been properly clean in ages!" She leaned back and closed her eyes, giving his hand a grateful squeeze before letting go and dropping that hand into the water, too.

She submerged and scrubbed at her hair, letting the strands flow around her face. Dim noises filtered through the water, and she surfaced. Swiping water from her eyes, she peered around the cabin and found him at her side, hands behind his back and a wide grin on his face. She smiled back and raised her eyebrows, trying to sneak a peek at whatever he held.

He brought his hands around, and she clapped in delight at the sight of soap and a washcloth. Better than gold.

"Ooh, thank you." She reached out to take them.

He shook his head and said, "Let me," as he knelt by her side.

He rolled his sleeves past his elbows then dipped his hands in the water to lather the washcloth. As he ran the soft cloth over her weary body, she sighed in contentment. "Life doesn't get much better than this."

Then his mouth covered hers and swallowed her gasp as he found that private part of her she would have sworn was too sore to be aroused so soon after last night. To her surprise, his skilled fingers brought her quickly to an explosive climax, which left her pleasantly drained and relaxed.

"Oh my." She breathed, and then laughed at the smug expression on Nicholas's face. "Proud of yourself, hmm?"

He laughed in response. "Yes," he said and lathered her hair.

As he gently massaged her scalp, her mind drifted in and out of focus. "Do you think anyone will notice that I've taken a bath?" she asked, wondering what people might think and not caring in the least.

He snorted and picked up a bucket of clean water from the floor beside him.

She missed his response as water cascaded past her ears. "What did you say?"

"I said I doubt anyone will care that you're clean. They'll be too busy wondering how they never realized you're a woman."

She tensed as she realized what he was saying. "How will they find out?"

"I think they will figure it out when you move into my cabin and stop working with them," he said, amusement evident in his tone.

"And what makes you think I plan to do either of those things?" She tried to keep the anger out of her voice as she asked the question.

His hands stilled on her shoulders, and she turned to look him in the eye. It probably never even occurred to him she'd be anything but thrilled at the idea. He wanted her at his beck and call. No point in taking her feelings into account.

"Of course you will move in here." He smiled and patted her shoulder. "Don't worry about how the crew will act once they know about us. They would never question me or mistreat my mistress. And they won't think any less of you; they know I'm pretty hard to resist." He gave her a cheeky grin. "Besides, you will barely have a chance to see them. With fair winds, we will arrive in London within the week. I plan to monopolize all of your time from now until then. Once we arrive, I will find a nice place for you to live, and I can begin showering you with the beautiful gowns, rich furs, and expensive jewelry I long to see you in."

She couldn't believe what she was hearing. How dare he plan her future without talking to her, as if she was bought and paid for with no say in the matter. Were all nineteenth century men so domineering, or was she just lucky?

"Oh, so I'm your mistress now, am I? Or should we just say whore? Get your hands off me you pompous ass. It's like dealing with a dinosaur!"

She pushed his hands off her shoulders and tried to stand. Unfortunately, rather than her vision of a dramatic, graceful exit reminiscent of a naked Venus rising from the surf, her right foot landed on the bar of soap at the bottom of the tub, and she lost her balance, falling backward with a large splash and hitting her hip and elbow in the process. She let out a loud yelp and cradled her aching arm gently while rocking back and forth.

"Are you hurt?" He reached for her, but she flinched away.

She winced when her movement pushed her bruised hip into the side of the tub. "I'm fine," she snapped. "Hand me a towel, please," she gritted out between clenched teeth.

He handed her the towel and grabbed her arm to help her safely out of the tub, where she dried herself with rough, jerky motions while he watched.

"What is a dinosaur?" he asked finally.

She stopped in the midst of wrapping herself in the towel. "You're joking, right?" When he simply continued to look at her without responding, she finished covering herself and set to work drying her hair with a second towel. "You know—Great big lizards, roamed the earth millions of years ago, extinct..." She trailed off.

Had dinosaurs been discovered yet? She couldn't remember, but judging from the confused look on his face, apparently not. "Well, don't worry about it. Just trust me when I say it was not complimentary. You're behaving like a jack-ass. You do know what they are, right?" She turned away to look for her clothes.

He grabbed her arm and swung her around to face him. She quailed at the look on his face but refused to be intimidated and glared back at him.

"What exactly did you expect would happen after we made love? Did you expect I would just walk away and not speak to you again?"

He abruptly dropped her arm, walked away, and then whirled back to face her once there was a little distance between them. She could tell it was taking quite an effort for him to keep control of his temper.

"You cannot judge all men by that scoundrel you once knew. I would never treat you that way."

He wrenched the door open, pausing to look back at her. "We will discuss this, but I do not have the time now. Be back here tonight. And I warn you, I do not tolerate disobedience on my ship."

He walked out, slamming the door behind him.

****

Alex shivered in her damp towel for a few moments before sinking into the nearest chair, burying her face in her hands and crying. She struggled to keep her sobs quiet so none of the crew would hear her distress.

It took a while before she was able to pull herself together, drying her tears on the towel. As she pulled on her clothes, she went over and over the morning in her mind and didn't understand what had come over her.

Why did he affect her this way? Her reaction had been completely over the top. His assumption that their lovemaking would lead to something wasn't unreasonable. In fact, wasn't it nice that he would want to continue to be with her? Weren't her friends always complaining that men ran the minute sex ended? Granted, she wasn't thrilled with the word *mistress*, but then again, casual dating wasn't exactly the norm at this point in time.

Dating! What was she thinking? She wouldn't be dating this man. Dating implied a future, and they had none. She didn't belong in this time, and he sure as hell didn't belong in hers. They would arrive in London in a few days, and they would part. He would take up his new title and responsibilities, and she would find her sister and return home. She'd already arranged to accompany Evelyn to her house. As luck would have it, her mother worked for a family with ties to Alex's ancestors, the Creswells.

Her plans for their arrival in London were set. Probably why she was so upset and had acted so insane. When Nicholas started to detail his plans for setting her up as his mistress, she was only slightly insulted. The idea didn't appeal to her because she was too independent to be taken care of in that manner, but he didn't mean it as an insult, and she didn't really see it that way. But speaking of the future brought it home to her that they had none.

So why was she so upset at the idea of parting from him so soon? After all, they'd known each other less than a month. It's not as if they were in love or something ridiculous like that.

Her stomach plummeted. *Oh no. Love.* She was in love with Nicholas. How had this happened? When had it happened? This was a disaster. Once they arrived in London, they would never see each other again.

Why hadn't she seen this coming? She'd been in love once. She should have recognized the signs. But no, she was completely blindsided. Nothing had prepared her for this.

She shook herself and used the damp towel to dry her hair. It didn't matter how it happened. The important question was—what was she going to do?

She should just cut herself off from him and try to minimize the damage. But could she do it? She wouldn't be able to avoid him. *The Reliant* was his ship after all. He was in complete control here. She'd have to make him want to leave her alone.

Her hands stilled, and she dropped the towel on a chair. Or, she could just enjoy the little time they had left. She would be devastated when they parted whether it was today, tomorrow, or next week. They could at least create a few memories for her to cherish when she returned home.

Yeah, that's what she would do. No need to suffer more than necessary. She would just avoid discussions of the future and not promise anything. When they arrived in London, she would certainly be able to slip away in all the confusion of their arrival.

She tied back her hair and wiped her face once more to dry her tears. She straightened her shoulders, lifted her chin, and then left the cabin to begin the day.

****

Nicholas stormed out of his cabin and went straight above deck. A long look at the endless ocean usually worked to calm him whenever he was upset, but this time it did nothing to ease his aggravation.

That woman was going to drive him insane! They spend an incredible night together, and then she acts offended when he speaks of a more permanent arrangement. In all his experience with women, he had never experienced a problem such as this.

His life at sea precluded keeping a long-term mistress, but there were several women, in both America and England, whom he visited regularly whenever he was in port. He paid them handsomely, and everyone benefited from their arrangement. Any one of them would have been thrilled with the proposal he had just made.

Proposal. Was that it? She could not possibly have expected a marriage proposal, could she? She wasn't some simpering little society miss on the market for a husband. She acted completely uninterested in any relationship with a man, let alone marriage. And while Evelyn was convinced Alex was a lady, there was no real evidence. The few glimpses he had of her past would indicate otherwise.

No, that could not be the problem, but he was at a loss to understand her anger. She had such strange ideas. No telling what she was thinking.

He had to admit he didn't know much about her, and this bothered him tremendously.

He tensed as someone approached from behind, hoping she had followed him to apologize and beg his forgiveness, but knowing that was wishful thinking. The step was too heavy and the looming shadow too large. He glanced angrily behind him, saw Grayson approaching, and turned back to the railing, unsure whether he wished to speak with anyone.

Grayson grabbed hold of his shoulder and swung him around to face him. "What did you do to her?"

"What are you talking about?" Nicholas replied, although he knew the answer well enough.

"I just saw Turner, and she's obviously been crying." Grayson looked angrier than Nicholas had ever seen him.

"We had a disagreement."

"A disagreement? Hah! You seduced her, didn't you? I cannot believe you would do such a thing. And I just sat back and allowed it to happen. I had my suspicions, but I didn't care to believe it of you." Grayson shook his head and paced the deck, speaking in a low voice, so only Nicholas could hear. "I was an idiot. I should have protected her, but I didn't want to think I needed to protect her from you. So what are you going to do now?"

Nicholas flinched at the scorn lacing his best friend's question. "I don't know." He must have sounded as forlorn as he felt, because Grayson stopped pacing and took a sharp look at Nicholas's face.

"She wasn't just some conquest, was she? You actually care about her." Grayson sounded amazed.

"Yes. I believe so. But I am at a loss to figure out

how to handle the situation in which I find myself."

"Sounds like we need a plan. Let's go." Grayson grabbed his arm and dragged him back to his cabin. They passed the galley on the way and grabbed a bottle of scotch. A good plan could always use the help of good scotch.

Chapter Fourteen

April 23 (36 Days Remaining)

Alex went about her duties in a daze, heartbroken and embarrassed. She wasn't sure how she was going to face Nicholas that night.

Could she just blow off discussions of the future or would he insist on finalizing everything? He wasn't the kind of man to let things go, but she didn't want to lie to him any more than necessary. She really hoped she could get him to drop the subject.

These thoughts occupied her throughout the day, but she pushed them aside when Evelyn joined her at the rail in the late afternoon. She couldn't bring herself to discuss her love life with a fourteen-year-old girl, even if she was the closest thing she had to a friend in this time.

"Are you all right?" Evelyn asked quietly.

"I'm fine," she replied in surprise. "Why? Don't I look okay?"

"To be honest, you look a little pale and not quite yourself."

"I guess I'm just a little preoccupied. Don't worry about it. I'll be fine." To distract her, Alex asked, "Are you sure no one will mind if I come with you when we arrive?"

When Alex had mentioned the Creswell name,

Evelyn had jumped in delight. She knew the family well, if only from the distance of servant to employer.

Alex had said the Creswells were distant relations whom she'd never met. Evelyn had understood her reluctance to show up on their doorstep unannounced and had suggested they travel to Evelyn's home together before deciding how she should approach the Creswells, if at all.

"It will be fine. My mother will love you, and the Thorpes are a wonderful family. They're much nicer than most peers. They won't mind if you spend a few days there until you find a place to stay. Besides, mother will find you a place in the servants' quarters, so they may not even notice you, if that is your wish."

"That would be great. I—"

Evelyn continued chatting, not noticing Alex had started to speak. "The Thorpes are very well connected. They know everyone and are on intimate terms with Lord and Lady Downing. Their sons are close friends. If you wish, I am sure they could arrange an introduction. They have always been so kind to my mother and me…"

Alex smiled at her, barely listening as she rambled on. Evelyn obviously adored this Thorpe family and couldn't seem to sing their praises highly enough.

When Evelyn stopped to take a breath, Alex asked, "Why did you ever leave?"

Evelyn's smile faded, and she glanced out at sea for so long, Alex thought she might not answer.

"It's rather a long story. Suffice it to say, it felt as though the time had come for me to set out on my own. I managed to secure a position with Miss Elizabeth." She paused and a tear came to her eye. "She was a lovely girl. I was happy with her for a while, until she married that scoundrel. He swept her off her feet. She was so in love and happy, but the moment they were married and he had her money…" Tears ran silently down her cheeks.

Alex put her arm around her shoulders, squeezing gently. "I'm so sorry. I didn't realize you were so close. It must have been horrible."

Evelyn nodded. "Yes, I…" She paused, looking at something behind Alex with a queer expression on her face.

Alex turned to look, and her jaw dropped. Nicholas and Mr. Grayson struggled up from below deck. They argued as Mr. Grayson attempted to hold Nicholas back.

Something was odd about Nicholas. He moved strangely, and Alex had never seen him argue with Mr. Grayson before. Brief snatches drifted to where Alex and Evelyn stood, looking on in amazement.

"Wait until you're…" said Mr. Grayson.

"I am not…" Nicholas replied.

"Now's not the…"

"I will not wait any…"

Their words wavered in and out as the ocean waves slapped against the hull. Mr. Grayson appeared to give up, shaking his head and walking away while Nicholas stood peering around, his arms outstretched slightly as if trying to maintain balance.

"What do you think's going on?" Alex asked Evelyn. "Nic… uh, the captain looks as if he's about to fall over."

"Foxed, looks like," Evelyn replied.

Alex did a double take. She should have

recognized the signs, she'd worked as a bartender long enough, but somehow it seemed completely out of character.

A moment later, he caught sight of her and made his way to her side. "Alex."

She stared back at him, waiting for him to say something and hoping he wasn't about to embarrass the hell out of her, but somehow pretty sure he was. When he didn't say anything, "yes?" she prompted.

She thought he was about to fall, but suddenly he reached out and pulled her roughly to him. There was nothing clumsy about his kiss. Shocked, she leaned against him, unable to break away. And not sure she wanted to.

A gentle coughing slowly reached her ears, and Nicholas pulled back, though he didn't release her.

When she looked around, she saw they had gathered a crowd. All along the ship, people had stopped working to gawk at the spectacle of their captain embracing a young boy.

"Oh, God," she said. "What must they be thinking?" She hid her face in Nicholas's chest and groaned.

"Go back to work." She reared back to stare and her jaw dropped as Nicholas waved a hand and spoke to the watching crowd. "Alexandra and I have some important matters to discuss."

She caught a brief glimpse of Mr. Duff staring at her as he paused in his work on the rail a short distance away. She hadn't noticed him as she talked to Evelyn. The look on his face made her shiver.

Nicholas tugged at her hands, forcing her to follow as he led her back to his cabin. His smile was reminiscent of a young child who had accomplished some great feat of daring, clearly expecting everyone to be overjoyed with his success.

"What the hell was that all about?" she demanded the second the door slammed closed behind her.

He tried to pull her toward him, but she snatched her hand away and dodged across the room so she could glare at him from a safe distance. The crumpled sheets brought forth memories from the night before, and she averted her gaze, trying to focus on her humiliation. Not as pleasant, but much smarter at the moment.

He fell into a chair and leaned back with a sigh. "I told you we needed to talk."

"You can't seriously have been expecting me so soon. It's still daylight."

"I may be a little foxed and not thinking too clearly at the moment." His words slurred slightly.

All her anger drained away, and she had to laugh. "I think that's a bit of an understatement."

She went over and knelt in front of him, peering up into his handsome face. "Well, I'm here now. What did you want to say?"

"I can't remember," he whispered as he reached for her.

****

Alex spent the next few days sequestered in Nicholas's cabin, too embarrassed to face the rest of the crew. He tried to ease her mind by saying the crew had taken the news of her gender well, but she wasn't sure if this was true or if he just said it to ease her discomfort. He certainly didn't object to her remaining in his cabin as he left to inform Mr. Grayson he would be in charge for the duration.

By some mutual unspoken agreement, they didn't discuss the future, although all other topics were fair game. The days passed swiftly as they spent the time getting to know each other better.

All too soon, they heard the cry, "Land ahoy!" and Nicholas left to see to his ship.

The news brought mixed feelings for Alex. She was anxious over her sister and eager to begin her search, but the thought of leaving Nicholas brought fresh tears to her eyes as she sat in his cabin thumbing through one of his books.

She looked up at a quiet knock on the door and quickly dried her tears. "Come in."

"Did you hear?" Evelyn asked as she walked through the door. "They've spotted land. We'll be home soon."

"That's great." Alex forced a smile.

Evelyn sat across from her and leaned over to take one of her hands in her own. "Do you want to talk about it?"

"About what?" Alex feigned innocence.

"I may be young, but I'm not an idiot." Evelyn sat back and folded her hands in her lap. "Do you still wish to leave with me?"

"Of course, nothing's changed." *Only her whole world.*

****

Nicholas finished tying his cravat and looked over at Alex lounging naked under the covers. "I will return as soon as I can. I have to take care of a few matters myself, or I wouldn't leave you." He grinned widely and moved toward her. "I certainly do not care to leave while you present such a tempting picture." He sat on the edge of the bed and leaned into her, savoring the silken warmth and delicate scent of her skin as he trailed kisses down the length of her arm.

Her hand came up to trace the scar along his cheek, and it surprised him to find he didn't mind.

"Does it hurt?" she asked quietly.

"No." He hated the scars. Women viewed his face with horror and repugnance, men with fear. His crew saw it as a badge of honor, a reminder of his actions in the war. Hardly anyone took the time to look past the scars to see him.

Not Alex. With her, his scars no longer defined him. She didn't flinch away in revulsion, and that pleased him. The pride of his accomplishments overrode his hatred of his disfigurement for the first time.

She gazed at him as if trying to remember every detail of his face. A small tremor of foreboding caused him to frown, but she pressed her lips to his, and all thoughts receded as he lost himself in the sweet delicacy of her kiss.

He broke away reluctantly and laughed, albeit a bit shakily. "I had better leave, or you might tempt me to remain here all day." After one last, longing look he turned and headed out the door.

****

Alex breathed a sigh of relief. That had been much harder than she'd thought it would be. She still wasn't sure how she had managed to keep from breaking down and begging him not to leave. She was lucky a kiss could so easily distract him, even if it had left her weak in the knees and wondering how she would find the courage to walk out of his life.

Quickly. That was the key. She rushed to get dressed. Before long, Evelyn knocked and entered, carrying a bag with all their belongings. She looked excited and happy, but a touch nervous as well.

"Are you sure they won't stop us?"

"They have no reason to. I think Nicholas has made it pretty clear you're forgiven, and, well, I'm not sure what they think of me, but they have no reason to stop me either." She shrugged and tried to look casual, as if every fiber of her being wasn't screaming out in pain.

****

Alex squinted in the sun as she came up from below deck, stepping hastily to the side as a sailor rushed past carrying a heavy wooden crate. Finally. They could get off the ship. When she got home, she'd never again complain at the time it took to get off a crowded bus.

Everywhere she looked, sailors raced to and fro, going about the business of unloading cargo and finishing their work as quickly as possible, eager to head to shore. Spirits high, they joked around as they worked, but their ribald comments died away when they saw her and Evelyn. As one sailor nudged another to draw their attention, work momentarily halted as all eyes focused on them. Then quickly, as if it had never happened, work resumed, though with fewer bawdy jokes.

She tried to ignore it all as she strode to the gangway, hoping she looked more confident than she felt.

Just as they stepped onto the dock, a voice she had dreaded spoke from the rail above, "Where are you off to?"

She looked back at the Adonis as he started toward them. "I just have a few errands to run."

"Surely it can wait until the captain gets back. I'm sure he would be pleased to accompany you."

"No," she said, a little too quickly. "That's not necessary. I don't wish to waste his time, and I know he had plenty to do today." Was that suspicion in the first mate's eye?

"You should have someone with you. It's not safe for a lady on the wharf."

Oh, so that was it. The whole *women are too delicate and must be protected at all times* crap. "I can handle myself. Besides, as far as anyone can tell, I'm a man, escorting a young girl. Don't worry we'll be fine." Before he could say any more or insist on sending an escort, she pulled Evelyn along and walked away from the ship, trying not to look as if she were running away.

Evelyn looked back over her shoulder briefly. "I don't believe he's following."

Alex sighed in relief. "That was close. I was worried he was about to insist on having someone escort us. Now. How do we get out of here?"

****

Nicholas leapt down from the carriage and gazed at his townhome. His. Hard to believe. He could remember the day Lucius had dragged him out and taken him to the docks. He hadn't been back since.

Not nearly as big and imposing as he'd remembered. Of course, at only ten and three, he'd been much smaller then.

The door swung open before he made it past the newly-painted, light blue gate at the entrance. His sister fairly flew down the three steps, skidding to a stop directly before him and sinking into a graceful curtsy. He bowed in response, laughed, and pulled her into his embrace.

"Meghan! You know I do not abide such formality." He smiled into her glowing blue eyes. How she'd grown. "Who is this lady that stands before me? Where is the little minx I left?"

She tilted her head in a regal manner to look down her nose. Not as effective as it could be as she stood a full foot shorter than he. "It has been five years, Oakleigh. Our brother did not approve of my reckless behavior."

He frowned at her use of his title. "I may be Lord Oakleigh, but I am still your brother."

She grinned, and her eyes twinkled as they had when she'd been a child, before their father's untimely death. Her spirit was good to see.

"Oh, Nicky. It's so good to have you home." She placed her hand gently upon his arm and urged him toward the house. "Come. Mother is waiting."

The butler stood at attention by the door. He bowed as Nicholas passed and stood by to receive his hat and greatcoat. Nicholas had dressed for the occasion. He knew his mother would expect it. It had been too long, and he wished to please her. She'd been through enough at his elder brother's hands.

"Mother is in the drawing room. We watched you arrive. I simply could not wait to greet you."

He followed Meghan up the stairs. The house looked to be in the midst of refurbishment. Everywhere he looked were signs the house had been on the verge of ruin prior to the recent improvements.

"Meghan." He reached out a hand to halt her midway up the stairs. He nodded to the wall where half the paper had been stripped away. He ran his hand over a piece of the faded, dirty paper still remaining. Tools littered the upstairs corridor. "Mother is refurbishing the house?"

"Yes." She looked around. Was she avoiding his eyes? "We were surprised when we received your message that you had arrived so soon. We had hoped to have the house complete before your arrival. Mother wished to make your homecoming as grand as possible."

He took a closer look at her dress. It looked new. "Is that a new dress?"

She nodded and continued up the stairs without saying anything further.

His mother stood to greet him as he came through the door into the drawing room. She held out her hands, and he rushed forward to take them in his. "Nicky! It is so good to have you home."

"It is good to be home, Mother." He kissed her hands and embraced her. He held her lightly, lest he crush her frail form in his arms. "Are you well?"

"Of course, darling." She lowered herself to a settee and patted the spot beside her. "Please, sit. I have sent Yates for refreshments. You must be hungry after your journey."

He sat and looked around the room. It too had signs of recent repairs. "I see you are redecorating."

His mother stiffened. "Yes. I do hope you don't mind, Nicky. We wished to make sure your home suited your new station."

Meghan twisted her hands in her skirt and sat in a

chair opposite them. "Don't be angry, Nicky."

"Angry?" What did they think of him? "Why should I be?"

Meghan hung her head and spoke in a whisper, "Because of the expense."

"Never mind the expense. We are quite wealthy." He peered into his mother's face. "What I would like to know is why the house needed refurbishment so desperately? From the state of the old wallpaper, it appears as if the house was in a shambles."

His mother and sister stared at each other a moment before Meghan answered. "It was."

"Why?" He jumped up and paced the room. While everything was new and decent quality, there were very few decorations. He paused at an empty cabinet on the far wall. "Where is your figurine collection, mother? I seem to remember cabinets full of the tiny little statuettes."

"I found I no longer enjoyed them and disposed of them."

"Father bought you many of them." She would never get rid of those horrible artifacts. "You loved them."

"People change, Nicky." She shrugged as if it did not matter, but her eyes told a different story.

He shook his head. "We shall discuss that later. Answer my other question. Why was the house in disrepair?"

Meghan squeezed their mother's hands, which lay quietly on her knees. Odd, his mother had always been so full of life. His memories of her were of constant motion, not this deathlike stillness. He found he preferred movement.

"He will find out, Mother. Isn't it preferable for us to prepare him before he is confronted with the truth at the first society function he attends?"

Mother sighed, squared her shoulders and looked at him. "I did not wish for you to know the truth of how we have lived these past few years."

He sat in a chair across from her, his hands on his knees and leaned forward to keep his eyes on hers. "My understanding is that my brother was quite wealthy."

"Yes. As are you now. However, he did not feel obligated to drown his father's widow in luxury, as he claimed your father was wont to do."

Meghan gave a most unladylike snort. It pleased him to hear it. Some things had not changed so drastically. "Meaning, he did not feel it necessary to spend a penny to support us."

"He did not provide you with an allowance? I understood from father's will that you were to be taken care of to the end of your days." He forced his hands to unclench. His brother's neck was quite far beyond his reach.

"However, the will did not state in any direct terms the extent of that allowance." Mother shook her head and smiled sadly. "Your father believed your brother would gladly take care of us all. He fell quite short of my expectations."

"Bastard!"

"Nicky!" Mother gasped. "You may be used to such rough language on board your ship, but I will not tolerate it in my drawing room."

He grinned. "Ah, Mother. It's a pleasure to be back in the fold. I haven't been chastised in years."

Her lips quirked, and Meghan put a hand over her

smile.

"I am so happy to have you finally at home," Mother said. "It is awful of me, yet I could wish your father's eldest son had drunk himself to death years ago. Then perhaps I would not have had to give up my own son to satisfy Lucius's spiteful nature."

"Lucius drank himself to death?"

"Essentially," she replied. "He made the foolhardy decision to ride a horse he could not manage when sober. He was thrown. I confide in you, my son, but that knowledge is not to be discussed. It would be a dreadful scandal."

He nodded. He could not manage to dredge up any regret for their loss, other than a wish to inflict on his half-brother some measure of the pain Lucius had inflicted on his mother and sister, not to mention himself. "I am sorry, Mother. Meghan. I did not realize your troubles. I imagined Lucius's grievances were confined to my person. I had always planned on returning when I amassed a large enough fortune to keep you in the lifestyle in which I believed you were accustomed. Had I realized..."

"It isn't your fault, Nicky," Meghan chimed in. "We saw no reason to burden you."

"There was nothing you could do, in any case. Lucius was appointed Meghan's guardian. He never would have allowed you to take her. And I would never have left her to his care."

Meghan grinned. "Your gifts came in quite handy in recent years."

"I would have sent more."

Mother shook her head. "Lucius would have found out and taken it away." She waved her hand. "Enough.

We will discuss it no more. Let us discuss the future."

He wasn't sure he liked the sound of that, but he returned the wide grins his family sent his way.

It was good to be home.

Chapter Fifteen

April 30 (29 Days Remaining)

Alex looked up at the elegant townhouse as she walked under the wrought iron archway, Evelyn beside her. She started up the few steps leading to the front door, but Evelyn put a hand to her arm, holding her back.

"Oh, no. We need to go down here to the servants' entrance, not the front door," Evelyn said, a slight frown on her face. She squinted her eyes and scrutinized Alex before leading her off to the side.

"What's with that look?" Alex followed Evelyn down a steep set of stairs.

At the bottom, Evelyn led her to a door on their right. She paused, turning to look at her. "It's just..." She hesitated. "...the way you naturally went to the front door. I knew you were quality the moment you mentioned your relation to the Creswell family. You are, aren't you?"

"I have no idea what you're talking about."

"You're quality, a noble, not a servant like me." She smiled. "It's okay. You have your reasons for keeping it secret, I won't pry." She turned and knocked on the door as if satisfied she had her answer.

Almost immediately the door swung open, and a young woman about Evelyn's age answered, "Can I help you?" When she got a good look at them, she let out a squeal of delight. "Evie!"

"Louise!" Evelyn shrieked. The girls fell together, hugging and laughing like the young women they were.

Louise started a stream of chatter whose speed surpassed any radio advertisement disclaimer Alex had ever heard. As the girls caught up on each other's lives over the past few months, Alex's attention wandered to her surroundings. A small hatch behind them seemed to lead out under the street, and she wondered what it could possibly be for, but the girls had moved, still chattering, and she followed.

Servants rushed back and forth everywhere. She flattened her back against the wall as someone rushed past, a foul smelling bucket in her hands. *Eww.* She recognized a chamber pot and prayed the girl didn't run into anyone as she rushed about with the thing. "Is it normally so busy around here?"

"Oh, no miss. It's just my lady is having a small dinner party tonight, and we're a bit short handed." She glanced at Evelyn before continuing. "Young Mr. Thorpe has become engaged, and his betrothed's family and a few close friends are celebrating the announcement of their union tonight."

Evelyn looked crestfallen but visibly pulled herself together before asking, "How can we be understaffed? The Thorpes have always kept a large household. Certainly enough to handle a small dinner party. Is something amiss?"

"A few of the maids have taken ill and…" Louise rambled off a list of the household woes. The girl could really talk.

"I can help," Alex chimed in, trying to cut Louise

off before she fell over from lack of oxygen. Alex had yet to see her take a full breath.

"No, don't be silly." Evelyn perched her hands on her hips and frowned.

"Why not? I may not be able to cook, but I can help with the cleaning or other manual labor." Keeping busy might help keep her mind off other...things.

"But, but, it just wouldn't be proper!"

"Nonsense, I want to help. Maybe I can borrow a change of clothes? Then I can get right to work."

****

Soon enough, dressed in borrowed clothes, Alex sent Evelyn off to be reunited with her mother and set to work assisting one of the upstairs maids. The shy young woman barely spoke except to point Alex to her next chore, which left Alex plenty of time to think.

Her thoughts dwelled on Nicholas. What was he doing? Did he realize she wasn't there? Her heart ached as she thought of him coming back to the ship to find her missing. She had left a short note, but it didn't explain anything.

She couldn't explain, not really. She had simply said she'd gone to begin the search for her sister and wished him well. Heartless, but all she had been able to manage. The truth was impossible.

The truth! They would lock her up in an insane asylum if she tried to tell anyone the truth. And yet, somehow, she had been tempted to tell Nicholas. She had started to write it out but had come to her senses and ripped it up.

The afternoon wore on in a daze of menial chores, the hardest part of which was doing it while wearing a full-length skirt. She kept tripping over it. She thought that was why the servants kept giving her odd looks until Evelyn explained what was bothering them.

"They all know my theory that you're a lady, and they're wondering what you're doing here," Evelyn explained. "They're all quite intrigued by you and have been pestering me with questions. Why are you here? Why were you dressed as a man when you arrived? They can't stop talking about it."

"I hope I haven't caused any problems for you or your mother?"

"Oh, no, not a bit. They're thrilled. They live for gossip. Even Mr. Dobson." Evelyn led her down a narrow, winding staircase to the basement servant level.

"Mr. Dobson?"

"The butler. He was scandalized, of course. But I've known him since I was a young child, and he has a soft spot for me. Once I told him what you did for me, he was willing to overlook your unusual arrival. Now, come and meet my mother."

She led Alex to the kitchen, toward the back of the house. As far as possible from the main house in case of fire, Evelyn explained. All work stopped as everyone looked around at her entrance but quickly started again. Still too much work to be done for the party.

A woman about the same height as Evelyn but twice the width stood from the table and stepped forward to greet her. She had brown hair liberally streaked with gray and a kind smile. "There you are! I have been so looking forward to meeting you. My daughter's savior." Her eyes twinkled and her smile widened. "Yes, she told me about what you did for her, and I am so grateful." She pulled Alex to her, kissing both cheeks and then stepping back to get a good look at her. "Now, sit down and have a little something to eat. You are much too skinny."

Alex sat at the long table.

Evelyn's mother—"Call me Maggie, dear"— placed a huge plate of food in front of her and another for her daughter.

"We're informal here in the kitchen, probably not what you're used to, but with all the preparations for the party, we nibble a little here and there when we have a moment."

"No, this is great, thank you. I'm starved." Alex dug into the huge meal, wondering how she could possibly manage even half.

"So tell me how I can help. Evelyn tells me you're on a bit of a quest."

"I'm trying to find my sister. I have distant relations in London and plan to start with them. However, I don't want to just show up on their doorstep. I'm not really sure whether I'd be welcome." Alex stifled her guilt at all the lies she had to tell these nice people. "If I could stay here tonight, I would appreciate it." She smiled at Maggie's nod. "Tomorrow I'll find a hotel and maybe start by contacting the authorities."

"You should seek an audience with Lord Thorpe. He has many connections and may be able to help you, without bringing the authorities into it." She tapped a finger against her lip, her brow wrinkled. "You would not wish to create a scandal if it can be avoided. Lord Thorpe will know how to handle the thing properly."

"I'm not really concerned about scandal. Once I find my sister, I'll be leaving, so it doesn't really matter what people think of me."

"What about your sister? What if she minds? Or the rest of your family?" Maggie asked. "No. You will start by speaking with Lord Thorpe. After that, if you still wish to go to the authorities you may." She nodded as if the matter were settled. "Are you finished with your meal, dear? It's time to get back to work."

****

Alex had placed a huge arrangement of flowers on a table in the drawing room when the door opened behind her. Two gentlemen walked in, completely absorbed in their conversation.

"She's an angel. Wait until you meet her," the shorter of the two men said in an animated tone of voice, his excitement spilling over not only in his voice but in his agitated gestures and eager posture.

Alex coughed slightly to let them know she was in the room and went to walk past them with a muttered, "Excuse me." Unfortunately, she still wasn't used to walking around in such long skirts and tripped on her hem just as she reached the door.

The taller of the two men caught her arm, steadying her. He looked into her face and turned deathly white. "What...Who...Who are you?"

She looked back at him in surprise. "My name's Alex. I'm helping out today."

He turned even paler when she said her name.

"If you'll excuse me, I should be getting back to work." Confused at his reaction, she made to continue out of the room, but he wouldn't release her arm. She glared at his hand and raised her eyebrows. "Let go," she said, in as authoritative a voice as she could manage. *What's wrong with him?*

"Alex. Alexandra?"

"Creswell? What's wrong?" the other man asked. He grasped his friend's shoulder and gave Alex a once over.

She stifled a gasp at the man's name. Evelyn had thought it likely the family would attend tonight. Alex had planned to hide in the servants' quarters during the dinner. Maybe sneak a peek into the dining room when no one was looking and catch a glimpse of her ancestors. This was too much.

"Can't you see it? She looks just like Mary. A little older and her hair's darker, but the resemblance is astonishing." His head swiveled back and forth between Alex and his friend as if seeking reassurance he wasn't hallucinating. "And her name is Alex."

"You don't think she's…"

"That's exactly what I'm thinking!" He turned from his friend to look at her again. "But what are you doing here? How did you get here? Where did you come from? How long have you been here?" He paused for a fraction of a second. "Answer me, damn it!"

His friend gasped.

A feverish light shone in the man's eye. Even his friend seemed alarmed at his behavior.

She hadn't thought anyone would think she was part of the Creswell family. She should have done some research on them before she came. Too late now. Now, she just wanted to get away from them. She'd have to bluster her way out of this. "I'm sorry. I don't know what the problem is, but I should be going." She tried to pull her arm from his grasp, but he tightened his hold.

"No. You can't go. Answer me," he demanded.

"Creswell, calm down," his friend interrupted. "Let her go. You're frightening her."

The crazed look faded from Creswell's eyes, and he seemed to come back to his senses. He dropped her arm but moved to stand between her and the door, effectively keeping her there all the same. "I'm terribly sorry. This has been a bit of a shock. Please sit." He waved her to an ornate sofa positioned on the far side of the room next to a huge fireplace.

"What's your problem?" She cast him a scathing glare. "Never mind. I don't care. Just move, I'm leaving. Now." She tried to walk past him, but he didn't budge.

His friend stepped out the door and called down the stairs, "Dobson, please come up here right away." He stepped back inside. "We'll ask Dobson about her. He knows everything that goes on around here."

This wasn't going to be as easy as she'd hoped. She should at least try to use Creswell's shock to her advantage. "Does this have something to do with my sister? Do you know where she is?" She threw caution to the wind. Maybe she could learn something while she figured out how to get out of here.

"Your sister?" Creswell's hands shook, and he fell back a step. "Charlotte?"

This time Alex paled. She hadn't expected that reaction. "You do know something! Where is she? What did you do to her?" She grabbed the man by his jacket and tried to shake him, too freaked out to think clearly. The man topped her by about half a foot and looked to be solid muscle. He didn't move an inch.

He threw his arms around her and hugged her tightly to his chest. "Alexandra, it is you!" Tears ran silently down his face. "I can't believe it. After all these years."

She pushed against him and finally freed herself. Shit. She couldn't let him think she was his missing sister. Could she? "I'm sorry. I don't know who you think I am, but there's obviously been some mistake."

Just then, Mr. Dobson walked in and bowed slightly to both men. "Sir?"

The second man, Alex hadn't heard his name, but guessed he must be the young Mr. Thorpe she had heard so much about, said, "Yes, Dobson. Who is this young woman, and how did she come to be here?"

"Ah, yes, sir. She joined us today, along with Evelyn, the daughter of Lady Thorpe's abigail. She volunteered to help ready the house for your dinner party this evening and has been helping the maids for most of the day."

"Fine. But who is she?"

The butler began to look nervous. "Is there a problem sir? Has she done something egregious?" He cast Alex an evil glare, then pulled himself up straight and faced his master. "I am to blame, sir. I should not have permitted her to stay. I allowed myself to be deceived in her character. Because of a very kind service she performed for our little Evelyn, I assumed she was of the highest moral character. Please allow me to escort her out and contact the authorities." He moved to grab her arm, but Mr. Thorpe pulled him back.

"No, nothing like that." He waved aside this concern. "We simply need to know who she is."

The butler visibly relaxed and opened his mouth to answer.

"It's really none of your damn business," Alex chimed in, annoyed they were standing around discussing her as if she weren't in the room. Mr.

Dobson gasped, and both men looked at her in surprise. "I don't know who you think I am, and I don't really care. I just want to leave."

"Alexandra, it's me. Gregory. Your brother."

****

Alex glowered at him. "I don't have a brother."

"Don't you remember me?" He shook his head with a sad smile. "You must have suffered some injury to not remember your family. That would certainly explain why you have not returned to us. Tell me where you have been all this time and what brought you here. What's this about Charlotte? Is she here too?" His face lit with an inner joy Alex didn't understand.

"Excuse me, my lord," Mr. Dobson interrupted. "From what I understand, the young woman has recently arrived from America. She is searching for her twin sister, who, she believes, is in trouble."

"Charlotte's in trouble? What kind of trouble? Do you know where she is now?" The happy smile had faded, replaced with a worried frown. "What can I do to help?"

"Look, you must have me confused with someone else."

"I am not mistaken. The resemblance is uncanny. There can be no other explanation. I was thirteen when you and Charlotte disappeared from our garden. You were ten. It was a horrible time, but I remember you well." He gave himself a little shake, but then looked at her and smiled. "But here you are. It's a miracle."

Alex took a good look at him. Now that he'd calmed down and stopped scaring her out of her wits, she realized he was quite handsome. Maybe a couple of inches over six feet, he had a strong face with large green eyes and brown hair that fell over his forehead in a casual way that belied his formal attire.

He wore light colored pants with a dark green coat that brought out the color of his eyes and fit snugly over his wide shoulders. She couldn't imagine how he managed to keep his waistcoat and shirt so brilliantly white in a time before washing machines and even her untrained eye could tell his cravat was expertly tied. At least, she could picture it on any of the actors she'd watched play Mr. Darcy on TV.

She studied Gregory's face, noting their resemblance. Something about the eyes and their hair color was similar. Yup. Definitely one of those ancestors she'd intended to keep an eye on. Though certainly not from this close up.

Who would have thought the resemblance would be so remarkable so many generations later? She should have, that's who. Why, oh why, hadn't she gotten out of sight before the guests started to arrive? She'd known he might be here.

She shook her head. How was she going to talk her way out of this one? She needed time to think. "I'm sorry. It's just not possible. I'm sorry for your loss, but I can't possibly be who you think I am."

"Please. Stay. Our parents will be here in a short while. Meet them. We don't have to figure everything out now. We can take some time, but please, don't leave." He stood in front of her, his arms crossed over his chest, an audible tremor in his voice as he pleaded with her to stay.

Our parents—That sounded really good. If only it were possible, but it wasn't. Her parents had died when she was a child.

Still, they were family, of a sort, weren't they? Alex sank onto the sofa and looked into the depths of the fire burning low on the hearth, the smell of coal strong in her nose.

She pressed the heels of her palms into her eyes and tried to focus. What should she do?

****

That question was answered when they heard a knock on the front door. Mr. Dobson left to answer it and a noisy group entered.

"That's them; I hear mother's voice," Gregory exclaimed. "Wait here; I'll only be a moment."

Alex fought back a wave of panic and leapt to her feet, wringing her hands. Gregory rushed out the door, but his friend stayed behind and watched her warily. She thought of pushing past him, but after a quick glance at his stance next to the door, she thought he seemed prepared to stop her.

While she tried to think of the best course of action, Gregory returned. With him came an older man she realized must be his father. They had similar builds and the same strong face, though the elder had more wrinkles and was heavier in the midsection. His gray hair was cut close to his head, and he dressed as impeccably as his son. Alex would have felt quite intimidated by him, if not for the kindness that shone in his blue eyes.

It appeared Gregory hadn't explained his theory regarding her, because after greeting Mr. Thorpe, he looked around inquiringly and following a kind smile in her direction, turned to his son. "What was it you wished to speak with me about in such an urgent manner? You were quite rude to your mother and our hosts." He frowned at his son.

"I'm sorry, Father, but I felt I should bring this to your attention first, on the off chance I am mistaken. I would not wish to upset Mother."

"And just what is it that would be so upsetting to your mother?"

He gestured toward Alex. "Her."

The man smiled kindly. "You will have to excuse my son. It seems his mother and I have failed to impress on him the importance of good manners." He stepped toward her with a slight nod of his head. "I am Lord Downing." He stopped within a foot of her, and his eyes widened. He stared at her face and found the explanation for his son's odd behavior. He looked to his son for confirmation.

"Father, this is Alexandra. Our Alexandra, I believe. She arrived in London this morning."

"Alexandra," Lord Downing whispered, as he reached out to her.

Alex anticipated his intention and dashed out of reach. "I'm truly sorry that my appearance here is causing so much confusion. I wish I could be the person you think I am, but it's just not possible." She chewed her bottom lip in indecision, a vague sense of— something—in the back of her head. She shook herself to clear it. She couldn't quite name the feeling and didn't have time to figure it out, with this man staring at her thinking her his dead daughter brought back to life.

For a brief moment, she flirted with the idea of going with it—she could use the help. But much as she hated to dash their hope, letting these people think they had regained their long lost daughter only to leave would be cruel, and she immediately dismissed the idea.

Lord Downing followed her with his eyes. "I don't know what is going on, but we will figure it out together. You, young woman, are going to sit down and tell me all about yourself. And I will tell you all about us and the tragedy that befell our family fifteen years ago."

****

Alex's thoughts rioted about in her head. The easiest emotion to deal with at this point was anger at being treated as if she had no say in the matter, so she latched on to that anger in an attempt to keep her sanity. "I'm tired of everyone acting like they can order me around," she lashed out. "I can't deal with this. I have other things to do, and I'm leaving. You can get out of my way on your own, or I can make you move. Your choice." She glared at Mr. Thorpe, still standing quietly in front of the exit.

His eyebrows shot up into his hairline, and he smiled, which enraged her further. She started toward him, but Lord Downing intervened.

"I am Marcus Creswell, The Earl of Downing, and as such, I may indeed *order you around*, Miss...?" He left the sentence hanging, clearly waiting for her to insert her name.

"Turner," she replied tersely, unsure of her standing. How could she have forgotten for even a moment that women didn't have the same rights in this day and age as they did in her own? Did an earl, or his son, have the right to detain her if they wished?

She had a sneaking suspicion they did.

"Thank you. Now, if you please, have a seat." He looked at Alex and then over at Mr. Thorpe and sighed.

"I am sorry, Mr. Thorpe. We are quite ruining your engagement dinner."

Mr. Thorpe interjected before he could continue. "Not to worry at all my lord. This is an amazing discovery. I am quite thrilled to be a party to such a wondrous occasion. Miss Hawkins will quite understand when I explain the circumstances."

"Thank you. I—"

"This appears to be a bad time for everyone," Alex interrupted, thinking to buy some time to sort out her thoughts before the interrogation she knew was coming. "And I, for one, could really use some rest. I've been up and working since before dawn. Maybe it would be best if we talked tomorrow." She tried to look tired, let her shoulders droop and avoided Lord Downing's eyes.

"Working?" He frowned and looked at her again, taking in everything from her ill-fitting and dirt-streaked dress to her work-reddened hands. "I beg your pardon, you must be exhausted. Perhaps it would be better if we continued this in the morning." He looked at his son. "See that she gets home safely. I will make your excuses." He started to leave but turned back. "I think it best if we not mention this to anyone else until we have a chance to settle affairs tomorrow."

After his father left, Gregory turned to Mr. Thorpe. "Can you ensure this remains between us?"

"Certainly. I will simply inform Dobson that if any information on Miss Turner escapes this house, the person responsible will be turned out—without references."

"You can't do that!" Alex objected. "I don't want anyone to lose their job over me. Besides, I've been here all day, and the way I arrived was pretty juicy gossip. It's probably spread all over town by now."

"What do you mean?" Gregory asked.

"Well, from the reaction I got when I arrived, I take it women don't usually show up at the door wearing men's clothing. Not even at the service entrance."

"Men's clothing! Why?" He shook his head. "No. You can explain yourself tomorrow. It's time I got you home."

Chapter Sixteen

May 1 (28 Days Remaining)

Alex awoke from a delicious dream involving Nicholas and a bottle of whipped cream. She sighed and stretched luxuriously, wondering what woke her, and whether it would be possible to get back to her dream. She'd tossed and turned half the night, trying to make sense of everything, and was still tired.

The bed curtains parted and sunlight streamed in from the window, momentarily blinding her. "What's going on?" She rubbed her eyes and tried so see past the colorful spots left from the dazzling light.

"It's time to get up, my lady."

"Evelyn?" Alex blinked, and Evelyn's smiling face came slowly into focus. Alex sat up and swung her legs over the edge of the bed. "What are you doing here?"

"I just arrived this morning." Evelyn beamed. "It took me awhile to find out what happened; the staff is under strict orders not to discuss it, but I finally spoke to Mr. Dobson himself and he told me." She cast Alex a self-satisfied smirk. "I knew you were quality. Didn't I tell you so? I knew you were more than merely a distant, unwelcome, poor relation. Daughter of an earl. Isn't it just wonderful, my lady?"

"I'm not an earl's daughter," Alex mumbled. "And stop calling me, *my lady*."

Evelyn ignored her. "Well, first thing this morning I made my way here and presented myself to the housekeeper as your abigail." For the first time since entering the room, her smile faded, and she turned away. "That's if you want me. I—I understand if you feel you need someone with references." She peeked at Alex through lowered lashes.

Alex stood and put her hands on Evelyn's shoulders. Looking straight into Evelyn's eyes, she smiled. "I couldn't ask for anyone better than you. You've been a great friend. I really appreciate it." She paused. "So what's an abigail?"

Evelyn's smile returned full force, and she bobbed down into a quick curtsey. "Oh, thank you, my lady! I promise you will be very pleased with my skills. My mother taught me everything she knows." Ignoring her question, she moved around Alex and placed a dress carefully on the bed. "The earl asked that I deliver this morning dress and undergarments for your use until you have your own. They belong to your sister." Alex frowned and she broke off, but then continued swiftly, "to his daughter, Lady Mary."

Alex glanced at the gown nervously. "I don't want to impose. I'll just wear the clothes from yesterday or my—"

"No, you can't. I already returned them and had the other burned," she said with a shudder. "Besides, they're not suitable for the daughter of an earl." Shaking her head, she observed Alex shyly from beneath lowered lids.

Knowing her as she did, Alex suspected she had something on her mind, so she nodded her encouragement. "Go on, say what you're thinking."

"It's just that..." Evelyn took a deep breath. "You should try to accept what's happening, rather than fighting against it. I know you are accustomed to doing everything on your own, but you don't have to now. You have a family to help you. They have welcomed you with open arms and are truly thrilled at your presence. The Creswells are a highly respected family; you should be proud to be one of them."

Alex blinked back tears and turned away before Evelyn could see. "But it's not true, and I don't want to deceive anyone." But oh, how a part of her wanted it to be true!

"Mr. Dobson told me the family resemblance is astounding. And think about it, you have the same name as their daughter and a twin sister named Charlotte. That can't be coincidence."

"I guess we'll just have to wait and see." How could she explain she hadn't been born until the nineteen eighties, and rather than being one of the earl's twin daughters, she was a distant descendant named after the original who went missing? It sounded like a crazy sci-fi soap opera.

Evelyn cleared her throat and bustled around the room. "We better get you dressed properly. Lord Downing wants to see you."

Alex groaned. She had forgotten for a moment what she faced this morning. "Maybe I could just slip out the back."

Evelyn laughed. "Don't be silly. Come now. Get dressed. I think this shade of blue will be quite becoming."

Alex fingered the delicate fabric of the gown and realized she was completely at a loss to know how to get dressed 'properly.' "Um…" She paused, blushing and uncertain how to ask for help without revealing how little she knew of the clothing of the time. She had muddled her way through dressing in the maid's outfit yesterday and had worn her own padded corset, but this 'Lady's' outfit seemed a bit more complicated. And Evelyn apparently wasn't going to let her get away with wearing her own undergarments.

Evelyn came to the rescue, without even knowing it. "Hurry up now. Take that off, and we'll get you into a nice clean shift." She held up a long white shirt from the pile on the bed and looked Alex up and down disapprovingly. "Didn't they have someone help you undress last night? I would have thought they would have provided you with proper nightclothes, rather than forcing you to sleep in your shift." She looked nervously at the door and gestured at Alex impatiently. "Go on now, we don't have much time."

Relieved Evelyn was going to stay and see her through the intricacies of a nineteenth century morning dress, Alex quickly complied. After a dizzying number of hooks, buttons and ties, she looked the part of a proper earl's daughter, or so Evelyn said as she stood behind her fastening the dress.

For her part, Alex thought modern push-up bras had nothing on a nineteenth century corset. She tried to pull the dress up a bit to cover the amazing amount of cleavage on display and sighed in relief when Evelyn added a little scrap of lace that transformed the gown from indecent to demure.

"It's just a simple morning dress, but the color does look lovely on you." Evelyn smiled fondly, and then with a quick slap at Alex's tugging hand said, "Quit fussing, you're all done." She motioned Alex toward a small table and chair set against the wall. "Now, we must do something about your hair."

****

Alex walked cautiously down to the library after Evelyn declared her fit to be seen. By family and close friends only, of course. She smiled, recalling Evelyn's parting words of advice.

"This is a morning dress, so remember, you mustn't go out anywhere."

The look on Evelyn's face warned her that she took this quite seriously, so Alex stifled the laugh that rose to her lips as Evelyn continued her lecture.

"You may receive visits from close friends, but other than that, this dress is strictly for around the house. I'm sure your family will see you have appropriate attire for the rest of the day. Come back to your room after you meet with the family, and I'm sure I'll have something for you."

She actually looked forward to it, in a way. She smoothed the front of the high-waisted gown with its dainty pink and green flower pattern. She could feel the stiffness of the corset that had her breasts pushed up practically to her chin, but with all the layers, it wasn't visible to anyone else. She felt all fancy and dressed up, like a child trying on her mom's clothes pretending to be all grown up. She couldn't imagine how she'd look in a gown Evelyn considered *appropriate*.

She wouldn't feel like herself that was for sure. And sometimes she thought that wouldn't be such a bad thing. For a little while at least. She could almost lose herself in this place, with this family. Except she didn't really belong.

The thought brought a frown to her face. She couldn't afford to like it here. She'd be leaving soon. She had to focus. Find Charlotte and get out. She was becoming too attached already. First Nicholas and now the Creswells. Evelyn too.

Thinking of Evelyn had her smiling again. She was lucky to have met the girl. She would have been lost without her. While Alex had always loved reading historical romances, she'd leaned toward highlanders and medievals rather than regencies. They didn't begin to prepare her for this.

That had been obvious when Evelyn had felt it necessary to give her a lecture about clothes. Luckily, Evelyn had assumed her lack of knowledge came from being raised away from her true family. Alex hadn't had to think up some plausible excuse, and she had Evelyn as a guide for the ins and outs of polite society.

Alex paused outside the library. Her smile faded as she heard the rumble of raised voices beyond the slightly open door. She knocked and the voices silenced.

A deep voice commanded, "Come in."

She pushed open the door and stopped dead, her mouth hanging open.

****

"What are *you* doing here?" she asked.

Nicholas turned his fierce gaze in her direction. The look on his face caused her breath to catch in her throat. She had known he'd be angry, she just never thought she would actually have to face up to it.

Even so, it was the worry in his gaze that affected her more than anything and had her moving toward him before she was even aware of her own intentions.

"I'm fine, Nicholas," she said softly. She stopped a few feet in front of him and looked up into his smoldering eyes, golden sparks flying within their hazel depths. "There was no reason for you to worry. I can take care of myself."

"You can take care of yourself, can you? Is that what you're doing?" He glowered at the earl and his son, whom she had barely noticed and ignored now as she devoted her attention to Nicholas. His gaze softened as he put one hand on her shoulder and cupped her face with the other, looking deep into her eyes.

"Take your hands off her!" Gregory moved to intervene, but she waved him off.

"Are you all right?" Nicholas caressed her cheek with his thumb. "Did he hurt you...force you...?" His eyes closed and voice trailed off as if he couldn't bear to finish the sentence or hear the answer.

"Force me to what?" she asked, not immediately grasping his meaning. Her face flamed a second later as his thoughts became clear.

"Grayson had you followed. He told me how that boy..." He glared briefly at Gregory, then returned his gaze to her. "...forced you into a carriage. It took us a while to figure out who had you, or I would have been here sooner." He lowered his forehead to rest against hers. "Am I too late?" he whispered.

Gregory grabbed Nicholas's arm to pull him away, but only succeeded in bringing Nicholas's wrathful gaze his way. "How dare you come into my home and imply that I—that I—"

Lord Downing interrupted, "Gregory, do sit." His voice left no room for argument, and Gregory spluttered to a stop. "We appear to have a number of misconceptions to set to rights, and I will not allow this to erupt into violence."

Nicholas ripped his arm out of Gregory's grasp. "Listen to your father, puppy. I'll deal with you later."

Gregory stalked over to a chair and threw himself into it, his hands clenching and unclenching continually. "Call me puppy...arrogant bastard...," he mumbled under his breath.

"And you, Lord Oakleigh, will kindly take your hands off Lady Alexandra and have a seat." He waved toward another chair. He walked to Alex and took her hand gently in his own. Seeing that Nicholas had declined to sit in favor of leaning on a corner of the desk with his arms crossed, he led Alex to the chair and motioned for her to take it. "Alexandra, we have much to discuss, but first we need to deal with this—person."

Alex could sense Lord Downing was upset even though he kept his face neutral. Remorse surged through her at the pain her presence caused this nice man, and she patted his hand before taking the offered seat. "Please don't worry about me. You all seem very nice, but as I told you last night, I'm not who you think I am."

"We'll get to that later, but first, does this man have some claim on you?"

"Yes," Nicholas said.

"No," Alex said at the same time.

"She's mine," Nicholas stated.

"Excuse me?" Alex exclaimed. "I don't belong to anyone, thank you very much." She glared at Nicholas, the nerve of the man. She opened her mouth to continue.

"Stop. Both of you," Lord Downing held up his

hands. "So we have a difference of opinion, apparently. Are you saying the two of you are betrothed or married, Lord Oakleigh?" He fixed Nicholas with a hard gaze.

"No." He appeared a bit unsure of himself for the first time. "But I fail to see what business it is of yours."

"Lady Alexandra is my business. Since you have no claim on her, I'll have to ask you to leave."

"I'm not leaving her with you and the puppy," Nicholas practically growled the words. "You're eager to inquire into my business, but you have yet to explain what claim *you* have on her."

Lord Downing gave Nicholas a considering look, and then nodded his head as if coming to a difficult decision. "I will explain, as you appear to have Lady Alexandra's best interest at heart, but I ask for your word to not repeat any of this outside this room—at least for the moment." As Nicholas started to protest, Lord Downing continued, "I can promise you that I am also looking to protect Lady Alexandra. We would never hurt her."

"Fine," Nicholas grunted through clenched teeth. "You have my word, provided my silence will not hurt Alex."

"Thank you." Lord Downing nodded.

"Excuse me, but has everyone forgotten that I'm in the room?" Alex asked through gritted teeth. "I really hate people talking about me as if I have no say in the matter."

"You don't," Nicholas stated with a flash of his usual grin that made Alex's pulse flutter even as the urge to strangle him nearly choked her.

At the same time, Lord Downing said, "We need to

rectify this misunderstanding, Alexandra. Would you prefer that Lord Oakleigh and Gregory finish this with pistols at dawn?"

Alex fell back in her seat and tore her gaze away from Nicholas. "Pistols at dawn? That's insane." She wanted to scoff at the absurdity of it all but deep down realized how deadly serious they were.

"Did you believe I would not defend your honor?" Nicholas demanded. "If this puppy hurt you, I won't rest until he pays for his crime."

"Fine." Alex huffed and looked at Nicholas. "Lord Downing here thinks I'm his long lost daughter. I keep telling him he's wrong, but he won't listen to me. So, no. I didn't come here willingly, but Gregory hasn't hurt me. Far from it. He thinks I'm his sister."

"We brought her here to find out where she has been all these years and to convince her that she is, indeed, my daughter. I am certain of it."

****

"Your daughter?" Nicholas repeated in astonishment. "How is that possible?" He looked to Lord Downing for the answer. Alex had clamped her lips together and was studying her nails. He didn't think she was prepared to answer.

"Our twin daughters, Alexandra and Charlotte, were kidnapped fifteen years ago," Lord Downing began, a pained expression on his face as he recalled what must have been a tortuous time for the obviously devoted father. "They were taken right out of our own garden on their tenth birthday."

Nicholas frowned. "That was your family? I do not recall the details, but there were rumors the kidnappings were politically motivated."

"Yes. Someone threatened myself and a number of my fellow lords in order to influence a vote during Parliament that year. I was one of the leaders in favor of the bill." Lord Downing looked at Alex, his eyes suspiciously bright.

A wave of pity for the man washed over Nicholas.

"Can you forgive me, darling?" Lord Downing asked her. "I should have taken the threats more seriously. I never should have allowed you and your sister out of the house. It was my fault," he whispered.

Tears slipped silently down Alex's face. Nicholas longed to hold her close and wipe away her pain, but he simply watched in silence as Alex reached out her hand and Lord Downing grasped it between his own. "You can't blame yourself for what some madman did."

As he watched the tender moment play out between father and daughter, he turned his thoughts to his next course of action.

He had been enraged upon learning of Alex's desertion when he returned to *The Reliant* late the night before. Then, when Grayson had reported she had been forcibly removed from a house in Berkeley Square, he had been frantic with worry. They searched all night, his mind tortured with thoughts of her suffering. He'd blamed himself for not settling the future with her before he had left her alone. He wouldn't make that mistake again.

His brother's death had altered his world drastically. The rules of polite society reached out to muddle his thoughts and make his options less clear. He didn't know what to do anymore or how to act. His impulse was to grab Alex and drag her home. It had taken all of his control not to engage in fisticuffs with the puppy when he arrived a half hour ago, and they had refused to admit Alex was there.

He was used to taking what he wanted and damn the consequences, but he had a position in society that demanded he conform to certain modes of conduct.

His mother had made this abundantly clear when he visited her yesterday. "You are a marquess now, not a ship's captain. It is your responsibility to uphold the honor of our family name. I understand it will be difficult, but your sister and I will help you reestablish yourself into society. You will be welcome. Your title is impressive and your wealth substantial."

She had given him a stern look. "However, the *ton* likes nothing more than a good scandal, and having been absent from society for so long, your return is already the latest *on dit*. Your sister will make her debut this year. It is long overdue, and we do not want a scandal to ruin her chances of a happy match." She had looked at him fondly then and smiled. "The young debutants will flock to you, as will their mothers. I can foresee no difficulty in finding you a brilliant match before the season ends." He hadn't had the heart to tell her he wasn't interested in looking for a wife, when he had his lovely mistress waiting for him on *The Reliant.* Or so he had thought at the time.

Instead, he had spent one of the longest and most miserable nights of his life, dealing with Alex's abandonment and subsequent kidnapping by some rich nabob. Now the revelation she was not only safe, but possibly an earl's daughter, was almost too much to comprehend. Abducting a young woman, an earl's daughter no less, would cause a scandal even his mother couldn't imagine, and he wouldn't do that to her. Only now, his course of action remained unclear. The feeling was unfamiliar and most unwelcome.

He watched her fidget in her seat. God, she was beautiful. He had known she would look fantastic in proper clothing. He had, in fact, borrowed a dress from his sister, unbeknownst to his mother, and had been looking forward to taking Alex shopping for a new wardrobe. As much as he was furious at her desertion, it didn't change the fact he wanted her in his life. One way or another, she would be his.

****

Tears trickled down Alex's cheeks and fell unheeded as she reached out for Lord Downing. She wanted to ease this man's grief but didn't know how. "You can't blame yourself for what some madman did."

"Oh, but I can. I ignored the threat and continued to seek support for my position. I was arrogant and naïve. So sure in my belief I was right and no one would dare to hurt me or my family." He squeezed her hand and then smiled brilliantly at her. "But now here you are! We thought you dead these many years. Where have you been?"

Alex squirmed and looked away, wiping the tears from her cheeks. Her glance fell to Nicholas, watching in silence. To avoid the current subject, she turned her attention to him. "So. Nicholas. As you can see, I'm in no danger, so feel free to leave whenever you're ready," she said, ruining the chilly tone she tried to adopt by sniffling in the middle.

"I'm not leaving."

"What do you mean, you're not leaving?" Alex asked, her voice squeaking embarrassingly. Trying not to sound too guilty or worse, regretful, she cleared her throat and continued in a slightly stronger voice. "Look, I'm sorry if you got the impression I was planning on staying with you. I tried to tell you it wasn't possible, but you didn't want to listen."

"So you just left, without even a fare-thee-well. I would never have thought you to be a coward."

Alex's spine stiffened. "I'm not a coward," she said. "I just chose to avoid a little unpleasantness." Her excuse sounded lame even to her own ears.

Apparently he felt the same, for he snorted and repeated, "coward."

Lord Downing cleared his throat, and Alex returned her attention to him. He didn't look pleased at what he was hearing. "Alexandra, what exactly is the nature of your relationship with this man? How do you know him?"

"Alex was one of the sailors on my ship, *The Reliant…*" Nicholas stated calmly. An undercurrent of amusement tinged his voice, which faded and turned angry as he continued, "…and she did not have permission to disembark."

"I beg your pardon? A sailor?"

"I felt it best to travel in disguise." Alex blushed as both Lord Downing and Gregory gaped at her in astonishment. "I was traveling alone and thought to avoid certain situations…" She let her voice trail off, unsure how to continue in the face of their obvious dismay.

"What about your abigail? Did she not travel with you?" Lord Downing asked. "She seems quite devoted. I assumed she had been with you for some time."

"Actually, I met Evelyn on board. I helped her out

of a small situation so she's just..." Alex shrugged. "...grateful."

Lord Downing turned to Nicholas. "Were you aware of her true nature?"

"Not at first, no. I thought she was younger than she claimed. It didn't occur to me that a woman would be capable of such a ruse."

"Most of the men didn't look twice at me, convinced as they are of their own superiority. The disguise worked very well, for a while."

"I expect you did not have the wherewithal to purchase passage, hence your sojourn as a sailor?" Lord Downing asked.

"*The Reliant* was the first ship leaving for London and wasn't willing to take me as a passenger. I didn't have time to wait for one that did."

"You say the disguise worked well *for a while*. How and when did your masquerade unravel?"

Alex winced at the suspicion evident in Gregory's tone. She had been hoping no one would notice that small slip of the tongue.

"As I said, I helped Evelyn out of a little trouble, and in the anxiety of the moment, she let my secret slip." Alex kept her words vague and hoped they wouldn't pry deeper, not wanting to go into details. She hadn't counted on Nicholas's perverse sense of humor.

"Yes, it was quite something. There I was watching Alex beating Mr. Duff senseless, and enjoying myself immensely as Mr. Duff richly deserved a beating, when the little minx Alex had been hiding in the hold comes running up to me, demanding that I not let Mr. Duff hurt *her*. Imagine my surprise." He chuckled, clearly enjoying the effect his story caused.

Alex wanted to slap the evil grin from his smug, handsome face, but thought Lord Downing and Gregory had probably suffered enough shock. "I'll explain the whole story later. It's, uh, not as bad as it sounds." She satisfied herself with casting Nicholas a killer glare, which didn't faze him in the least. "Suffice it to say, Nicholas and the first mate discovered my disguise and that was that." Would they leave well enough alone?

"What *exactly* did you do with this information, Oakleigh?" Lord Downing asked, the ice in his voice freezing Alex in her chair.

"I merely changed her *duties* to accommodate her new found status." The inflection of his tone led no doubt about the nature of those duties.

Alex stared at Nicholas, her fingers itching to wrap around his throat. *What was he trying to prove?*

The smug look on his face didn't fade a bit, even when Gregory leaped up from his chair, fists clenched at his sides. "You—You—Scoundrel!"

Furious that Nicholas seemed set on embarrassing her, she ground out, "He means that he took me off some of the more dangerous jobs—like taking a turn in the rigging."

With a quick glance at her and a wicked grin, "I meant," Nicholas said, "I assigned her tasks that kept her—shall we say—close?"

This was apparently too much for Gregory. He launched himself at Nicholas and let fly with his fist. But Nicholas was too fast. He ducked and landed his own fist in Gregory's stomach, doubling him over. Lord Downing stepped between the two.

"Gregory, have a seat. I shall handle this." As Gregory slouched into a chair, still clutching his stomach and gasping for air, Lord Downing considered Nicholas. "I find it curious that you would make such crude suggestions, when your purpose for being here was to wrest Alexandra from our *nefarious* clutches." He walked calmly to sit behind his desk. "So, shall I assume you are prepared to obtain the special license?"

"I should have it in a week."

"Ah, I thought so."

Alex looked from one to the other in confusion. "What are they talking about?" she whispered to Gregory, who ignored her as he watched the bi-play between his father and Nicholas. "Would someone please tell me what's going on?" Alex hated the whiny note that came into her voice, but it was too late to fix that now.

Lord Downing looked at her and asked quietly, "I dislike embarrassing you this way, but I must know the truth. Lord Nicholas has implied that the two of you have been—intimate. Is this true?"

Alex gasped. "That is really none of your business!" Heat consumed her cheeks when she darted a glance at Nicholas, afraid the truth was written on her face.

Apparently, her fear was well founded. Lord Downing sighed and said, "I'll have the papers drawn up immediately."

"What papers?"

"Settlement papers. For your marriage."

Chapter Seventeen

May 1 (28 Days Remaining)

Alex stormed back to her room, startling Evelyn when she slammed the door.

"Whatever is the matter?" Evelyn's voice carried a note of concern.

"Are all men in this day and age arrogant, domineering jackasses?" she demanded. "I'd like to know, because I've yet to meet one who isn't. Why does every man believe they have the right to tell *me* what to do? I'm not an idiot; I can make my own decisions." She paced around the room. "If one more person tells me they know what's best for me—I think I'll scream!"

"My lady, what has happened to put you in such a foul disposition?"

"They've decided I *need* to marry Nicholas." Alex sat abruptly on the bed and whispered, "You should have seen the look on Lord Downing's face when he realized I had been with Nicholas." She sniffed and tried to hold back the tears gathering at the corners of her eyes. "He was so disappointed…"

Evelyn sat and wrapped an arm around her waist, pulling Alex's head onto her shoulder. "It will be all right, my lady. He is probably most upset to think of losing you to a husband after having only just found you again."

"I doubt it. He just thinks I'm a slut."

Evelyn giggled. "Oh my, I don't believe I shall ever get used to your cussing. My mother would box my ears if she heard me speak such words."

Alex grimaced. "I've been trying to cut back, but I keep forgetting." She wiped a stray tear from her cheek.

"Well, no matter what Lord Downing thinks of your behavior prior to now, so long as you marry the captain, all will be forgiven." Evelyn comforted her with a pat on the shoulder.

Alex sat up and looked at Evelyn. "I don't need to be forgiven. I haven't done anything wrong, and I'm not marrying Nicholas."

Evelyn gasped. "Of course you must marry him. Setting aside the scandal of not marrying a man with whom you have been intimate, it would be a brilliant match. He's a marquess!" she exclaimed, as if this was reason enough to marry anyone. "Why would you not marry him?"

"Because I'm going back home as soon as I find my sister. And I'm not tying myself down to someone who doesn't..." The tears returned full force, and the last few words came out in a whisper. "...love me."

Evelyn pulled her back to her side. "Are you so sure he doesn't?"

****

Several hours later, Alex sat quietly in the back parlor, an area she had been told the family used as a gathering place whenever they spent time amongst themselves.

The room was cozy, with a roaring fire, slightly threadbare furnishings and a hint of lavender in the air.

Sheets of music lay propped open on the piano, books lay open on a table next to the built-in bookcase, and knitting overflowed a basket by a fireside chair. She could picture the family going about their individual pursuits while enjoying each other's company. She imagined they were a close-knit group.

Lord Downing had asked her to wait in this room while he gathered his family to break the news of her miraculous *return*. Nothing Alex said could convince him she wasn't his daughter.

She felt desperately sorry for the man. He wanted her to be his daughter so badly he refused to believe anything else. She could hardly blame him.

She stared into the fire, lost in her thoughts. She was tempted to believe it herself, but she clung to the thought of her father who had sacrificed himself to save her all those years ago. He had saved her and died trying to save her mother and sister from the fire that had burned their house to the ground. She couldn't forsake him, no matter how much she wished for a living, breathing family of her own.

"You look lovely tonight, Alex," Nicholas said.

She bolted from her chair. "I didn't hear you come in! What are you doing here?" Her heart skipped a beat then ran wildly as she watched him saunter into the room.

"Your father thought you might appreciate a familiar face tonight." His gaze raked her from head to toe. "You are beautiful in those clothes, but I must say, I prefer the way your arse looked in breeches."

"Nice. And Evelyn blushes at the things I say." Incredibly her heart raced even faster at the look in his eyes, and she turned toward the fire to calm her nerves.

"It was nice of you to come, but unnecessary. You don't need to stay if you don't want." *Please stay.*

She started as his arms wrapped round her waist but quickly melted back into his solid form.

"I'll stay," he whispered. His mouth brushed against her ear and sent shivers down her spine.

"Thank you," she said and her tension began to ease. Something about him inspired confidence. Now that he was here, she could handle whatever was about to happen this night. *It's so strange, this effect he has on me.*

They stood together for several minutes gazing into the fire before the door opened and Nicholas released her, stepping back quickly. She whipped around toward the door, wishing for a return of Nicholas's solid comfort against her back.

Lord Downing entered first, a beautiful, fragile-looking woman hanging on his arm. She scanned the room quickly, taking in Nicholas's presence with a brief glance before finding Alex and staring at her with wonder, tears falling silently from green eyes so like Alex's own. She made to rush forward, but Lord Downing had a firm hold of her hand and kept her at his side.

Gregory entered next escorting a young woman of about seventeen or eighteen. Alex stared. They did look amazingly alike. No wonder Gregory had been so taken with the sight of her.

Lastly came a young man, perhaps a year or two younger than his sister. He was tall and gangly, though not yet as tall as his brother. He tripped slightly as he entered, and his face turned beet red. Alex smiled at him, but this seemed only to increase his embarrassment.

"Lord Oakleigh, Alexandra, may I present my wife, Lady Downing," Lord Downing said as Lady Downing nodded her head at each in turn, though her eyes remained focused on Alex's face. "You have already met our eldest son, Viscount Creswell." Gregory bowed. "This is our youngest daughter, Lady Mary and our son, Myles."

Unsure of how she was supposed to act, Alex attempted to curtsey, but again, her skirts got in the way. She stumbled slightly, but Nicholas caught her arm and steadied her. Embarrassed, but grateful, she caught his hand and squeezed, holding it clasped between her own. The warmth of his palm spread to hers, and she took a deep, calming breath before greeting everyone, "It's nice to meet you all."

A moment of silence filled the room as they stared at one another, no one sure of how to act. What exactly should be said in such a circumstance?

Lady Downing stepped tentatively forward, one shaking hand stretched toward Alex. "Please, child. May I look at you?"

Nicholas squeezed then released her hands, smiling encouragingly as Alex nodded and moved toward the beautiful woman who claimed to be her mother.

The shaking of both their hands seemed to subside only when clasped together, face-to-face. The love and joy radiating from the woman before her was a palpable thing. Alex should reiterate her disbelief in their relationship but couldn't resist putting the inevitable aside for a brief moment to bask in this wonderful thing she had been denied her whole life, a mother's love. When Lady Downing drew her into her warm embrace, she closed her eyes and breathed her in.

Reality came crashing back at the tear-choked sound of the lady's voice, "Oh my darling daughter. How I have missed you these many years."

Alex pulled back slowly and wiped her eyes, smiling sadly at the woman. "I'm so sorry to disappoint you ma'am, but as I have already explained to your husband, I'm not your daughter."

"Nonsense." Lady Downing touched Alex's cheek gently. "I can see the truth with my eyes and feel it with my heart." She sighed. "However, I can see that you have not yet accepted the truth. I will not push you."

The lady returned to her husband's side. He smiled and held her hand as she sat, then moved to stand behind her, his hands resting lightly on her shoulders. "We will not push you to accept us," he repeated. "However, we will insist you stay with us as we help you locate your sister." When Alex opened her mouth to protest, he held up his hand to forestall her. "I have already instigated a search, and your help may be required. It would be most convenient for you to be here should you be needed."

Lady Mary spoke in a quiet, yet excited voice, "Oh, please won't you stay? It would be ever so nice to have you here. This is my very first season, and I am dreadfully nervous. It would be glorious to have a sister—a friend—to share confidences."

"Yes. Then she would have someone else to bore with all her talk about bonnets and other such silly girl things," Myles teased, poking his sister in the waist.

She turned and swatted his hand away. "Perhaps she can teach you how to talk with a woman without blushing and stumbling over your own feet," she replied tartly and smiled triumphantly as he blushed to the roots of his hair. She turned back to Alex. "And you must come to our ball. It's only a few weeks away."

Before Alex could respond, Lady Downing clapped her hands, "What an excellent idea, Mary! Of course you must come."

Silent so far, everyone turned to stare as Nicholas interrupted, "I'm sorry, but I won't allow it."

"Why ever not?" asked Lady Downing.

"I fear it may pose some danger for Alex," he said slowly, his brow knitted. "She looks exactly like her sister, and we already know Charlotte is in trouble. I wouldn't want to expose Alex to the same danger. I think it best she stay in the house. Or, better yet, with me."

"Humph." Alex snorted. "I'm here to help Charlotte, and that won't happen if I'm stuck in my room like a naughty child." She tapped her lip with the tip of her finger. "Now that you mention it though, it might not be a bad idea." She paced before the fire. "A ball might be just the place to flush the perp out."

"Flush the perp?" Lord Downing narrowed his eyes and tugged on his ear, his head tilted a bit to the side. "I'm afraid I don't understand."

Alex blushed. "Sorry," she mumbled. "Too many late night TV shows." Realizing they would have no idea what she was saying, she was quick to add, "It may amount to nothing, but someone kidnapped your girls all those years ago. If, like you, they mistook my Charlotte for your daughter, they may have kidnapped her to keep her quiet. Maybe they saw her and were frightened she would recognize them. If they see me, they may feel desperate enough to try something, and we'll be able to figure out who they are and have them arrested."

Everyone started talking at once, practically shouting to be heard. Nicholas overrode them all and spun her around to face him. "That is out of the question. I will not allow you to place yourself in danger."

Bristling at his tone, she replied, "It's not up to you now, is it?"

"It most certainly is. As your future husband, you must do as I say."

"Hah! You're—"

Luckily Lord Downing interrupted her, because she was so angry she had no idea what she had been about to say. "Her idea actually has some merit, Oakleigh," Lord Downing said quietly.

They swiveled to gape at him in unison. Alex couldn't have heard him right. She had been sure it was going to take a whole lot of convincing before she got her way.

"Excuse me?" Nicholas asked, his voice cold and lethal as he focused his full attention on Lord Downing.

"We always suspected whoever kidnapped our girls must have been someone I knew." He squeezed his wife's shoulder when she let out a small gasp and turned to face him more fully in her chair. "But were unable to determine the guilty party."

"You never told me!" Lady Downing accused in a trembling voice.

"I'm sorry, my dear. I thought it best not to upset you further. You may recall you were *enceinte* at the time."

"We shall discuss this later," she said, the ice in her

voice chilling even Alex from across the room.

Lord Downing winced, but nodded. "As I was saying, if Alexandra were to attend the ball and should the criminal be in attendance, she may possibly recognize him. We could finally bring the scoundrel to justice. She would hardly be in any danger in the middle of a crowded ball with all of us surrounding her." He turned to Nicholas. "As her betrothed, you would naturally be with her the entire evening and could personally see to her safety."

Before anyone could reply, Alex remarked, "I won't be able to recognize anyone, seeing as how I'm not actually your daughter. However, if the person were to fear recognition, like I said before, they may become desperate, and we'll figure it out when they try something." She smiled brightly. "So when is this party?"

"The evening of the twenty-eighth," Lady Mary said, her voice bubbly with excitement.

Alex's heart skipped a beat before hammering against her chest. The twenty-eighth. The night before Charlotte's murder.

****

After all arguments over her attendance at Lady Mary's ball ended with the assurance that she *would* be going, Lady Downing had swept her out of the room to begin preparations. With only a few weeks to go before the big event, not a moment was to be lost in outfitting Alex appropriately. They had spent the evening making lists and taking stock of Alex's meager belongings before Lady Downing had insisted Alex go to sleep early to rest for the morrow.

The next day passed in a blur as Alex got to know

the Creswell ladies. In the morning, they headed to the Burlington Arcade. Lady Downing assured her that while this was relatively new, it was still *the* place to go for all the latest fashion trends.

Had she not felt tremendously guilty at all the expense and hassle she was putting these wonderful people through, Alex would have enjoyed herself immensely. As it was, she would manage to relax for short bursts of time—until someone would ask a question about her life she couldn't possibly answer truthfully. Shame would return full force and slam her in the chest.

She had little in common with the two ladies, but she liked them never-the-less. They were kind and considerate and simply overjoyed to be with her. Even though Alex knew they must find her strange with her complete ignorance of the rules of the day, they never let slip they found her anything less than *delightful*— which seemed to be one of Lady Downing's favorite words.

The state of Alex's wardrobe shocked them, and she marveled at the amount of clothing they considered mere essentials. The day passed in a whirlwind of fabrics, ribbons, hats and shoes. Never in her life had Alex experienced such first rate service. They merely stepped foot into a shop when no less a personage than the owner would be at their side, seeing to their every desire and assuring Lady Downing those items that could not be created on the spot, dresses and such, would be completed without delay and delivered to their townhouse as soon as possible. Lady Downing and her daughter must be very good customers.

Not only popular with shop owners, the ladies

stopped frequently to greet an astonishing number of acquaintances. Shopping was apparently a favorite daytime activity during the season.

They introduced Alex as their American friend visiting for the season. Lady Downing couldn't hide her disappointment when Alex refused to allow her to introduce her as their long lost daughter.

She got over it quickly enough as she explained the importance of the social season in London. "We spend most of the year at our country estate. While we visit with our neighbors and often entertain close friends as guests at our home, our social circle is very limited. So when Parliament is in session, we come here with Lord Downing and have a chance to greet all our friends and meet others. It's also the best opportunity for young people to find a suitable match."

"What exactly makes a match *suitable*?" Alex asked, surprised at her interest.

"The two young people should have similar backgrounds, fortunes, and be of good family..." Lady Downing began.

"Don't forget about love, mother," interrupted Lady Mary. "I refuse to settle for anyone whom I do not love."

"Of course not, darling. Be sure the man to whom you give your affection is worthy of that honor. As the daughter of an earl, and a wealthy one at that, you will attract the attention of unsuitable persons trying to improve their station in life by marrying above themselves."

"You can't help who you fall in love with, though," Alex said. "Love doesn't work like that."

"Of course you can, dear," Lady Downing replied.

Mouth agape, Alex just stared for a moment, and then asked, "How?"

"Close your mouth, dear. It's most unbecoming." Her smile took the sting out of her words, but the smile was sad and a trifle shaky. "Your upbringing has been most unusual. How I wish I had been there for you. To teach you such life lessons as you grew up." She dabbed daintily at her eyes with a lacy handkerchief she pulled from her reticule. "Now, let us get back to the subject of love with a suitable gentleman. This is why a season in London is so important for a young lady's future. It is her opportunity to meet a variety of eligible young men with whom to fall in love. It is the responsibility of a young lady's parents or guardian to see to it she not meet any young men of unacceptable backgrounds. She is then free to fall in love without worry."

Alex burst out laughing but stifled her outburst as best she could when she realized Lady Downing was completely serious. "I'm sorry to laugh, but how exactly do you manage that?"

The two ladies looked curiously at Alex. "Why should that be at all difficult?" Lady Mary asked.

"How do you keep her from meeting someone unsuitable?" Alex asked again. "You can't tell me every single person at every event you attend is some paragon of virtue, wealth, and title looking to get married?"

"That is true, depending on the event there are often undesirable people in attendance, rakes, fortune hunters, and the like. However, we simply deny those gentlemen an introduction."

"I'm sorry, I don't understand. Deny an

introduction? How do you do that—ignore someone when they introduce themselves?"

"Introduce himself! Why such a thing is never done. It would be the height of impropriety, and that person would never be invited to another social event," Lady Mary exclaimed, blushing and apparently scandalized at the very thought.

"Really. Jeez, you people have more rules," Alex muttered, taking it all in.

"What was that, dear?" Lady Downing asked.

"Nothing," Alex said quickly. "Where to next?"

"We should return home. We have to get ready for this evening. Are you sure you won't accompany us, Alexandra?"

"No, thank you. I think it best if I just have a quiet evening to myself."

She had no reason to suspect this was not going to happen.

Chapter Eighteen

May 1 (28 Days Remaining)

After dinner, Alex selected a book from Lord Downing's library as the family got ready to go out. She stared at the shelves, her mind refusing to focus and settle on a book. She brought her hand up to cover her mouth as she yawned. Who knew shopping could be so exhausting.

The night was much too young to just go to bed though. Having worked as a bartender for so long, she rarely got to sleep before three or four in the morning and hadn't managed to kick the habit except when completely worn out on *The Reliant*.

She came across a copy of Jane Austen's *Pride and Prejudice* and pulled it gently from the shelf, reverently stroking the spine. To think, this wasn't one of a gazillion reprints. She held her breath and prepared to open its crisp new pages, but a knock at the open door interrupted her.

She looked up to see the butler waiting for her acknowledgement.

"A young lady has come to call and wishes to speak with you, my lady." He held out the tray in his hand for her to see.

A card, slightly larger than a modern business card, revealed the name—"Lady Meghan Somerville." *Oh, no. Nicholas's mother. It must be. What in the world is she doing here?*

"Shall I tell her you are not at home to visitors at the moment?" the butler, Preston, if she remembered correctly, asked.

"No, that's okay. Do the Creswells bring visitors in here or...?"

"I shall show her to the drawing room. Shall I send for some tea?"

"That would be great. Thanks, Preston."

The butler returned her nervous smile fleetingly as he left.

The precious Jane Austen book remained clutched tightly in her hands as Alex checked her hair in a mirror hanging next to the door. Dressed in another borrowed gown, she admired the way the fabric flowed gently from the high empire waist to the floor. Never having worn such fancy clothing in her life, she had to admit she liked the way she looked. She felt almost graceful, at least while she stood still and couldn't trip over the long skirts. Would she ever get used to the damn things?

This dress was in Mary's favorite shade of light pink, a row of lace around the hem was matched by a little lace collar contraption that covered her chest up to her neck and tied tightly under the dress below her breasts. Overall, she thought she looked nice, even if the color was a bit childish. Lady Downey had nixed all her requests for a basic black dress, insisting that since she was not in mourning, black would be completely inappropriate. Apparently, the slimming effects of black were not yet known in the regency.

After sneaking a quick peek at the front door to

make sure the coast was clear, she started up the stairs, and only realized she still held *Pride and Prejudice* when she was half-way there.

She faltered a second, wondering if she should return it to the library but decided against it. After all, if conversation failed...she had read the book for a literature class in college not that long ago. She could probably hold her own in a discussion. Of course, maybe his mother hadn't even read it. It may be a classic in her time, but now, it's just another book.

Bringing her attention back to the moment, she entered the drawing room to see a beautiful young woman standing next to the window, looking down on the street below. She quickly adjusted her thinking. The woman was young. She couldn't possibly be Nicholas's mom. She had been expecting his mother but found herself facing his sister instead. Her relief was short lived.

Alex cleared her throat and smiled as Meghan turned to face her. "I'm Alex. Preston said you wanted to see me?"

Meghan curtsied briefly, "So you are the—bird of paradise—whom my brother is making a cake of himself over."

Alex stumbled out of her attempted curtsey, a little flustered at her clumsiness and the fact she had no idea what Meghan just said. She stared a moment before saying, "Excuse me?"

In an extremely haughty voice, Meghan stared down her nose at Alex and said, "I may be unrehearsed in the use of such language, but I do believe I have managed to use the term accurately."

"I'm sorry, but I have no idea what you said. I've

never heard the term *bird of paradise* before. Unless you're talking about a Hawaiian flower—and I somehow doubt it. What does it mean?"

Meghan's face turned beet red, and she stammered, "Why it...it refers to someone...someone like you." She took a deep breath. "Someone of loose morals. A harlot," she finished in a rush.

Alex's muscles clenched, and she drew herself up straight. She hadn't expected Nicholas's family to love her, but she hadn't anticipated an outright attack either. "Well, Nicholas didn't mention his sister was such a bitch," she snapped back.

Meghan gasped. "How dare you!"

"You come here and call me a whore; you don't think that's a tad uncalled for?" *I will never understand these people. Seriously, the nerve of the bitch, she calls me a whore and then gets all indignant when I respond in kind.*

Meghan sank down onto the sofa and put her hand over her eyes. "Oh my. I am all at sixes and sevens. This has not gone at all as I planned."

What in the world? "Are you all right?" she asked, a little concerned now. The girl looked like she might faint. Nicholas acted like his sister walked on water. She could just imagine telling him the girl had collapsed after a mere five minutes in her company. *Just great.*

Alex strained to hear the feebly muttered, "I am fine, thank you." Meghan stared at her hands clasped tightly in her lap and said quietly, "Please, I must beg you will forget I ever called. It was uncommonly rude of me."

Alex stared at her. "Why did you come exactly? I

thought you were going to a play with Nicholas and your mother this evening. You just wanted to get your insults in without him around to see?"

Meghan finally looked up at her. "I slipped out," she admitted, albeit reluctantly. "I simply desired to keep you away from my dear brother. He has not been in society much of late and does not realize how a union with one such as you would negatively affect our entire family. It would be a dreadful scandal."

Alex snorted. "You say that as if you thought I would say *thank you* for informing me and simply walk away." *This girl is seriously delusional.*

"I must admit, I did indeed imagine something of that nature would occur." She returned to staring at her hands. "However, I have made a complete bumblebroth of the entire situation."

Alex tried to hold back a laugh, but it burst forth anyway, and she sank down next to Meghan on the sofa, tears streaming from her eyes while Meghan stared at her as if she were insane. She slowly brought herself under control, wiping at her cheeks. "I'm sorry. This is all just so crazy."

Meghan stood up stiffly, making Alex wonder if she actually had a wooden rod stuck up her a—her back.

"I am pleased to have provided you with such amusement. I shall see myself out."

Still chuckling slightly, Alex grabbed her arm. "No, please. Don't go. I'm not really laughing *at* you. I'm new here and everything seems so...unreal, sometimes. I think if I didn't laugh I would scream." She waited until Meghan's arm relaxed slightly, and then let go. "Preston sent for some tea. Won't you please stay? We can start all over again."

"That would be lovely, thank you."

From that point on, Meghan apologized repeatedly and launched into a long-winded explanation centering on her half-brother Lucius Somerville, the recently deceased Marquess of Oakleigh, who had apparently been such a tyrant Meghan had been practically locked in her room from the day their father died. She uttered expressions like *ape leader* and *tabby* with such a look of horror Alex knew this was a fate to be avoided like the plague.

When she finally realized Meghan was afraid she would never get married, Alex almost laughed. Until she thought about what that would mean for a woman of this century. Without any money of her own and no marketable skills, she would be forced to live off the generosity of her brother for the rest of her life. And while Alex was sure Nicholas wouldn't mind and would probably give Meghan anything she wanted, Alex could definitely see why she would prefer to get married and have a life of her own.

So instead of laughing, she reassured Meghan she had no intention of actually marrying Nicholas. Meghan said goodbye shortly after and left Alex with the feeling there was more to Meghan's animosity than she let on.

She was also more disappointed than she would have expected. Even though she had told Meghan the truth and had no intention of marrying Nicholas, it was depressing to realize that—even if she wanted to—she wouldn't be a welcome addition to that family.

Alex sat for a long while, listening to the clip-clop of horses' hooves and the rattling of carriages riding past in the street. She shivered and moved closer to the fire. How had she managed to make such a mess of everything?

Here she was living *the dream*, the one she'd had her entire life. The dream every orphan cherishes—where it turns out you're not really an orphan after all. A mistake had been made and a warm, rich, perfect family claims you as their own. Of course, *this* dream was a bit wacky, what with the time travel and all, but that hardly mattered. What did matter was that it was all a lie, based on the hopes and fears of a family that had already suffered so much and sooner or later, she was going to add to their suffering. Would they ever forgive her after she left? She had known them for such a short time, but she already cared about them.

What would they do when she disappeared—from their point of view—again? And what about Nicholas? Oh, God. Nicholas. What would *he* do? What would *she* do?

****

Lost in her thoughts, she looked up in surprise when the door opened and Nicholas came in, followed closely by Preston.

"Really, my lord, you must not. It would be more proper for you to wait in the hall until I can be reassured that my lady is able to receive visitors." Preston appeared flustered for the first time since Alex had entered the house. "I must apologize, my lady, I was unable to restrain his lordship."

Nicholas just grinned. "Don't worry yourself. It would take more than one man to keep me away from Alex." He tried to gesture Preston out of the room, but the butler refused to move and looked to Alex for guidance.

"Shall I summon some footmen to oust this scoundrel from the house, my lady?" He had regained his composure.

Alex fought back a grin and replied, "No thank you, Preston. I'll be fine."

"Very good. I shall inform the master that the gentleman is visiting."

"No need for that. I wanted a few minutes alone with Alex."

Preston left the room but made a point of opening the door as wide as it could go. He then made his way up the stairs, obviously on his way to inform Lord Downing Nicholas was here.

"Well, I don't think you've got much time." Alex let loose with a quiet chuckle. "Preston doesn't seem to approve."

Nicholas gathered her in his arms, stealing her breath away. "Then I had better be quick." And his mouth descended on hers in a blistering kiss that for all its brevity left Alex weak at the knees.

Her hand trembled as she lifted it to her lips after Nicholas released her. "What was that all about?" she asked, breathlessly.

"I missed you." He watched her with a look in his eyes that told her how much he wanted her. Right now, right there. But he restrained himself. They both knew they would not be alone much longer.

Sure enough, a second later, Lady Downing came rushing into the room, her hand held out to Nicholas. "Lord Oakleigh, you should be ashamed of yourself! Had we known you were to visit us this evening, Lord Downing and I would have been here to receive you properly."

Nicholas took the offered hand and kissed the back lightly. "I am afraid I was rather impulsive in my desire to see Alex this evening. I beg you will forgive me?"

Lady Downing melted at his words. She looked fondly between Alex and Nicholas. "I suppose I can allow for a young lover's feelings. I was young once myself." She smiled at Alex. "As you are engaged, I see no harm in allowing you a few moments of privacy. However"—and her gaze became stern—"the door will remain open, and Lord Downing and I will be right across the corridor." With that warning, she left them alone.

Nicholas took Alex's hand in his and brought her to the sofa, pulling her gently to sit at his side. "Please, I would speak with you a moment."

"Sure." Alex shifted to face him, moving further away in the process and placing her hands in her lap. She needed at least a little distance in order to think straight. She couldn't get the thought out of her head she would have to leave soon and would never see him again. *Could he hear her heart creaking with the strain?*

"My sister informed me of her visit here tonight. She would not reveal all of your conversation, but I did manage to find out you said you will not marry me." He frowned, and Alex thought he was angry with her, but he continued, "I was not pleased with her interference. I hope she did not say anything to upset you?"

"No, it was nothing. She just wanted to meet me, I guess," Alex lied.

Nicholas raised an eyebrow and peered at her. "I have a feeling there is more to it than that, but we shan't discuss it at the moment." His expression softened as he smiled and gathered her hand in his. "It has occurred to me that I may have never *asked* you to marry me. Assumed, demanded…"

"Ignored altogether?" Alex interjected.

"Ignored altogether." Nicholas brought her hand to his lips and kissed her fingers, one by one. "I have been terribly remiss." Kiss. "Please accept my apologies." Kiss. "And know that I will endeavor to never again ignore your desires." Kiss. "My life will, in fact"— kiss—"be devoted to fulfilling your each and every desire." Kiss. "Will you marry me?"

The tears came to her eyes, and she pulled her hand from his grasp. "No." She turned away to avoid watching his face.

"No?"

Alex winced at the coldness of his voice. At least he was finally hearing her.

"I'm sorry," she whispered. He rose from the couch and she turned to see him almost out the door.

He stopped and stood, gripping the door handle so tightly she feared it might break. He turned back toward her slowly, his face a blank mask. If not for the slight whitening of his lips pressed firmly together, she might have thought him completely unaffected by her rejection. "May I ask why?"

His voice was tightly controlled, but Alex could practically feel the tension.

"I've tried to tell you from the beginning, but you just wouldn't listen," Alex said. "I have to leave as soon as I find my sister. I can't possibly marry you."

"Are you married? You have to return to your husband, is that it?"

"No! Of course not." Alex shook her head. "I can't

explain it to you, I just have to leave."

"I see. I thought you were different. Yet you are like all the rest, you are simply a better actress. You had me fooled." He laughed bitterly.

"What are you talking about?"

"You don't want to leg-shackle yourself to someone who looks like me. You don't want to wake up every morning and face a monster."

She jumped to her feet, hands clenched. "Ooh! You are the most annoying, pain in the a—" She reached out as if to choke him, but shook her fists at him instead, and then propped them on her hips, threw her shoulders back, and glared. "Stop putting words in my mouth and listen to me for once. I love you. I don't care about a few scars. The only thing the scars show me is that you're brave and... Why are you looking at me like that?"

As she'd ranted, Nicholas's face had undergone a transformation, and he now eyed her with the oddest expression on his face. What had she said? Oh God. She'd just said she loved him. The man drove her crazy. She hadn't meant to admit to that!

"You love me?"

"Yes," she admitted, waiting on tenterhooks for his reply.

His face lit up, and he pulled her back into his arms, crushing her to his chest, his mouth devouring hers. Gradually, the kiss lightened, and he gently nibbled her lower lip, before trailing kisses along her jaw and sending shivers down her spine as his hot breath grazed her ear. "Then say you will marry me," he whispered.

Alex reared back and stared at him. "You're

impossible. I told you, I can't. It doesn't matter how I feel about you, I can't stay."

It was Nicholas's turn to stare. "Why not?"

Oh, God. He's gonna think I'm nuts. Alex took a deep breath. Time to admit the truth. "Like I said, I have to leave as soon as I find Charlotte. But…uh…" She paced before the fire. "I don't know how to explain this. You're going to think I'm crazy, but I'm telling you the truth."

"I should hope you will always tell me the truth, and I have faith in you. I could never believe you insane."

Alex snorted. "Wait 'til you hear me out." She stopped and faced him. Picking a spot on his right shoulder to stare at, she burst out, "I'm from the future. I traveled back in time to find my sister, who was stranded here while doing research on our ancestors. I haven't even been born yet. I won't be born until nineteen eighty-five. Once I find Charlotte, we'll both go through a time portal and back to the twenty-first century."

Nicholas just stared.

"Well? What do you have to say about that?" she asked nervously.

"I don't know whether to be amused or outraged. That is the most ridiculous story I have ever heard, and I don't understand what you are about."

"I told you so."

He cupped her face in his hands and forced her to look him in the eye. "You obviously don't feel you can trust me. While I am disappointed, I understand. Trust does not come easily to me either. The fact-of-the-matter is that we have not known each other long, and you are going through a difficult time right now. I cannot begin to fathom how difficult this must be for you." He kissed her ever so gently. "I will wait. I will help you find your sister, and you will learn to trust me. You can continue this ridiculous tale all you like. I will not be deterred. But just remember, in the end, we will be wed, and you will tell me the truth." He looked at the door. Alex could hear footsteps out in the hall. "I must leave now. I will come by to visit you tomorrow. Goodnight."

At first Alex thought the pain that stabbed her heart was caused by his refusal to believe her, but she had never expected him to, not really. No one would. No, that wasn't it. What was causing her chest to tighten and eyes to tear was she had admitted to being in love with him, and sure, he had been pleased, but he hadn't told her he loved her back.

****

The faint murmur of voices outside the door gave Alex less than a second warning before Lord and Lady Downing entered the room. Lady Downing sat next to her on the sofa and pulled Alex's hands gently into her own. "My dear, is there something you wish to share with us?"

Alex started. "Uh…no…why?"

Lord Downing answered, "What my dear wife is trying to say is we heard every word of your conversation, and she would like to discuss it with you."

Alex sat up straight and glared at the two of them, ripping her hands from Lady Downing's grasp. "You were eavesdropping? How dare you! You had no right." Being angry right now was easier than dealing with her pain. Alex tried hard to hold onto that anger, but the ache was already creeping over her heart.

"I am so very sorry, but you were not precisely quiet, and we worry so for your welfare…"

"You were worried, my dear. I am an excellent judge of character, and I trust that Lord Oakleigh will do nothing to hurt Alexandra."

"He looks so fierce most of the time. It's not the scar, though that adds to the impression. It's those eyes. I get chills when he looks at me with those piercing eyes."

Alex sighed. "Yeah, me too." At Lady Downing's knowing look, she blushed.

"Our point, Alexandra, is we heard your rather unusual reasoning for turning down Lord Oakleigh's proposal of marriage." He paced as he talked and looked like he was preparing to deliver a long, fatherly sermon. "I must say I feel honesty would have been a much wiser course of action. To make up such a blatant falsehood is unbecoming of a young lady of your position."

Before he could continue, Alex decided to put an end to this debacle. "Lord Downing, please stop." Alex rose and gestured for him to take the seat next to his wife. "I know you can't believe what I told Nicholas, but it's the truth. I really did travel back through time from the twenty-first century. I'm not your daughter, and when we find Charlotte, I will be returning to the future where I belong." She looked at their stunned faces and felt like crying all over again. It was so unlike her to cry, but she felt like that was all she was capable of lately. Would she ever get back to herself again?

Yes. As soon as she was back in her own time—to

her *real* life.

Thinking of her life brought her real parents to mind. She reached into her pocket and pulled out the small, neatly folded newspaper clipping of her parents' death. She opened it carefully and smoothed it out. "Here." She held the paper out to Lady Downing. "*This* was my family. Read it."

Lady Downing took the paper and read with Lord Downing looking over her shoulder. It didn't take them long, and they seemed more interested in the photograph than the article.

Lord Downing spoke first, "The date—nineteen hundred ninety-nine. It's not possible."

They studied the proof of her incredible story. Her fingers ached, and she realized she'd been squeezing them tightly into fists. She straightened her hands and smoothed down her skirt, before folding them lightly in front of herself.

"All right then, my dear. If you insist you are telling the truth, and this article does appear to support your claim, we believe you." Lord Downing looked at Lady Downing as he talked, and she nodded her head slightly in agreement.

Alex's jaw dropped, and she found herself completely tongue-tied. Did he just say they believed her? As proof went, she didn't think the newspaper clipping was that infallible.

"Believe what?" asked a male voice from the doorway.

Alex turned to see Mary and Gregory enter the room. Both were dressed in elegant evening clothes, like their parents. As dressed up as Alex felt in her borrowed finery, she felt plain compared to the rest.

"Alex has decided to trust us with some information on her past. Her story is quite amazing, and she feels sure we will be unable to believe her. I was assuring her that we believe *in* her and will do our best to put our skeptical natures aside and trust she would not lie to us."

"Why of course we will believe you, Alexandra! We are your family." Mary came up and gave her a big hug. "You look marvelous in that dress, by the way. I just knew it would suit you beautifully."

"I agree. I am pleased to learn you have decided to trust us with your past. We all would like to help you in whatever manner possible." Gregory took her hand and gave a slight squeeze before releasing it. "I believe we have time before the play is scheduled to begin; shall we all have a seat and listen to Alexandra's story?"

"You're all insane. You can't possibly believe me." Alex looked from one to the other in disbelief, but as they looked back at her, she saw simple acceptance on all their faces. Never in her life had anyone trusted her like this. She didn't know what to do, except tell the truth and see what happens.

"Alexandra has just explained that she comes to us from the future. The twenty-first century, in fact." Lord Downing handed the paper to Gregory before he continued, "This is as far as she has had a chance to explain thus far. Please Alexandra, continue."

Mary and Gregory looked stunned but quickly rearranged their expressions to show polite interest as they studied the paper between glances at Alex. Belief was easier said than done, apparently.

Not sure where to begin, Alex started at the beginning with Charlotte's phone call and disappearance. All four stared at her intently, but with such interest and compassion in their eyes, she could have wept.

"So, I came through the portal to find Charlotte before that newspaper article can come true. When I do, we'll be going home."

"This is quite extraordinary." Lady Downing held one hand to her head as if trying to ward off a headache. "And I am sorry to hear of the death of your parents, my dear. Were you taken in by relatives upon their demise?" Lady Downing asked, a slight tremble in her voice.

"No. My entire family died in that fire. Until Charlotte called me, I had no one." Alex wasn't used to talking so much. She swallowed, holding back her grimace at the pain in her throat as she reached for a cup of tea. The perfect hostess, Lady Downing had served the refreshments as soon as she had realized they would be staying for a while.

"Oh my, how dreadful!" Mary exclaimed, her hands covering her mouth. "What a terrible memory that must be for you."

"Actually, I don't remember anything." Alex shrugged, trying to act nonchalant about the extremely painful void in her memory. "I was injured during the fire and spent about two years in a coma. The first memory I have is waking up in the hospital."

A small noise brought Alex's attention back to Lady Downing, and Alex was surprised to see her look happier than she had all evening. She stared radiantly at her husband, and Alex saw the same joy reflected in his face.

"I have to admit, your reaction is not what I

normally get when I tell people my family's dead and I suffer from amnesia." Alex spoke a bit harshly, hurt that these two kind people could be so callous over her suffering. Not that she wanted pity or anything, but unalloyed joy was a bit much.

Lady Downing's expression fell. "I do not mean to belittle your suffering, child. I would do anything to be able to take away all the pain you must have suffered. It near breaks my heart to think of you, all alone, thinking your family dead."

Lord Downing handed her a handkerchief, and she dabbed at her eyes. "However, you must see that this all supports our belief that you are, in fact, our child."

Alex's brow furrowed. "How, exactly?"

"Don't you see? It all fits. Doesn't it, my lord?" Lady Downing turned to her husband and seemed encouraged by his expression. "Please, darling. Won't you explain?"

"Of course, my dear." He gave her hand an encouraging pat and looked Alex in the eye. Gregory and Mary sat nearby, watching with rapt attention. "You say time travel exists, that you were sent to this time by a man that could not give you a satisfactory answer as to why he required *you* to take part in your sister's rescue. Do you not see the answer? He sent you back because you belong here. They must have lied to you when you were a child. Mayhap in a misguided attempt to protect you. I do not begin to understand their reasoning.

"Your family did not die in a fire, because we are your family. You and Charlotte must have stumbled through the time portal when you were children, and you were raised in the future. Thank goodness you did, or you may not have survived. The fiend who kidnapped you may have killed you had you not managed to escape. While I mourn all the time we lost, I can rejoice in your presence now."

Alex stared. A roaring sounded in her ears, and she suddenly found it difficult to breathe. The light dimmed but for tiny flashes at the corners of her eyes. She tried to lean over and put her head between her knees but was unable to bend due to her corset. The long ruler-type thing in the middle, Evelyn had called it a busk, prevented her from having anything other than perfect posture. She felt like ripping it out, but was sure she couldn't manage on her own, besides which, she had shocked her family enough for one evening.

Her family! Oh my God. Could it be true? It actually made a weird kind of sense. Well, more sense than the crazy story Sawyer had fed her. The one she had gobbled up—hook, line, and sinker.

She looked around the drawing room then closed her eyes, the images of their kindly faces burned to her brain. She forced herself to breathe deeply, though she wanted to gasp and cry or simply let the light fade entirely and sink back into the couch unconscious. She had never fainted in her life and wasn't about to start now.

Chapter Nineteen

May 3 (26 Days Remaining)

Alex spent the next day alone in her room. Well, not entirely alone. Evelyn refused to heed Alex's request for privacy and watched over her as if she were on her deathbed, rather than simply overwhelmed by all that had transpired the day before.

Evelyn spoke in whispers and insisted on keeping the curtains shut and a fire blazing. Alex gave up reasoning with her and gave in. It wasn't all bad. Being coddled and cared for like a child was kind of nice for a change. She couldn't remember ever having anyone make such an effort on her behalf.

In fact, her head ached from trying desperately to remember something, anything about her family before the fire. She couldn't, even though she had spent half the night trying.

She had tossed and turned thinking through all the crazy conversations she'd had the previous evening. She went over and over everything that had been said. And not said. It was almost more than she could bear.

If only Nicholas loved her, how happy she would be! Instead, she was in this stiflingly hot room, wallowing in self-pity. If only she could get past her feelings for Nicholas and deal with her family.

Sometime in the middle of the night, she'd finally

come to the conclusion the Creswells were indeed her family. Hard to believe, but it actually fit the facts better than the story she'd been told. She should have been overjoyed. Instead, she just wondered what she was going to do.

Up until accepting the truth last night, everything had seemed clear. She would find her sister, and together they would return to the present, or future, or whatever.

She had never really considered Nicholas's offer seriously, because she couldn't accept it. She had no idea what she should do. Going back home was no longer the easy answer, because now she had two homes.

She could return to her life back in the twenty-first century. Back to hot showers and electricity, cell phones, and cars. Back to her lonely apartment and late nights working the bar while trying to avoid the octopus-like tentacles of horny college boys. Back to where Nicholas and her family would be but a memory, long since dead and buried.

Or she could stay. Stay where women were little more than property, hygiene was a fashion trend, and she would be forced to marry a man who didn't love her.

****

"You must get up now, my lady! One day is quite enough for you to stay in your room and sulk."

Evelyn's commanding voice woke Alex the next morning. She had fallen asleep in the wee hours of the morning, completely exhausted and still unsure of what she was going to do.

"I was not sulking; I was processing," Alex

grumbled, shutting her eyes tight against the bright light flooding through the window. Evelyn moved around the room, muttering to herself. "What was that?"

"I said you most certainly were sulking, and it was not at all becoming, my lady," Evelyn replied tartly. "Your family is sick unto death about you, and they have enough to worry them at the moment, what with your sister missing as well. I would think you would not wish to cause them further pain."

Alex opened her eyes and blinked until she was able to focus properly, and the white spots had faded from her vision. In a quiet voice, she asked, "Are they really that worried? I didn't mean for them to be. I just couldn't handle seeing anyone. I thought they understood."

"They do understand, but that does not mean they don't worry all the same," Evelyn said in a gentle voice. "The captain, Lord Oakleigh, has been here as well. He was most reluctant to leave yesterday without speaking with you."

Alex sat bolt upright in the bed. "Nicholas was here? What did he say?"

"He simply wanted to see you. He said he had told you he would be paying you a visit."

"Oh, yeah, that's right. I forgot." She sank back into the feather mattress and sighed. "Did he say whether he was coming back today?"

"Of course he will come today. Don't you remember? You are to have dance instructions. He will be your partner during the lesson." Evelyn took hold of a corner of the blanket and twitched it back, leaving Alex to shiver at the sudden chill. "Now, time to get up if you wish to be properly dressed in time."

Alex stood and looked over the dresses Evelyn had pulled out to show her.

"These new dresses arrived today. My, they are lovely." Evelyn smoothed a hand down a sage green dress and looked shyly back at her. "I am glad you have finally accepted your place here. I know it has been difficult, but I am confident you will be very happy, in the end. It's just like a fairy tale—and they all lived *happily ever after.*" She sighed dreamily.

If only Alex could be so sure.

****

Knowing how much the family had worried about her, Alex practically ran down the stairs to meet them for her dancing lesson, an apology on the tip of her tongue.

She stopped short at the door. Nicholas stood in the corner talking to Gregory. She had known he would be there, but that didn't stop her heart from tripping at the sight of him. She wondered what they were talking about. Gregory seemed a bit on edge.

"Good morning, everyone," Alex said from the doorway, her voice squeaking. She cleared her throat. "I'm sorry if I kept you waiting."

Nicholas stepped forward and looping her right arm over his left, escorted her into the room. "You are worth the wait. You look lovely, Alex."

She blushed. "Thank you." A fist squeezed her heart, and she took a deep breath to calm herself. She would get through this. She didn't need to worry about hiding her feelings now. He already knew how much she cared.

In fact, everyone in the room knew just about everything by now. She could actually relax, truly relax, for the first time since she arrived. She didn't have to worry about what she said or how she acted. Everyone knew she wasn't from here, so they wouldn't wonder if she didn't know something she should.

"Father and mother will be joining us in an hour or so. They asked that I give their apologies for being late. There has been a slight issue with the planning of Mary's ball, and mother needed father to help deal with a difficult merchant." Gregory bowed slightly in Alex's direction.

"Are you feeling better now?" Mary asked. "You look much improved."

"Yes, much better, thank you." Alex smiled. She was feeling better all of a sudden. True, Nicholas didn't love her. Now. But he was obviously attracted to her, she could build on that. Maybe, given a little time, she could make him love her.

She turned to Nicholas and grinned. "So, you're going to help me learn to dance?"

He gave a little half bow, without letting go of her arm. "It will be my pleasure."

She gripped his arm a little tighter and leaned into him. "And mine." She let go and turned to Mary. "So, are these dances very complicated? I've never really been that great a dancer, and I have a feeling the kind of dancing I'm used to is nothing like yours."

"Ooh, Alexandra. Please show us some of your dances. I would love to see how people dance in the future." Mary clapped her hands and bounced lightly up and down.

Alex caught Nicholas start and frown out of the corner of her eye, so she was prepared when he leaned in close to whisper harshly to her, "You told them that ridiculous tale you told me the other night?"

"Yes. I did. And *they* believed me." She tossed her hair and turned away from him to cross the room and stand next to Mary. "I don't think our parents would approve my teaching you the kind of dancing I'm used to," she said, shaking her head.

"That makes it even more interesting. You must share this with us," Mary said, the excitement plain on her face.

"Yes, Alexandra, please do," Gregory chimed in. "It must be fascinating in the future. While dancing is not my main interest, art in its many forms can tell a great deal about a culture."

"What is your main interest in the future?" Alex asked curiously.

"Science! What improvements have been invented to improve the lives of everyday people?" His face lit with enthusiasm.

"Oh, jeez. I could go on forever. Cars, AC, Television. The list goes on. I would have a hard time figuring out what makes the biggest change. But I have to say, I miss hot and cold running water the most." She sighed and glanced at Nicholas. A pang twisted her heart from the look on his face.

"You actually believe this preposterous story?" he asked.

Gregory looked angry as he answered, "Of course we do. She is our sister after all, and what reason would she have to lie?"

Alex gave Nicholas a triumphant glare. Of course, glaring at him was probably not the best way to win his love. And maybe showing him a small hint of the future might not be such a bad idea. "On second thought, maybe a small dancing demonstration wouldn't be completely out of order. I'm afraid it might look a little odd without music."

"I can play for you!" Mary volunteered. "What would you like?" She ran over to the piano and sat.

"I don't even know how to begin to explain the music. Let me think for a moment." Alex paced, trying to come up with a song she could remember well enough to sing or hum. She needed something that would get Nicholas's attention but not make anyone drop dead from shock. The first thing that came to mind was the twist. *Way too embarrassing.*

She pictured the bar and a classic rock song came to mind. The college boys went wild when the girls danced to its beat. *That'll have to do.* She'd try a little dirty dancing next time she had Nicholas all alone.

She started moving, the song playing in her head. She sang the words quietly to herself as she closed her eyes and memories of her last night on board *The Reliant* with Nicholas played in her mind. The song and memories of Nicholas naked made her heart beat faster and her movements seductive. The soft fabric of her dress caressed her skin, and she imagined Nicholas's hands replacing her own as she ran her hands along her sides and up to lift her hair off the back of her neck.

She opened her eyes to see Gregory and Mary staring at her, mouths open. She stopped dancing. "Okay. So maybe I should have gone with my first instinct and not shown you anything."

"Oh no, Alexandra. It's just I have never seen anything like it." Mary tried unsuccessfully to keep the shock from her voice.

"Well, of course you haven't. It won't be around

for more than a hundred and fifty years or so." She shrugged. "It probably looks pretty ridiculous without the music, and I really can't explain the music, or eighties' hair bands for that matter. Anyway, I have absolutely no musical talent."

She finally took a look at Nicholas, but his back was turned. *Had he even seen her little performance?*

He turned around and her breath caught in her throat. The fire in his eyes told her the answer.

****

Nicholas couldn't keep his eyes off her. He was livid she stuck to this ridiculous lie and had somehow managed to convince her whole family it was true. *Why couldn't she be honest with him?* Since the beginning, it had been one lie after another. Would he ever be able to trust her?

Why had he promised to listen to this nonsense without judgment? What secret did she hide from him? She refused to tell him anything about her past, and her lies were becoming more and more elaborate. How could he gain her trust and win the truth?

All thoughts left his head as she started singing, poorly. He cringed as the thankfully quiet sound assaulted his ears, but her lack of musical instruction barely registered before she started moving. Her hands caressed her body as her movements seduced him into a frenzy of need. *Was she trying to kill him?* Because he certainly felt he would die on the spot if he couldn't get her in private in the next few minutes.

Her sensual movements brought with them visions of the last week on board *The Reliant* and their passionate lovemaking.

All he wanted was to spend time alone with her,

while she was locked up in this house as surely as if she were the innocent maiden most assumed her to be. Leaving him rather frustrated. Their wedding, particularly their wedding night, couldn't come soon enough.

Thankfully, her dancing didn't last long. Judging by the looks on the faces of the others, he wasn't the only one floored by the past few moments. He turned away and struggled for control lest he embarrass himself.

When he turned back he caught her looking at him and from the look in her eyes, she wanted time alone as much as he did.

He cleared his throat. How he was going to survive this lesson was anyone's guess. He walked toward her, drawn like a sailor to the sea. "Perhaps we should continue with the lesson." He wanted nothing more than to drag her from the room to gain the privacy he desired, but there was no chance of that. The next few hours were bound to be hell, close to her, touching her, yet forced to keep his distance.

The prudent course of action would be to cancel the lesson until he regained control, but he'd be damned if he could walk away from her. No matter how sensible it might be.

"We do not have a large amount of time to teach you to dance well enough for the ball next week. Although I can see you have a natural talent." He gave her a wink and led her into the middle of the room. "Perhaps we should start with the waltz." His desire to get his hands on Alexandra spurred the suggestion rather than experience or knowledge of the requirements of a London ball.

"No," was the immediate and suspicious denial from the puppy. "While the waltz has become quite popular, other dances are more appropriate and will take more time to teach. Therefore we should start with the cotillion."

Nicholas hated to admit it, but he knew the pup was most likely correct. Young though Viscount Creswell was—his experience in London society far surpassed Nicholas's own. It would also be unwise to get so close to Alex. Self-restraint did not come naturally.

They spent the rest of the afternoon with the dance lessons. Unfortunately, when Nicholas left the Creswell home at the end of the day, his exhaustion did nothing to dampen his desire to drag Alex to the nearest bedroom and not release her for days.

His suppressed desire set his temper on edge. His restraint in not taking out his temper on Alex's brother, who had clearly not gotten over their initial meeting, was remarkable. Not that Alex had noticed his control. She'd reprimanded him repeatedly for the most minor of comments.

Nicholas told his coachman to take the carriage home without him. He could use the fresh air to clear his head. He strolled down the street lost in thought.

****

Alex's heart rate didn't return to normal until after she returned to her room. The dancing was nothing like what she'd expected. Instead of elegantly gliding around the room dazzling her partner with her witty conversation, she had whirled and stomped about, barely able to catch her breath. Anytime she tried to slow down, the others would tease her she was supposed to be dancing, not strolling along the garden path. Those Jane Austen movies she had watched from time to time had done nothing to prepare her for reality.

The only dance that had met her expectations was the waltz. It was glorious—gazing into Nicholas's soul searing eyes while his arms wrapped possessively around her. At least, in one of the versions of the waltz they had shown her. She had never realized there were so many ways of dancing the same dance.

The only problem was it made her hunger for Nicholas grow until she could have devoured him whole. If she were home, no one would care who she slept with, but here, her family seemed determined she and Nicholas not spend another moment alone until they were married. Which wasn't going to happen—unless she could get him to fall in love with her.

How she was going make that happen, she had no idea. At least the chemistry was there. Boy was it there. That was no problem. But sex wasn't enough on which to base a marriage. Especially not when it meant leaving everything she knew behind. She didn't know anything about this time in history. She had read a few books, so she knew the basic struggles and the big events, but that told her nothing about what it would be like to live her life here. To raise a family.

Her face heated, and her heart swelled in her chest. A pleasant thought. Having Nicholas's kids. *If* she stayed. *If* he loved her. That would make all the difference.

She had been doing fine so far. She honestly didn't miss all that much from modern times. True, a hot shower would be nice, but baths were very relaxing. She certainly didn't miss her job at the bar, but she hadn't planned on doing that for the rest of her life. She had hoped to have a career some day when she got her college degree. She'd worked hard to get as far as she had. She hadn't cruised through like so many of her classmates.

What would she do if she stayed? She didn't even know if she'd be allowed to work.

The *allowed* part was what really got to her. She had grown up believing a woman could do anything she wanted. But that wasn't true here. People would insist her place was in the home. Not her home either, but that of her father or her husband. Never her own, not really. She would never be allowed to get a job. Maybe she could get involved with some kind of charity, but only if her husband or father approved. Her life would be dependent on the men in her life. Could she handle that?

Well, maybe. It all depended on what that home was like. If she had a husband who treated her like a person rather than property, than yes, she could deal with it. Nicholas could be that kind of husband, *if* he loved his wife. If not, well, he would never be cruel, but he wouldn't be able to understand her, and that would be even more painful, feeling the way she did.

Giving it time wouldn't work either. Dating wasn't an option. Her parents would have her married within the month. She had pretty much sealed that deal when she admitted to having sex with Nicholas. In her father's mind, the only way for her to redeem herself was to marry the man who had ruined her.

Ruined her. She snorted. What a load of crap. Yet they actually believed it, as if she wasn't worth as much because she'd had sex with a man who wasn't her husband.

After marriage? That was a different story, apparently. From what little she'd read, it wasn't unusual for a woman to have an affair after she'd provided her husband with an heir, and it was pretty much expected of a man. Nicholas had even mentioned how hypocritical society was in that respect. He, at least, hadn't seemed to mind she hadn't been a virgin when they met.

Fidelity was a must when she married. She would never cheat and wouldn't accept a cheating husband. At home she would have the option of divorce. Here she wasn't even sure if that was possible.

Nicholas could be faithful. Loyalty was an important quality to him. But again, he might not see having an affair as being disloyal. Adultery was a fact of life in these times—expected almost—for a married man. But if Nicholas loved her, it would be a different story.

So how was she going to make that happen? In modern times, they could date for a while and see how things developed. She didn't have that kind of time. Her family would not accept a long courtship. In their view, time was of the essence to repair her fall from grace.

She and Nicholas weren't even allowed to be alone together for any length of time. How in hell were they supposed to get to know each other well enough to know if they could make a marriage work?

****

These thoughts consumed her through the next few weeks as she attended more dance lessons, fittings, and spent time getting to know her family. The Creswells had a busy social calendar, but they cancelled as many of their engagements as they could to spend time with her. They graciously welcomed Nicholas into the fold and invited him to all the family gatherings. Though she longed to find time to spend alone with him, she cherished the time with her family.

She had spent her childhood hopping between foster homes. While most of them were very kind people, some of them were not, and none of them cared for her as this family did. Her mother was especially interested in all those families, but Alex wasn't sure how much to share. While there had been times when she'd been happy, more often she'd been miserable, alone, frightened and struggling to survive.

She didn't want to hurt them. This whole business of having a family to worry about was new to her, and she didn't know how to act. But her mother pushed her for information, and Alex didn't want to lie. Though maybe that would have been best, as she learned one night after dinner.

The women moved into the sitting room, while the men stayed behind in the dining room to smoke and drink brandy or some liquor deemed not suitable for ladies.

Alex drank a bit too much wine. Her head spun and her thoughts drifted. While the ladies didn't drink much in the way of hard alcohol, they seemed to drink wine as if it was nothing. Besides a lack of money to spend on booze, Alex had always been behind the bar serving. She'd never developed a tolerance for it.

She'd relaxed in a pleasant daze staring into the fire so had lost track of the conversation, when Mary turned to her and asked, "How about you, Alexandra? Did you ever fall off a horse and break any bones when you were a child?"

She blinked in confusion for a moment, bringing the room back into focus. "Break any bones?" She wrinkled her brow. "Sure. Broke my arm and a few ribs once."

Her mother gasped. "Were you in a terrible accident?"

"No," she answered as the men walked into the room. "One of my foster fathers got drunk one night, and he preferred to take things out on the foster kids rather than his own. I just happened to be in the room." She shrugged; it was just a distant memory and hardly the worst thing that had happened in her childhood. She didn't notice the silence that fell on the room.

"What did he do to you?" Nicholas asked in a cold voice.

Alex looked up, still a little foggy. "Oh, it wasn't all that bad. It was my mistake for trying to fight back. When I made a clumsy attempt to strike back, he grabbed my arm and twisted it behind my back until I went down. Broke my arm and ribs when he kicked me as I lay curled up on the ground. He probably would have just punched me the once if I hadn't defied him." She shrugged again. "At least they transferred me to a new home when I got out of the hospital." She grinned. "The new home was one of the nicest I'd been to. She was such a sweet lady." She thought back to the few days she had spent with them, before being moved again. "She actually made me a cake for my birthday; no one had ever bothered before."

"How old were you?" Lady Downing asked in a whisper.

"Oh, I think I was thirteen or fourteen." She

suddenly realized everyone was staring at her in horror. "What? What did I say?"

Lady Downing had tears in her eyes. "The way you talk about the future, we thought it must have been such a wonderful place. We thought you were happy, and that made us feel better about not being there to protect you." Her husband walked to her side and handed her a handkerchief. She wiped her eyes delicately. "I think I need to lie down for a moment. If you will all excuse me?"

"Let me assist you to your room, my dear." Lord Downing placed his wife's hand over his arm. "I shall return in a moment."

Nicholas moved to stand behind Alex's chair and rested a hand comfortingly on her shoulder while she watched her parents leave.

"I'm so sorry. I don't know why I said all that. I certainly never meant to say any such thing. It just sort of popped out." She turned to Gregory. "Will she be all right?"

"Yes, of course she will." Gregory's voice wavered and he ran a hand down his shirt front. He cleared his throat and sat beside her. "I am sorry you had to suffer through such experiences, Alexandra. I wish there were some way I could make it up to you."

"Don't be stupid! It's not your fault. I wasn't trying to gain your sympathy or pity or anything. I never would have said anything, but I'm a little out of it right now." She put her hand to her forehead. "I don't normally drink so much. Wine goes straight to my head."

Lord Downing came back into the room. "Lady Downing will be fine. She asked me to convey her apologies for leaving so abruptly."

Alex nodded. "I'm sorry I upset her. It was really no big deal. She shouldn't let it bother her."

"It does bother her. Of course it does. But that does not mean we do not wish to know all you went through in the years you spent away from your family." He smiled and patted her gently on the shoulder. "Please do not feel you cannot share everything with us. We are aware you did not have an easy life, if we can ease that burden in any way, please allow us to do so."

"Thank you. I'll keep that in mind." She smiled at him. "It doesn't matter anymore. I'm here now." She was surprised to realize she meant every word.

Chapter Twenty

May 28 (1 Day Remaining)

The day of the ball finally arrived, and butterflies moved in to take over Alex's stomach. She was surprisingly nervous over a simple dance.

But it wasn't simple; it was much more than that. Tonight was their last ditch effort to find Charlotte. Lord Downing's search hadn't turned up any clues. All their hopes hinged on scaring an unknown kidnapper into making a desperation move and revealing himself.

Although a long shot, it was their only hope of finding Charlotte. According to the article from Sawyer, Charlotte would be killed tomorrow unless they did something to prevent it. *Why didn't she insist on more info?* She was such a fool.

What if her sister wasn't in any danger? Sawyer could have faked the news article and made the whole thing up as a way to trick her into going through the portal. After all, he hadn't bothered to tell her she and Charlotte had come through the portal as children. But why? Why would he do such an awful thing?

She still hadn't come up with an answer when her mother insisted she take a nap so she'd be refreshed for the ball. Alex doubted she'd get any sleep; she was so keyed up, but it wasn't long before she fell into a fitful doze. It seemed only moments before Evelyn urged her gently to wake.

"It's time to wake up, my lady," Evelyn said shuffling around the room, laying out clothes for the evening.

Evelyn seemed more excited about the ball than anyone else in the family. She'd been fussing over the dress ever since it arrived the day before. She couldn't wait to show off *her lady*.

Alex suspected it was a chance for Evelyn to display her skills as an abigail. She didn't get the opportunity often because Alex insisted on wearing her hair down or in only the simplest of styles. For the ball, however, Alex had given Evelyn free rein to fuss as much as she liked.

She would be in her glory because it would take a great deal of fussing to get Alex ready. But she was looking forward to it. Almost like going to the prom, she figured. She hadn't stayed in school long enough to go to her own. She might even be able to have some fun, if she could relax.

The dress was beautiful and fit her to perfection. Having clothes made to order was refreshing. Clothes off the rack always gapped awkwardly, either stretching too tightly across the breasts or sagging so much they resembled a potato sack and made her look huge and frumpy.

This dress was tight across the chest too, but it enhanced her appearance rather than detracted from it. She wasn't sure about the sleeves, but the dressmaker insisted it was the style. They were short and a little too puffy for her tastes. She would be cold; she was always cold, but they had insisted. Mary had explained it would get hot in the ballroom with all those people dancing and crushed together. Alex hoped she was right, because she was sure her delicate, little shawl was not going to be enough to warm her.

The dress flowed from the tight bust in graceful lines to the floor. It didn't cling, but it enhanced her figure in all the right ways. Instead of another of the pastels she had been wearing, the dress had beautiful black embroidery on a deep red silk of her own choosing that looked good on her. The dark color was a little unusual for an unwed woman, according to her mother, but Lady Downing had agreed it suited Alex.

Alex looked forward to Nicholas's reaction. He had admired her in all the dresses she'd borrowed from Mary the past week, but this dress was something special. She hoped his blood pressure, among other things, would rise the moment he saw her. It was as good a way as any to make sure his attention remained on her and gave him ample opportunity to fall in love with her.

What else could she do? She had never tried to make anyone love her. She'd fought tooth and nail against it, knowing she never stayed in one place long, and it hurt more if she cared about the people she left. So all she had to go on was the attraction between her and Nicholas. She hoped it would be enough.

****

The night of the party, Alex descended the stairs as Nicholas waited. Her heart did a spinning hook kick against her ribs at the sight of him. She thought his everyday clothes were very formal, and compared to what men wore around the house in modern times, they were. Nevertheless, his evening attire was certainly something special.

His jacket was a deep, midnight blue and looked spectacular against the crisp, pure white of his shirt and cravat. His hair was brushed back from his face, but he'd left it free of its usual tie to tuck it behind his ears. It gave him that slightly wild look that made her insides tingle.

And hadn't she wished at one point he'd wear tighter pants? Well, here they were. And she'd been right about the sight he'd present in them. Yum.

She watched him for a few moments before he realized she was there. He stood at the foot of the stairs talking quietly with Mr. Grayson and Preston. Probably going over security details for the evening.

In addition to the Adonis, several of her former crewmates were stationed throughout the house on guard duty. Alex had overheard Nicholas telling them that someone was to keep an eye on her at all times.

He looked up and stopped speaking mid-sentence. Mr. Grayson followed his gaze and smiled before motioning for the butler to precede him out of the hall.

Alex smiled and attempted to glide down the stairs as her mother did. She doubted her ability to pull it off as she held the hem of her dress up out of the way and watched every step. She'd tripped too many times to be careless walking down a full flight of steps. As she reached the bottom step, Nicholas held a hand out and she grasped it.

"You look lovely, Alex." Nicholas's eyes radiated a heat that scorched her where she stood.

"Thank you."

They stood still, his hold on her hand warm and inviting. Slowly a slight frown marred his features. "There's something missing." He smiled suddenly and put a hand to his pocket, withdrawing a gold chain. "I have just the thing. Turn around, please."

Alex turned and soaked up Nicholas's heat along the length of her back. His arms encircled her shoulders and a small weight dropped onto her chest. She looked down in surprise. Her locket. Her eyes misted, thrilled to have it back. She hadn't realized how much she'd missed it. "I thought this was going to some woman you know," she quipped, trying to mask the tears in her voice.

He snorted. "You thought no such thing. I only wanted to have something of yours to hold onto until I was able to convince you to end your charade and join me in my bed."

Alex swung around and stared, lips twitching. "I don't know whether to be outraged or flattered."

"Let's choose flattered, shall we? Outrage does not suit the mood tonight."

Alex laughed. "Only you would think you can command my emotions to your liking."

He grinned back. "Only I could do it," he said, and then laughed. "Are you ready for a night of dancing and merriment?"

"Yeah, I suppose."

"You overwhelm me with your enthusiasm," Nicholas said, a touch of concern in his voice. "Are you worried for your safety? I have taken precautions in that respect. Mr. Grayson is overseeing security for the evening. You should have no fear; I will not permit any harm to come to you."

"Oh, I know that." Her heart fluttered at his reassurances. Surely he cared more for her than just as a sex toy, or he wouldn't be going to all this trouble to make sure she not only was safe, but felt safe too.

"Alexandra?" called a voice from above, and her mother appeared at the top of the steps. "There you are, dear. Would you please come to my room for a moment? We need to select your jewelry for the evening."

"Oh, that's okay. Nicholas returned my necklace, and I think it goes nicely, don't you?" She held the necklace up to catch the light. She looked back up quickly when she heard her mother's gasp. "Are you all right?"

"The necklace! You still have it."

It suddenly came back to Alex why the necklace was so special to her—the only thing she had left from her parents. "Oh." She rushed up the stairs to where her mother seemed frozen on the landing. "Yeah, I still have it. It's always been such a great comfort to me, knowing that once upon a time, I had parents who loved me."

Tears glistened in her mother's eyes as she stared at the necklace. Alex barely heard her whisper. "We gave them to you and your sister on your tenth birthday, the day you disappeared. Your sister's pendant has an emerald. Your favorite colors." She looked up and met Alex's eyes. "It brought you comfort when you were a child?"

"Oh yes. I never took it off. So many of the other kids I ran into were taken from their homes because they were abused or neglected. I couldn't remember being loved, but I would hold the pendant and know that I had been at one time. So many never even had that."

Alex wanted to give the woman a hug, but she just

didn't know if it would be okay. None of her foster parents had ever encouraged any kind of physical contact; they were too afraid of lawsuits. The few that had encouraged it, needed to be sued.

Nicholas whispered in her ear, "Alex." She'd been so focused on her mother she hadn't realized he'd followed her up the stairs. "I think Lady Downing would welcome a hug from her daughter."

Alex looked into her mother's eyes and seeing the longing there, leapt forward and flung her arms around her. They held each other tightly for several minutes until Alex pulled back in horror. "Oh my God, your dress! I'm so sorry, did I wrinkle it?" She looked her mother up and down, but she looked stately and elegant, not a hair out of place.

"My dear, don't you worry about my dress. I would risk a thousand wrinkles for a hug from you." Her smile was radiant, if a bit watery. "Now. You have a necklace, but you could still use a few other accessories." She turned to Nicholas, "If you will please excuse us?"

"Of course, my lady." Nicholas bowed and left Alex to her mother's loving care.

****

The lights of hundreds of candles dazzled Alex as she entered the ballroom on Nicholas's arm shortly before guests were expected to arrive. Flowers covered every surface, and the floor gleamed with reflected light. She could imagine how the room would look with people crowding the dance floor, twirling and swaying to the music of the orchestra set up in the far corner.

Nicholas turned to her and bowed. "Would you care to dance, my lady?"

Alex laughed. "We might as well do it now, because there's no way I'll be dancing when there's anyone around to watch." She stepped into his arms, and he immediately swung her around into a waltz. He held her tighter than they had practiced and she nearly—*swooned*—she guessed was the word someone would use in this time. In Nicholas's arms, she could dance the night away, light as a feather and floating on air.

"I have missed holding you. We must either be married soon or run away together on *The Reliant*." His arms tightened around her so she could scarcely breathe, but he relaxed quickly, and she took a deep breath. Well, as deep as possible. Evelyn had been a little overzealous in tying up her corset this evening.

"I've missed you, too," Alex replied, a trifle breathlessly as they twirled around the dance floor, the only two people in the world.

Clapping brought the dance to an abrupt halt. She blushed as she turned to the door to see Mary and Gregory standing there, applauding. They made a pretty sight. Mary shone in her long, cream and pink gown with her hair piled high atop her head, and Gregory suited up to perfection.

"You look beautiful, Alexandra!" Mary exclaimed. "Your dancing has improved tremendously. You will be the hit of the party."

"Absolutely stunning," Gregory added. "Mother said you had chosen an unusual color for your gown, but it certainly does suit you. No one will be able to take their eyes off you."

Blushing even more furiously now, Alex returned the kind words. "You both look amazing, too. I doubt anyone will even notice me with you in the room, Mary, that dress is gorgeous. You'll have all the men standing in line for a chance to dance with you. And Gregory, you certainly are very dashing this evening." *I'm beginning to get a hang of the way everyone talks around here.*

Gregory bowed in acknowledgement of the compliment. "We should go receive our guests," Gregory said.

A knot formed in the pit of her stomach at the clatter of a carriage drawing up in front of the house. She held her head high and dismissed it. "Of course. That way we can make sure everyone gets a good look. If our kidnapper is among the guests, we want to make sure he notices me."

Alex ignored Nicholas's frown.

****

All eyes were indeed on Alex and Nicholas, but no one seemed hostile or shocked, just curious. Everyone wanted to be in on the latest gossip, and they were the most likely subjects. Alex inspected everyone, hoping for a spark of recognition, but it was no use. No one seemed familiar or showed any sign of alarm at her presence.

She got her fair share of interest, particularly from the young men, but nothing compared to the intense interest Nicholas garnered. He grabbed the ladies' attention and held onto it.

Apparently, society had awaited his homecoming for some time, ever since his brother's death. No one could remember ever meeting him; he had been so young when his father died and he joined the navy. All they knew was he had inherited a title, land, a fortune, and was single.

The mothers of the *ton* were obsessed with him, according to Lady Downing. They all hoped for the triumph of gaining such a son-in-law and were eager to make his acquaintance.

This proved accurate from what Alex observed, and she had a hard time keeping her temper with many of them. She could have happily executed a back-hand strike on a number of people as they openly stared at him like he was a museum exhibit. Some, mostly the marriageable daughters, even went so far as to gasp at the sight of his scars and shrink back from him. He took their reaction well, though the tension in his arm whenever he brushed against her, sent her nerves jangling.

That he was annoyed with her didn't help. Every time he glanced her way, she could feel his disappointment. He wanted her introduced as his fiancée, but Alex had refused. She won her argument by saying they needed to keep her real identity a secret. Their plan hinged on the kidnapper being shocked into revealing himself. If he were forewarned, he would have time to come up with a plan, and they'd be screwed.

But she had another reason for keeping the engagement to themselves. She didn't want to put him in the position of having to face the scandal of a broken engagement if things didn't work out. If she'd learned anything from hanging out with the Creswells, they took scandals seriously around here.

Lady Oakleigh was no exception. Alex had met Nicholas's mother on more than one occasion over the past few weeks, and they hadn't exactly hit it off. But at least Alex had one ally in her desire to keep her engagement a secret. Lady Oakleigh didn't particularly like the match.

Alex couldn't blame her. Nicholas had told her a little about how Lucius had barely provided Lady Oakleigh and Meghan with enough to eat, let alone the clothes and all the other trappings necessary for venturing out into society. They'd lived like hermits, barely getting by. Now the lady's beloved son had returned to take care of her, and some scheming hussy had already trapped him into marriage.

At least Alex didn't have to face another chilly greeting from the Dowager Marchioness or her bitchy daughter that evening. Nicholas had asked them to stay home, given all that could happen.

After what seemed like forever, she was released from greeting duty, and Nicholas escorted her into the ballroom to watch the dancing. As it was Mary's ball, she led the first dance, so they didn't miss much.

A swirling rainbow of color greeted her eyes, and she watched in awe as dancers practically flew in and out amongst each other in an intricate country dance.

"Wow." Alex mouthed the word, staring in amazement. "It's like watching a movie being filmed right in front of my eyes. People just aren't this coordinated as a group without rehearsing. I'd have bumped into at least a dozen people by now."

Nicholas laughed. "It's not as difficult as it seems. Besides, these people have practiced these dances since they were in the schoolroom. They could dance blindfolded." He looked down at Alex and placed his hand over the one she had curled around his arm. "Care to join them?"

Alex took the invitation to mean he was no longer annoyed with her, and a little of her tension eased. "Uh, no thanks." Alex smiled up at him and chuckled. "Believe me. You should be happy I'm refusing. Your toes would never survive." She looked around the room and pointed toward doors leading out into the garden. "Why don't we stand over there and watch the dancing. We'll be pretty noticeable from the door in case our kidnapper comes in late."

"I do not like using you in this manner," his voice gruff, as they made their way across the room.

She patted his hand. "Don't worry so much. What could happen? Besides, I can take care of myself, you know."

"Yes, I know." He smiled down at her. "But I *like* taking care of you."

Alex blushed and looked down, unsure how to respond as warmth seeped through her at his words. Surely, that was love in his voice? She looked away and spotted a gentleman bringing a drink to a young woman. She cleared her throat. "I could use a drink; how about you?"

He seemed caught off guard but quickly came to himself. "Certainly, I will fetch you some lemonade. Or would you prefer champagne?"

"A little champagne would be lovely, thank you." She started to follow him, but he put a hand out to stop her.

"I will get it. You stay here and enjoy the dancing." He made his way across to the refreshment room, on the way signaling a footman to keep an eye on her.

Damn, but the man looked good.

She looked away before she became too obvious

and started drooling. She focused instead on a delicate white flower that bloomed on the potted plant beside her. She leaned forward to inhale its sweet fragrance.

A hand roughly grabbed her elbow, interrupting her thoughts. She made to jerk her arm away, but the grip tightened. "Excuse me!" She put as much disdain into her voice as she could as she turned to face her detainer.

Her mind went blank as she stared into the face of a stranger, a face she suddenly realized she had seen before, a long time ago. His face triggered memories her mind had blocked, and she relived the day fifteen years ago when a happy ten-year-old's life had been ripped asunder.

"Alexandra, I'm scared," Charlotte whispered.

Alexandra groped about in the dark until she found Charlotte's cold, clammy hand and gripped it tightly.

She couldn't see Charlotte in the pitch dark, but it wasn't hard to imagine the look she would see on her sister's face. It would mirror hers exactly. Usually nothing alike, in this instance she imagined their thoughts were as identical as their looks.

Most people assumed this was the case all the time, a fact which never failed to annoy them. Only their mother seemed to realize that just because they looked alike didn't mean they thought alike. They were ten years old and had very distinct personalities. She wished her mother were there right now. She would know what to do.

Charlotte's admission of fear scared Alexandra even more. Charlotte was the brave one. Always trying new things and looking for adventures, while Alexandra tagged along pretending to enjoy herself.

She took a deep breath. She was used to putting on a brave face. Charlotte needed her to do that now. "Don't worry, it will be all right. Mother and Father will—"

"Shhh!" Charlotte's grip tightened. "He's coming back."

Light flared at the front of the cave, bouncing off the sharply jutting rocks and slowly moving toward them. Voices echoed off the high ceiling.

"They're back here, your lordship."

Alexandra recognized the voice. The scrawny little man with bloodshot eyes; a long, straight nose; and cruel, thin mouth had grabbed them from their garden earlier that day. His whiny, high-pitched voice surrounded them in the dark. A deeper voice answered, but he spoke so quietly she couldn't hear what he said.

"No, no problem nabbin 'em. They was playin' in their garden, just as ye said they would."

As the men came closer, she was finally able to hear the second man.

"Very good. I believe they have served their purpose. They mustn't be found."

She wrinkled her nose. She had heard that voice before, but where?

It came to her in a flash—her father's study just the other day. She'd been looking for Charlotte when she'd heard them arguing. She'd turned away before either of them saw her. She hadn't wanted her father to think she was eavesdropping.

Then she realized what he was saying. He was going to kill them! They had to get away now!

In the meager light shed from the approaching lantern, she could see Charlotte, who pointed to the

*back of the cave. Alexandra looked, then nodded, and
the two of them started inching their way quietly to the
deep black of the small opening visible because of the
approaching torchlight glinting off either side.*

*They slipped through the crack moments before the
men came into view. They stopped, clutching each other
for support, afraid the men might hear them moving
clumsily in the tiny dark space.*

*A cry of rage burst from the larger of the two men.
The flickering light of the lantern played across a face
twisted with fury and even their captor shrank back in
fear from the tall intimidating figure.*

*"Where are they?" he shouted, turning on the
cowering little man.*

*"I left 'em right here! They didn't have no light;
they couldn't have gotten away!" He looked around
wildly and finally spotted their opening. "There, they
must have gone through there."*

*Alexandra didn't wait to hear more. She turned
and fled down the narrow path in the pitch black, close
behind Charlotte.*

*Charlotte's hand ripped from Alexandra's grasp.
Her scream pierced Alexandra's ears as the path
ended, and she pitched forward. Agonizing pain seared
her skull. The last thing she heard before everything
went black was the large man's roar echoing off the
walls of the cavern.*

Chapter Twenty-One

May 28 (1 Day Remaining)

Alex felt the blood drain from her face as memories washed over her. She stood staring at the older man, whom she guessed was around sixty, with steely-gray hair and muddy-brown eyes. He'd probably been an attractive man once upon a time, but seen close up, his features were weathered and somewhat slack, as though he had recently lost a significant amount of weight. Bloodshot eyes gave Alex the impression he had gone days without sleep. The cold look in his eyes sent fear coursing through her veins.

Looks like her plan worked. What the hell had she been thinking?

His grip on her elbow tightened, and she winced in pain. "How did you get away?" He clenched his teeth in a mockery of a smile as he scanned the room.

"I beg your pardon. Let go of me!" Alex demanded. She needn't have bothered. The moment she spoke, he dropped her arm to stare at her, a look of shock on his face.

"You! The other one. You will come with me." He reached out to grab her arm again, but Alex stepped back and avoided his grasp.

"I don't think so. Take another step toward me, and I'll scream." She looked around desperately for

Nicholas but couldn't find him. Their position next to the patio door which she had thought would be highly visible, instead left them oddly alone in a room crowded full of people. A stand of flowers to her right gave them a wall of privacy she had treasured when standing with Nicholas but regretted with her current companion.

She sought a way out, but he blocked her path. A cool breeze came in through the French doors propped open on her left. He must have entered that way. He stood so closely he not only blocked the doors, but the ballroom as well. She couldn't get past without touching him.

No help for it. "If you'll excuse me." She stepped closer to the plant, its leaves scratching her arm and catching on her shawl.

His chilling voice stopped her before she could go any further. "Don't you wish to see your sister? She is under my care at the moment and is quite well—A situation that can change rapidly should you choose not to cooperate."

Alex quailed at the confident smile now plastered on his face.

"How do I know you're telling the truth?" she asked. "She could be safe and sound for all I know."

"You dare imply that I am lying!"

Alex could have laughed at the insulted look on the man's face, if the situation weren't so serious. "I'm not all that worried about hurting your oh so delicate sensibilities, you ass. Now tell me why I should believe you."

His face reddened, but he reached into his pocket and pulled out a necklace, showing it to her quickly before stashing it away again. That brief glimpse was enough to sink her heart to her toes. A brilliant emerald hung from the base of a heart-shaped pendant exactly like the one hanging around her neck.

"What have you done with her, you bastard?" She wanted to scream and hit him but her arms froze to her sides and her voice was barely audible.

"She is safe, as I said." He smirked. "You may remember the place, but I can assure you, she won't be making a miraculous escape this time."

The cave, Alex thought. "Who are you?"

"Forgive my poor manners. I am Lord Stone," he said with a small courtly bow, his composure regained, sure now he had the upper hand. "I do not wish to be seen over long in your presence; you will join me in my carriage around the corner at midnight." He waited for her nod before continuing, "You will come alone and will not tell anyone about me, or your sister will pay the price."

Alex fought to keep her expression neutral as she stared at his retreating back, wishing she had a knife.

****

A moment later, Nicholas returned, a glass of champagne in each hand, a frustrated expression on his face. "I have been trying to make my way back to you for two bells." He blew out a breath as he glanced around and handed a glass to Alex. "I don't know half these people, yet they approach me as if we are long lost friends."

She smiled tremulously, still trying to come to grips with what had just happened. "They must find you as fascinating as I do."

He smiled, but it faded quickly and changed to

concern as he got a good look at her face. "Is something amiss?"

"No. I'm fine." She took a sip of the champagne. "Mary told me it would get warm, but I didn't realize how warm. And I have to admit, I'm really starting to miss things like deodorant." She wrinkled her nose. The flowers next to her smelled lovely, but they couldn't mask the smell that had continued to worsen as more and more people joined in the energetic dancing throughout the room.

"Deodorant?"

"Never mind." She shook her head. "I'm feeling better already. This champagne is delicious." She took another sip. She couldn't afford to drink too much; she had to have her wits about her when she met up with Lord Stone later that night. But how was she going to get rid of Nicholas?

"Why don't we step outside and get some fresh air?" He placed a hand at the small of her back and guided her out the patio doors.

Lanterns flickered along the path, reminding her forcefully of the light reflected off that cave wall long ago. She fought back a wave of panic. Her grip on Nicholas's arm tightened and his warm, steadfast strength gave her courage. With him at her side, the lights flickered like a thousand Christmas tree lights rather than wavered like those long ago torches.

She hadn't lied about being overheated. The cool air soothed her skin. His presence, her spirit.

As they stepped out of view of the open patio doors, he pulled her to him and wrapped his arms around her. "Finally, a moment alone," he whispered before his mouth captured hers.

She melted into him, opening her mouth and meeting the thrust of his tongue with her own. Her arms circled around him, and she buried her right hand in the hair at the nape of his neck. He met her moan of longing with one of his own, and several minutes passed before they broke apart, both a bit breathless.

"I couldn't resist you another moment." He stepped back with a sigh. "We should return to the ballroom before we are missed." With a cocky grin, he asked, "Feeling better?"

"Definitely," she said, her answering grin as wide as his. They walked back up the path, her hand resting gently on his arm. She had almost forgotten about Lord Stone, but her anxiety returned full force as they entered the ballroom, and she saw him standing across the floor talking to her father. Her hand clenched Nicholas's arm involuntarily.

His eyes narrowed as he observed her tension. "Do you see someone you recognize?"

"Don't look now, but who is that man talking to my father?"

She wanted to tell Nicholas everything, but he would never allow her to make that meeting with Lord Stone. She couldn't take that chance.

But it would be extremely foolish to go without letting anyone know where she had gone. Her gut clenched as she tried to figure out what to do. For now she would make Nicholas a little suspicious of Lord Stone, without calling any particular attention to him.

They continued walking along the edge of the dance floor while Nicholas glanced casually at Lord Stone. "I don't know. I have spent so little time among the *ton*. We can ask your father about him later. Do you remember him? Could he be your kidnapper?"

"I don't know. He looks a little familiar, but we ran into so many people while we were out shopping the other day. It's possible I just met him then." She shrugged. "Let's not make him suspicious though by paying any special attention. If he knows my father, he shouldn't be hard to find later on."

Nicholas nodded. "I'll speak with your father, and we can investigate him later." He gave her hand a light squeeze. "So how do you—who the bloody hell is this?" he asked.

Alex followed the direction of his gaze and stared at the gorgeous blond man striding across the dance floor, his gaze intent on someone near them. She looked around but couldn't quite figure out who rated such intensity.

If she didn't know any better, she would have thought he was headed straight for her. But he didn't look familiar, and she would definitely have remembered meeting him.

He was just a little shorter than Nicholas, his long hair tied neatly back in a queue. A slight five o'clock shadow dusted his square jaw. Even at this distance, she could feel the intensity of his gaze and tell that his eyes were a light, piercing color.

The stranger marched up to her and looked straight into her eyes, his hands twitching slightly as though he fought hard against reaching for her. She saw the anger and concern in his gaze change quickly to confusion. He took a step back. "Excuse me, I'm terribly sorry to disturb you. I thought you were someone else."

"Do you mean Charlotte?" she asked, her voice squeaking slightly at the end. That would explain the way he looked at her as if he knew her.

"Yes. I thought you…" he trailed off, looking even more confused.

The tight set of Nicholas's shoulders relaxed the tiniest bit. She hadn't realized how tense he had been as the man approached.

"I believe this conversation would benefit from a smaller audience. We shall gather your father on our way." He had a hand at Alex's back, prepared to lead her to another room. He turned his gaze to the other man. "Would you come with us, please?"

The man nodded and followed quickly as they gathered Lord Downing and headed upstairs to find a room with some privacy.

****

Nicholas kept a surreptitious eye on Alex as they entered a small drawing room. Something bothered her, but he was damned if he knew what. She had been acting strangely since he left her to procure a glass of champagne. His heart felt heavy as he realized she did not trust him enough to speak of what bothered her. He had no idea how he could gain her trust.

And he definitely did not like the way she looked at their new acquaintance. As soon as the door closed behind Lord Downing, Nicholas pulled himself up straight to maximize the few inches he had on the other gentleman and rounded on him. "Who, pray tell, are you and what do you know of Charlotte Creswell?"

"Creswell?" the man replied. "Nothing. I thought for a moment the young lady was my daughter's governess, but I realize I was mistaken." He bowed in Alex's direction. "I beg your pardon if I startled you. It was not my intention." His brow knitted in confusion.

"The resemblance is uncanny."

"Is your governess's last name Evans?" she asked.

"Yes, it is."

Before he could say any more, Lord Downing chimed in, "I believe introductions are in order." He bowed slightly to the young man. "You are Lord Tyndale, I believe." At the young man's nod, he continued, "May I present to you, Lord Oakleigh." He gestured to Nicholas, who nodded. "And my daughter, Lady Alexandra Creswell."

Lord Tyndale's jaw dropped and his eyes widened as he glanced toward Alex.

"It sounds as though you know my other daughter, Lady Charlotte—Alexandra's twin. We have been searching for her for quite some time." Lord Downing continued to give a few details of their history and their search.

Nicholas watched Lord Tyndale as he listened to the story. He appeared to take in everything fairly well, though he looked a bit taken aback. "Miss Evans said she had family in London, but she refused to tell me your name. I had gathered from some of her comments you had parted on less than amicable terms." He glanced at Lord Downing, before looking at Alex with a huge grin on his face. "She worried she would never see you again. She will be thrilled when she discovers you are in London."

"Not on good terms?" Lord Downing asked, confusion evident in his voice, before he shook his head. "It is unimportant. Where is she now?"

"At my country estate. I asked her to accompany me to London, but she refused. I had an urgent letter from my younger brother requiring my presence in town. I expected to find him awaiting my arrival at our townhouse and was surprised to find he intended to attend your ball. I arrived at your home and was further shocked to see Charlotte, or so I thought, talking to Lord Oakleigh, when I had left her safe at my home."

"Safe?" Nicholas asked.

"Yes." Lord Tyndale frowned. "I am afraid there have been several attempts on her life since the moment she entered into my employ. I did not wish to leave, yet I had little choice. I left several men to guard her in my absence." He moved toward the door. "If you will pardon me, I would like to find my brother. His missive sounded quite urgent."

Nicholas moved to block his way. "You can find your brother in a moment. I want to know more about these attempts on Alex's sister." The danger to Alex appeared even greater than he had suspected.

"Why don't I have a footman escort your brother here?" Alex chimed in. Her gaze darted between him, Lord Tyndale, and the clock behind him.

"No, I think—"

Before he could stop her, Alex slipped out the door. Nicholas watched as her skirt swirled around the corner. Something certainly bothered her, other than the news they had just received. She appeared shaken, and it concerned him. What could have happened in the few minutes he had left her side for the champagne? Had someone contacted her, threatened her?

His blood boiled at the thought, and his hands clenched into fists. Whatever it was, she was scared, and he was going to find out why.

****

Alex rushed down the stairs. She only had ten

minutes to meet Lord Stone, and she needed to figure out how to let Nicholas know what she was doing. She sent a footman to fetch Lord Tyndale's brother as she made her way to the door.

She paused. Perhaps she could send a message through Tyndale's brother? She couldn't use a footman. None of them would let her leave if she told them of her intent. Nicholas had given them strict instructions regarding her, and even now a footman stood a few feet away, keeping a careful eye on her.

A young man came out of the ballroom, following the footman Alex had sent. She took a deep breath and walked up to him, pasting a smile on her face. "Good evening. Are you Lord Tyndale's brother?"

He was younger than she, maybe twenty or so. His smile widened as he looked her up and down. "Yes, I am. Sebastian Tyndale. I don't believe we have been introduced. I would surely remember a lady as lovely as you." He took her hand and brought it to his lips. "How may I be of service, Lady...?"

Alex tugged her hand out of his grasp and ignoring his question, turned to the footman. "Thank you. Could you excuse us, please?" When he was gone, she turned back to Mr. Tyndale. She spoke quietly so the other footman wouldn't overhear. "Could you please do me a huge favor?"

"Of course. It would be my pleasure to assist you in anything you desire." He reached for her hand again, but Alex stepped back.

"Thank you. Your brother is upstairs with Lords Oakleigh and Downing. Please let them know that Alex has gone to find Charlotte at the cave. Lord Stone has been kind enough to provide his hospitality and a carriage for the journey."

Being so vague was a risk since she had never discussed the cave with Nicholas. She hadn't even remembered it until this evening. She could only hope Charlotte had told Lord Tyndale. She got the impression he cared about Charlotte a great deal, perhaps was even in love with her. If Charlotte returned his affection, she may have put her trust in him and told the truth about herself and the location of the time portal in a cave. Alex couldn't be more specific since she didn't even know where the cave was located.

"A cave?" His mouth angled down in a slight frown and his tone was hesitant.

Alex could only imagine what he thought of her strange behavior. "Yes, the cave. It's important you tell him exactly what I said. Can you do that?" She needed to hurry; she didn't want to take the chance of Lord Stone seeing her and getting suspicious. He should be getting ready to meet her at his carriage any moment now.

Mr. Tyndale nodded his assent. "Of course my lady, I would be happy to oblige. Are you sure there is nothing else I can do for you?"

"I'm quite sure, thanks. If you could just deliver that message, exactly as I stated it." She motioned for the footman guarding her. "Please show Mr. Tyndale to the drawing room. Lord Downing has requested his presence."

The footman looked unsure. "Perhaps we should summon another footman. I have instructions not to leave you alone at any time."

"Oh don't worry about that. I'm going back into the ballroom." She smiled and headed that way, pausing in the door when she saw the footman leading Tyndale upstairs. As soon as they were out of sight, she headed to the door and let herself out, grabbing a jacket, or a spencer as they called it, on the way.

Chapter Twenty-Two

May 29 (Midnight—Day of the Murder)

Alex rushed down the street, shrugging into the spencer as she went. The chilly night air was nothing compared to the ice that encased her heart. What if Nicholas and Lord Tyndale couldn't figure out where she was? She didn't know where the portal was, how could they? She stopped dead for a moment before re-gathering her nerve and hurrying on.

Am I being a complete idiot?

She had no guarantee Lord Stone even had Charlotte. He could have stolen the necklace without actually having her. What if it had all been a bluff and she had fallen right into his trap?

No. He had Charlotte somewhere. According to that article, tonight was the night of her murder. Unless Alex could manage to find her in time. Or was she already too late?

She turned the corner and saw the carriage a few yards away. A coachman stood next to the horses' heads. He must have been on the lookout because he moved to open the door the second he spotted her. Shadows hid the interior, and her skin crawled at the thought of being stuck in the dark with the evil Lord Stone. But she was determined to see this through. She could see no other way to find Charlotte.

At least she had one thing going for her. This guy probably thought she was some silly high society innocent who would just do whatever she was told. He was in for quite a surprise.

****

Alex sighed with relief after the coachman handed her up into the surprisingly empty coach. Some of her tension left as she saw she was to have time to herself during the journey to join Charlotte. She would be able to think more clearly without that horrible man looming over her.

As the carriage jolted to a start, Alex frantically tried to figure out her next move as she watched the houses speed past. Once she found Charlotte, hopefully unharmed, they would need an escape plan. The ugly leer on the coachman's face as he helped her into the carriage told her there would be no help from that quarter.

Stealing the carriage was pretty much out of the question. She certainly had no idea how to control the horses, and she doubted Charlotte would either.

She also had no idea what condition Charlotte would be in. This Lord Stone character probably hadn't had her for very long since Lord Tyndale had only left her yesterday. Lord Stone claimed she was safe, but he wasn't exactly an unimpeachable source now was he?

She pushed those horrible thoughts aside. She would have to go under the assumption Charlotte was okay. She wouldn't be able to do much if she wasn't, so she would worry about that if the time came.

Assuming Charlotte was physically fit, what could she do to help the situation?

She tried to keep track of their route but quickly

lost track of all the turns they took through relatively quiet London streets.

She gave up and searched the carriage, looking for something to use as a weapon. Her hands scraped against rough warming bricks partially wrapped in a blanket under the seat. She unwrapped them all the way and picked one up, judging its weight in her hand.

It could be useful. Unwieldy, though. It needed to be smaller to fit in her reticule so she could keep it hidden. The element of surprise was her greatest asset.

She bashed the stone against the hard edge of her seat a few times until it broke into smaller chunks. She tucked some of these into her reticule and slid the cord around her wrist so she wouldn't forget and leave it in the coach.

That would be a nice surprise for Lord Stone. She pulled some of the decorative pins out of her hair and tucked them into her left sleeve where she could reach them in a pinch. If it came to a fight, she would have something up her sleeve—literally.

Winning their way free would be their first order of business. Then they would have to find someone willing to help two lost ladies. If chivalry were dead, bribery was always an option. Her jewelry was worth a pretty penny. She could easily trade it for a ride home.

Lord Stone had said Charlotte was at the cave, but she was only guessing he was bringing her straight there. For all she knew, he could be sending her to his house first. Maybe she'd be able to bribe Lord Stone's servants into helping her. The coachman was a lost cause, but surely all of Lord Stone's servants weren't so creepy. They might be afraid of losing their jobs, but she could promise them lifetime employment or enough of a reward they would never have to work again.

She hoped she would have the chance to try bribery. She could handle herself pretty well in a fight, but this dress was not meant for any activity more strenuous than a waltz. She stretched her arms out to get a good idea of her range of motion and found she had full motion back and forth but could only move them up as high as her shoulders. She'd have to keep that in mind, or she might try to overreach.

Her skirt clung to her legs, but she could move fairly well provided she didn't get the hem stuck on anything. A good knee shot to the groin was probably the best move she had. It wasn't much. She hoped lady luck was with her. She needed Nicholas to figure out her message and find her or track down Lord Stone.

Since Lord Stone wasn't with her, she assumed he had stayed at the party to avoid being implicated in her disappearance.

If Nicholas figured out what she had tried to tell him, he would be able to find a way to get Lord Stone to talk. He could be very convincing. No way anyone, let alone a weakling like Lord Stone, would be able to stand against him.

She couldn't count on it though. Too many things could go wrong in that scenario. Lord Stone could have gone into hiding rather than stay at the party, and she had no idea whether Charlotte would have told Lord Tyndale about the cave or their sorry history.

In fact, she didn't know anything about the adult Charlotte, though memories of their childhood were resurfacing. Charlotte had been a real adventurer when they were children. Was she the same or had the tragedy of their youth changed her irrevocably?

She could only hope her sister was still a fighter and would be a help rather than a hindrance. So the question of the day was, would Charlotte fight or faint?

****

"Where is she?" Nicholas demanded of the cowering footman.

"I don't know, my lord. She instructed me to escort Mr. Tyndale here."

"I gave strict instructions she was not to be left alone, even for a moment. Was I not clear?" He struggled to keep his voice even, though he felt like choking the man. They had all spent the last half hour combing the crowded ballroom for any sight of Alex, but she was nowhere to be found. She had gone off on her own, just as they had known she had as soon as Sebastian Tyndale relayed her message.

Bloody hell. He had known something was terribly wrong this evening, he should have trusted his instincts and not allowed her to leave his side. Lord Stone must have convinced her the only way to save Charlotte was to do it on her own.

"Yes, my lord. She was headed into the ballroom when I left her. She must have doubled back when I weren't lookin'. I'm right sorry, I am." He ducked his head, a look of remorse overtaking his fear. "She's real nice. I sure would hate to see anything happen to her."

Fear squeezed Nicholas's heart at the thought. "Find Lord Stone. Alert all the servants. If he is still here, he is not to leave under any circumstances. Bring him to me." When the footman left, Nicholas turned to face the room.

Lord Downing sat next to the fire, his head in his hands. "How did this happen?" he asked in a whisper, his voice strained and tired.

Lord Tyndale paced the room, looking just as anxious. "He must have sent that fake message from Sebastian to lure me away from my country estate in order to kidnap Charlotte. He then used her as a means of forcing Lady Alexandra to follow his demands." He shook his head. "Why is he doing this?"

"Obviously he's afraid the ladies can identify him as the man who kidnapped them fifteen years ago." Nicholas turned to Sebastian, who looked white as a sheet as he listened to the panicked men surrounding him. "Tell us again what she said."

"She simply said to let you know that Alex had gone after Charlotte, and Lord Stone was providing the carriage." He screwed up his face in concentration. "She didn't tell me her name, so I assumed Alex was a man."

He paused, and Nicholas watched him eagerly, hoping for some small clue that could lead him to her.

"Actually, she said to say it exactly as she did. Let me think." He closed his eyes and stood perfectly still, his mouth moving slightly. "She said Alex had gone to find Charlotte *at the cave*." He opened his eyes. "At the cave, does that help?"

Nicholas started to shake his head when Lord Tyndale gasped. "The portal! That's it."

"What?" Nicholas asked, hope rising in his chest. "Do you know where they are?"

"Yes. Lord Stone's country estate shares a border with mine. I used to explore the system of caves there when I was a child. That's where Charlotte..." his voice trailed off and he looked around. "What has Lady Alexandra told you about her life for the past fifteen years?"

Lord Downing spoke from his spot near the fire. "She told us everything. I gather Charlotte has confided her past to you as well?"

"Yes. And did you believe Lady Alexandra's story?"

Nicholas caught Lord Downing looking at him. "Lord Downing and his family did, yes. I have to admit to some doubt." He couldn't believe he was having this conversation now, of all times.

Lord Tyndale snorted. "Can't say I blame you. I had a time believing it myself. Time travel! The concept was too incredible to comprehend. Until she showed me her proof of course."

"Proof?" Nicholas demanded. "How could she prove her story to you?"

Her story couldn't possibly be true, could it? The first seed of doubt entered his mind. The knots in his stomach tightened. If it was true, no wonder Alex didn't trust him. Why would she put her trust in someone who didn't trust her?

"She had certain items that couldn't possibly exist. I found no explanation other than that they came from the future. They defied belief." He waved the thought aside. "That doesn't matter now. When the girls were kidnapped as children they were taken to a system of caves that lie along the boundary of my property and that of Lord Stone. He must have planned on killing the girls and hiding their bodies in the caves. Charlotte told me she and Lady Alexandra tried to flee but fell through the portal instead. Charlotte was forced back through that same portal two months ago. That is when I met her. Lord Stone or one of his servants must have seen her and made the attempts on her life. I am an idiot for not suspecting him in all Charlotte's troubles." He stopped pacing and looked directly at Nicholas. "We must hurry. If he brought them to those caves, he must be planning on killing them."

"We shall have to make sure we get to them first," Nicholas said as a knock sounded at the door.

"Enter," said Lord Downing.

Grayson entered, followed closely by the butler, who carried several great coats draped over his arms. "We have searched everywhere. Lord Stone left less than an hour ago. I sent two footmen around to his townhouse to look for his return there. If they locate him, I have instructed one to stay with him and the other to bring word back to us."

Nicholas nodded at his first mate to acknowledge his efforts. He couldn't bring himself to speak past the fury that threatened to strangle him.

"Excellent," Lord Downing said. "Preston, please have the carriage prepared. We have an idea where he may have taken Alexandra and will leave immediately."

"Yes, sir," Preston responded. He placed the greatcoats on the back of a chair and left.

"I believe it would be best if you were to wait here," Nicholas said to Lord Downing. He held up his hands to forestall the anticipated resistance. "Someone needs to wait here in case Lord Stone did indeed return to his townhouse. We also have no idea if Lord Stone has an accomplice keeping an eye on matters here. You have a house full of people and your absence would be difficult to explain. Besides which we would not care to upset Lady Downing unnecessarily."

Lord Tyndale turned to his brother. "Sebastian,

wait here with Lord Downing. If Lord Stone has returned to his townhome, I will need you to detain him. Make sure he does not have a chance to surprise us at the portal. We shall return as soon as we have Ladies Charlotte and Alexandra safe."

"I will contact some old *friends* of mine and see what I can discover about Lord Stone," Grayson said. "You should take this." He moved closer and held out a pistol. "It's primed and ready."

"Thank you," Nicholas replied, well aware of the nature of Grayson's friends. If Lord Stone had anything underhanded to hide, Grayson would soon discover it. Nicholas took the pistol and shook his friend's hand. Grayson nodded and left the room.

Lord Tyndale spoke a few quiet words to his brother and then turned to Nicholas. "Let's go."

Nicholas grabbed his coat off the chair, tucked the pistol into his pocket, and preceded Lord Tyndale out of the room.

Maybe Tyndale wasn't as bad as Nicholas originally thought. He looked as though he might be useful in a fight.

Nicholas had the feeling he was about to find out.

****

Alex figured it took about three hours before they reached the caves. She'd thought over her problems until her head spun and couldn't come up with anything new that could help.

She did manage to destroy the inside of Lord Stone's carriage though. It gave her a perverse pleasure to take some of her frustrations out this way. She'd heard her mother complaining about how expensive carriages were, and if she managed nothing else, at least she could give Lord Stone a little kick in the wallet.

Finally, the carriage rumbled to a stop. The coachman jumped down to lower the steps and helped her out. "You sure is one fancy lady." He looked her up and down. "You're right pretty too, like that other one." He motioned behind him with his chin. "Let's go join her."

He grabbed her elbow, and Alex jerked it out of his grasp. She did not want him touching her. He gave her the creeps. "I can walk, thank you. Now show me to Charlotte."

"Well, ain't we all high and mighty." He sneered. "Won't be so picky after a few hours in there. You'll be beggin' for me. No light, air so thin you can barely breathe."

Alex quailed at his description, the fear threatening to choke her. Until she saw the leer on the man's ugly face and anger saved her.

"Never," she said. "I'd rather be buried alive than beg you for anything."

His leer turned to rage, and he shoved her toward the cave mouth. He laughed when she stumbled. "So you already know the plan? That's good, much less to explain. Lord Stone wants to talk to you and that sister of yours first, so enjoy your last few hours."

Relief washed over her. Charlotte was alive. In the midst of all the horror of the situation, Alex felt a tingle of excitement. She was actually going to see her sister again.

Well, seeing her might be a bit optimistic, she thought as she made her way toward the dark maw of the cave entrance, the meager light from the coachman's lantern barely lighting the path. She stumbled over a root, and the coachman laughed softly behind her. *Jerk.*

He went to push her again as they neared the entrance, but anticipating his move she shifted to the side and stuck out her foot. His momentum carried him forward, and he tripped. She caught the lantern as it flew out of his hands and raced past him into the tunnel. She rushed around a corner and used her skirts to hide the lantern's light, hissing as her leg brushed up against the hot metal.

She could hear the coachman stumbling around and cursing her in the dark outside the cave. She waited for the shouting to die down and then made her way carefully into the tunnel, hoping there weren't any other lanterns in the coach. She didn't think the coachman was brave enough to follow her without a light.

"Charlotte?" she whispered. "Can you hear me?" Her voice hissed eerily in the enclosed space.

"Who's there?" a weak and terrified voice sounded from out of the darkness.

The sound echoed all around her, she couldn't pin point the source. "Charlotte? It's me, Alex. Where are you? Lord Stone's coachman is outside. We have to come up with a plan to get out of here."

The tunnel went steadily down. Loose rocks and dirt made it difficult to keep her balance as she slipped and slid down the path. She kept an eye out for tunnels, but there were none large enough for an adult to walk through. The tunnel grew narrower with her every step.

"Alex?" Charlotte asked, her voice laced with suspicion, but also much closer than a moment ago. "That's impossible."

"It's true. We spoke on the phone, remember?"

"Oh no! He got you too!" Charlotte sounded angry, her voice more recognizable now her spirit was back. She sounded like Alex, though with a British accent.

Alex was glad to hear the anger, it was much better than the weak and feeble sound of a moment ago. They were going to need all their strength to escape.

"I'm afraid so. Where are you?"

"I don't know. He didn't leave me a light, the bastard." Her voice vibrated with the force of her anger, but there was also a note of terror in her voice Alex recognized.

"I have a lantern; let me know when you start to see the light, and we'll know I'm getting close."

Charlotte called out after only a moment, "I can see some light. Keep coming; you're almost here."

The path narrowed drastically, and Alex stooped to continue. Not an easy feat in her party dress. She grabbed hold of her skirts in front and held them high to keep from tripping. The burn in her legs began almost immediately. She couldn't bend much at the waist because of her corset, so all the pressure of stooping was in her legs. Her breath came in quick gasps, and she paused frequently to rest against the rough wall.

Finally, the tunnel opened, and she groaned as she stood tall once more.

"What's wrong? Are you okay?" Charlotte's voice came from a few feet ahead. She sat with her back against a huge boulder on the opposite side of a decent size cavern.

"I'm fine. It's just this stupid dress. Looks great, but not meant for spelunking." Alex approached her sister. This wasn't how she'd pictured their reunion all those months ago when she first set up all those social media pages.

Dirt streaked Charlotte's pale face. Disheveled hair escaped from what had probably been a neat chignon. Her clothes were rumpled and torn. She had obviously not had an easy time of it. She squinted at the meager light from the lantern.

"Alexandra! It is you. But how?" Charlotte struggled to stand. Her arms were bound to her sides, her hands tied together in front. More rope lay on the ground where Charlotte had managed to untie her feet.

Alex put the light down in a smooth patch of dirt and went to help her. It took some time, but she loosened the ropes enough for Charlotte to slip out of them.

With a cry, Charlotte threw her arms around Alex, and they hugged each other with all their might. Fresh tears followed the path of the dried ones down Charlotte's dirt-coated face. Alex swiped a hand through a coat of sweat, tears, and dust covering her cheeks. She must look awful.

Charlotte pulled away first. "I just can't believe it's you! I thought you were dead for so long. When I saw that web page, I almost fainted. Then I got trapped here and thought I'd lost all chance of ever seeing you."

"It's a long story, and we've got to think of a way out of here, so I'll give you the quickie version." Alex gave a hurried description of the last two months, starting with Sawyer but leaving out many details that included her time with Nicholas. She couldn't afford to dwell on him.

Charlotte was a good listener, only interrupting when Alex told her the story Sawyer had given her about Charlotte's own disappearance. "That bloody bastard! I wasn't a client, and I bloody well didn't come here on purpose. He drugged me and forced me to come back here. I caused a cave-in when I tried to fight my way out of there." She closed her eyes and took a deep breath. "Just go on, tell me the rest. I'll tell you my sordid story later, when we have more time."

When Alex finished, they looked each other in the eye for a moment before Charlotte asked, "So what now?"

Alex sighed. She had hoped some grand plan would magically come to her once she found Charlotte, but she had nothing. "I have no idea. How about you?"

"No, nothing."

"Well, good thing I came, huh?" Alex snorted. "Hopefully Nicholas and Lord Tyndale got my message and will be able to figure something out."

"Lord Tyndale?" Charlotte asked. "How do you know him?"

Alex peered closely at Charlotte. Obviously there was something between the two, her whole face lit up at the mention of his name.

"He thought I was you and approached me at a party in London. He realized his mistake immediately, but we all went to a private room to find out what he knew about you. We've had people searching for you since I arrived in London.

"I wanted to leave some sort of clue where I had gone and who was responsible so I left a message saying I had gone to find you at the cave, and that I was using Lord Stone's carriage. I never told anyone about the London portal, but I was hoping maybe you did?"

"Yes, I did. We're actually on James's property. He got trapped in these caves once when he was a child, so he knows just where we are." Her face was hopeful. "I thought I would never see him again," she whispered. "He asked me to marry him, and I said no. Do you know what I've been thinking about most as I sat here in this damp, dark hellhole? I've been thinking about what an idiot I am. I had a chance to marry the man I love, and I said no. Do you think he'll ever forgive me?"

"I'm sure he will. Judging by the way he looked at me for that short time when he thought I was you, he's as much in love with you as you are with him." Alex smiled. "Thank God you told him about yourself." She hesitated a moment. "Did he believe you?"

"Yes. Well, not at first, but I had a bag full of modern stuff, so he didn't have much choice."

"Nicholas didn't believe a word I said. He's infuriating. He never listens. I get so mad at him, but then he turns around and does something wonderful…"

"Is Nicholas your boyfriend?" Charlotte asked.

"Yes," Alex admitted. "And I'm completely, totally, in love. I don't know what I'm gonna do." She lifted her head and shrugged. "Anyway, now's not the time. Lord Stone could get here any minute. We can't just sit here and wait; we have to come up with a plan."

"I'm afraid it is a little late for that, my dear."

Chapter Twenty-Three

May 29 (Day of Murder)

Alex gasped and swung around just as Lord Stone stepped into view. In her excitement at finally finding Charlotte, she hadn't noticed the light coming from the tunnel.

How could she have been so stupid, she thought as she saw the gun in his hand and the scrawny old man who followed behind. "Where's your coachman?" she asked, stalling for time.

"He is watching the horses, of course." Lord Stone dismissed his coachman as unimportant with a wave of his hand. "He is quite upset with you, Lady Alexandra. I have rarely seen him in such a temper." The man chuckled. "He is looking forward to dealing with you personally."

"Your coachman is a pig and should be kept in a sty," she replied tartly.

Lord Stone frowned. "You are an unusual girl. Your father should have taken a whip to you and taught you to mind your manners." He shrugged. "Too late now."

"What are you going to do with us?" she asked.

"What I planned on doing all those years ago. But first, I want to know where the two of you have been hiding all these years and whom you have informed of my involvement with your disappearance."

"I already told Mr. Timmons. I didn't tell anyone about you," Charlotte said angrily. "Until you walked in here, I never saw your face. You had nothing to worry about, you idiot."

Lord Stone bristled. "As unpleasant as your sister. It will be a pleasure to finally rid the world of the two of you."

Alex inched closer as he focused his attention on Charlotte. If she could only get close enough, she might have a chance to get the gun out of his hands. He would never expect her to attack and had no idea she could fight.

"Stop right there, if you please." Lord Stone focused on her and pointed the gun at her chest. "You wouldn't want your sister to be lonely now would you?"

Alex retreated to Charlotte's side and clasped her hand. The motion reminded her of the last time they had been in this cave. Could they possibly escape the same way? Sawyer must have this portal cleared by now.

Of course, if what Charlotte said was true, Sawyer might not exactly roll out the red carpet. Still, it might be worth a shot. Staying here wasn't much of an option.

****

The horses were about to drop. They needed to slow down and give them a rest, but every nerve in Nicholas's body called out to keep going, to get to Alex as fast as possible. He sighed. It wouldn't do Alex any good if the horse collapsed, and they had to walk the rest of the way. He signaled Tyndale, and they slowed to a walk.

"We had better let the horses walk." Nicholas dismounted and threw the reins over the horse's neck. He proceeded down the road, Tyndale at his side and the horses following, their breath heavy on his neck.

"I can't bear the thought that something may have happened to Charlotte. Who knows how long he's had a hold of her." Tyndale cursed beneath his breath. "We fought the last time I saw her. She refused to marry me."

"It must run in the family." Nicholas chuckled. "Alex is refusing to marry me as well, though she will eventually," he added confidently. "She loves me."

"Enough to give up her life, everyone and everything she knows and loves back home? Charlotte loves me, as well, but she has family and friends where she came from, and it's tearing her apart."

The smile fell from Nicholas's face. He hadn't considered that. "Women do it all the time. They leave their father's home for their husband's. It's the natural order. Besides, I own a ship. I could take her to visit any friends she may miss. She knows that."

"You can't sail a ship to their home. Besides, it's different in their time. They can reach out and communicate instantly with loved ones around the world." He snapped his fingers to emphasize his point. "They can travel distances much more quickly. A trip that would take us a month can be accomplished in less than a day with their technology. They can speak with someone across the ocean, without leaving their home." He shook his head as if he couldn't quite believe what he was saying. "The advancements science will make in the future are truly amazing."

Nicholas snorted. "Impossible. Are you talking

about this time travel nonsense? How can you believe in such a fairy tale? It is patently ridiculous to believe people can travel through time."

Alex had simply made up the story to avoid discussing her traumatic youth. It had to be. Nicholas ignored the tiny voice in his mind that asked how Alex and Charlotte had developed the same story though they grew up apart.

Perhaps they had fantasized about time travel when they were children. That was a possible explanation—though he admitted to himself it seemed weak.

"It's not nonsense. Charlotte proved it to me. She showed me technological inventions that couldn't possibly exist today. Once you get over the difficulty in believing the concept of time travel, it's the only logical explanation."

"Logical!" Nicholas exclaimed. "How can you call time travel logical?"

"I have learned to trust Charlotte. Do you not trust Lady Alexandra?" Tyndale asked. "Her family appears to trust her completely. They didn't have the evidence I had, and yet they believed her."

"Her parents are so happy to have her back they would believe anything she told them. They *want* to believe her. They *need* to. So do I." Nicholas took a deep breath.

Why he was telling this virtual stranger so much, he didn't know. He was so anxious about Alex, he couldn't seem to stop talking. At least it kept his mind off what could be happening to her.

"Yet I can't believe her. She has lied to me from the day I met her, all for good reasons I'll grant her. This is no different. I just don't know her reason—yet."

Tyndale looked at him with pity in his eyes. "You'll never truly win her if you don't learn to trust her."

Nicholas didn't respond. He resented the younger man's interference, perhaps because it was a little too close for comfort?

True. He didn't trust her. He found it hard to trust anyone, and she had never given him a reason to, had she? While he understood some of the reasons behind the lies she had told, it didn't make it any easier to place his trust in her.

Given her situation, dressing as a man to avoid the advances of every male within view was completely reasonable. It would have made more sense for her to hire a maid and book passage even if it had meant a delay of several weeks. But he could understand her impatience to continue on her journey as quickly as possible. Though her disguise hadn't held up under scrutiny, he couldn't fault her for trying. Under normal circumstances her disguise might have gone unnoticed for the duration of the journey. After all, how closely did one normally inspect boys hired on for one short journey?

He had more difficulty with her abandonment upon reaching London. Her betrayal infuriated him. However, if he were honest with himself, she had made a half-hearted attempt to warn him of her intention.

The reasoning behind all her lies had been fairly transparent, except for this one. He couldn't understand it, and he had given it quite a bit of thought.

But to think it could be true was insane. Alex couldn't possibly have expected him to believe her. He felt sure she hadn't, yet he had sensed her disappointment.

Was it some kind of test? Her way of seeing if he would trust her blindly? If so, he had failed miserably.

No. Alex wasn't the type to play games. She had valid reasons for all her lies. She must have one for this as well. He hadn't figured it out yet, but he would. He loved her, and there would be no more secrets between them.

Provided he got to her in time.

Nicholas patted the mare's sweat-soaked neck. She had stopped blowing her oat and hay-laden breath down his neck and showed increased interest in the grass at the side of the road. He pulled on the reins to keep her from stopping for a feast.

"I think the horses are sufficiently recovered, let's get going." He mounted and kicked the horse into action. Beside him, Tyndale gripped his reins in white fisted hands, a stony expression on his face. His horse grunted and tossed its head, but burst forward to keep the rapid pace Nicholas set.

They would reach the girls in time. They had to. The alternative was unacceptable. He couldn't possibly live the rest of his life without Alex; she was too important to him. Though he had known her a relatively short time, she had somehow become a vital part of his life. It appeared as though his new friend, Tyndale, felt the same about Charlotte. That was good.

He could use all the help he could get.

****

Alex shivered as moisture from the damp ground seeped through her gown to her knees. She leaned closer to share warmth with Charlotte huddled beside her.

The knots of Charlotte's bound hands stubbornly refused to give. Alex forced her chilled fingers to pick at the scratchy bindings.

She struggled in the pitch dark to feel whether she made any headway. One of the ropes gave slightly, so she redoubled her efforts. After several long moments, it slipped free. "Gotcha!" she exclaimed triumphantly. The bonds fell off, and Charlotte flexed her wrists.

"Brilliant, thank you. Give me a second, and I'll work on yours." Charlotte's indrawn breath hissed and she trembled as she shook her hands. "Pins and needles. Ouch. Bastard tied the damn rope so tight I lost circulation in my hands."

"Mine aren't that bad, the pig was distracted by my cleavage. He actually drooled on me." Alex shivered. "Yuck." She tested her bonds. There was a little play, but she couldn't quite get it loose. She stopped trying and waited for Charlotte. She didn't want to risk making them any tighter by struggling with them.

"Okay, give me your hands." Charlotte worked on the ropes. She had them off within minutes. "There you go." She paused. "Now what?"

Alex sat back and tried to think. What could they do? Without light they wouldn't get very far. "Should we try to make it to the portal?"

"I don't know if we'd be any better off. They might just push us right back. Or shoot us."

"No, they wouldn't, would they?" Alex asked in horror. She had a hard time reconciling what she now knew with the story Sawyer had fed her. She had thought it strange he needed her help but had never thought it would have come to force if she'd refused.

"I don't know," Charlotte's voice was thoughtful.

"They weren't about to let me walk out of there; that's for sure. Would they have shot me if they couldn't force me back? I just don't know. They wanted me back here, not dead. Not to mention, I caused a decent amount of damage when I left. I doubt they'd be too happy to see me."

"Yeah, but we might be able to buy some time. Convince them to let us stay a day or two before they force us back. Lord Stone and his people might think we escaped the same way we did last time and leave. Then we could make our way back and find a way to Lord Tyndale's house."

"Or Lord Stone might stumble through the portal." Charlotte laughed. "That could be fun. Lord Stone and those creepy servants of his at the business end of a couple of machine guns. With any luck the soldiers would shoot first and ask questions later."

"Humph." Alex chuckled. Passage through the portal had been a nightmare. And she'd been prepared. She could just imagine what Lord Stone would think. "Why was Sawyer so determined to send us back, anyway? I mean, it's been fifteen years. It's not like we just stumbled through the portal yesterday. We grew up there—uh, then—uh, whatever. Did he explain it to you?"

"No, not really." She sighed. "He said something about *cleaning house* and sending people back to their own time. He tried to tell me everyone was happy to go." She snorted. "I certainly wasn't. They had to drug me, and it still took a cave-in to push me through."

"They were a bit more creative with me. They went full court press to convince me to go willingly. They dangled you as the carrot to lure me here, but of course,

I thought I could always come back." She frowned as she thought about it. "I wonder what they were planning on doing when I returned."

"Maybe they didn't expect you to return."

Alex thought about it and shivered. "He said I could save you, and I believed him. He gave me the creeps. I should have paid attention to my gut and known everything wasn't what it seemed. I'm an idiot."

Charlotte clasped her hand tight and rubbed some warmth into her icy fingers. "You wanted to save me. That makes you heroic, not stupid. And if you'd never come, we would never have seen each other again. Nor would you have met your Nicholas and had a chance of living happily ever after with the man of your dreams," Charlotte said quietly.

"Do you think it's possible?" Alex asked.

"What?"

"Happily ever after." It occurred to her that Charlotte would be able to understand what Alex was going through. She was the only person who *could* understand. "Is it possible for us to live here, in this time, and be happy?"

"I've been thinking about that." Charlotte sighed. "I remember what it was like when we were kids. We were happy, but we didn't know any better. Had we been raised in this century, we would have accepted that our lot in life was to marry well and become dutiful wives and mothers. We were wealthy, so we wouldn't have had to face some of the harsher realities of this time. But now, we've been exposed to a different way of life. I don't know if we can go back so easily."

Charlotte sniffed, and Alex wondered whether she was crying.

"I'm a doctor. I went to work every day and made a difference, saved lives. Here, I can diagnose illnesses, but I have very little chance of actually helping. I lack the resources, and in most cases, they wouldn't listen to a woman anyway."

"But you could find a way to help within the strictures of this time." Alex thought for a second before continuing, "They have midwives. You could use your knowledge to help pregnant women. Think of the horror women go through to bring a child into the world now. You could make a huge difference."

"I would love that. *If* I were allowed…" Charlotte's voice sounded as bitter as Alex felt. "A woman's life isn't really her own here. I would need to have permission from my husband or father."

Alex winced. "Yeah. The idea of needing a man's permission to live my life drives me crazy. I've been taking care of myself since I was sixteen, and I resent the implication I'm not capable. I'm not even allowed to decide for myself who to marry." She wished she could see Charlotte's face as she asked the next question. "Do you think it's possible for a man of this time to accept us and not try to run our lives?"

"I don't know," Charlotte said softly. "My parents," she hesitated slightly. "My *real* parents, always discussed anything major, like when my mother wanted to go back to work when Steven, my brother, and I both started school. They argued a while, and in the end she waited a few more years before she started. I guess this wouldn't be all that different. James knows what I'm capable of. I think he would be supportive as long as I found a way to help without causing a scandal. If Nicholas loves you, he'll want you to be happy.

Surely you'll be able to work things out."

Alex let out the breath she hadn't even realized she'd been holding. "That's *if* he loves me." And if he could ever bring himself to believe her, to believe *in* her.

"Of course we have to get out of this mess first." Charlotte's tone turned bitter as she continued. "And hope our father doesn't decide to sell us to some other monster the minute he finds out we're still alive."

"What!" Alex exclaimed. She couldn't possibly have heard her correctly. "You think our father sold us to Lord Stone?"

"I know he did," Charlotte said, the anger in her voice apparent. "When we were kids, I heard Mr. Timmons telling Lord Stone our father had given us to him in exchange for some vote."

Charlotte's pain rang clear. No wonder she had been so set against coming back here. She thought their father was responsible for the whole thing!

"That's not true! Our family was devastated by our disappearance. Lord Downing blamed himself, but it wasn't his fault. He was a vocal proponent in the House of Lords of a bill to end the slave trade. He received a threat against his heir.

"He hired guards, but since the threat had mentioned Gregory specifically, they focused on him, and it wasn't too hard for Lord Stone's man to grab us. He killed the nurse who was watching us as we played in the garden that day."

Alex shuddered. She wished she hadn't regained that particular memory. She could remember how kind that woman had been, always helping them out of scrapes, bringing them sweets when they'd been sent to bed without supper.

Alex shook off the thought and continued. She had to convince Charlotte of their parent's innocence. "Our dad blamed himself for not taking the threats more seriously and backing down on the vote. He was young and cocky. He didn't think anything could possibly get to him or his family. He's had a virtual army of people out looking for you since the moment I came back and said you were in trouble. Please, you have to believe me."

Alex waited anxiously for Charlotte's response. Charlotte had spent a lifetime believing their father had betrayed them. Would she be able to accept the truth now?

Tears choked Charlotte's voice, "I don't know, Alex. I want to believe you, but I *heard* them."

"We were only ten. Maybe you didn't hear what you think you heard. Maybe it was just an expression, like *he practically handed them to me* because it was so easy for Mr. Timmons to grab us."

Charlotte sucked in a sharp breath. "Oh my god. Could I have misunderstood all this time?"

Alex pulled Charlotte close. Her shoulders shook with her tears. Alex patted her back comfortingly and rocked slightly back and forth.

"I've hated him for so many years. Everything I thought I knew has turned out to be wrong. What's next?" Charlotte gave a shaky laugh. "If Lord Stone doesn't kill me, I think I'll die from shock."

"Or cold." Alex let Charlotte go and rubbed her arms. "I'm freezing, and I'm getting a cramp from sitting for so long. I've got to move around a bit."

"Maybe we can make our way to the surface,"

Charlotte suggested. "They might not have bothered posting a guard. If they did, maybe the two of us can overpower him. Anyway, I'm with you. We have to do something."

"Okay. Let's go together. Grab my hand." Alex felt around until she was able to grab Charlotte's searching hand. "Now, grab on and follow me. I need my hands to make sure I don't bump into anything. The ceiling gets pretty low in spots." Alex put one hand to the wall and the other in front of her, and they inched their way slowly around the cavern.

****

Alex let her breath out in a long, slow whisper, trying to keep as quiet as possible. She tucked herself against the jagged wall of the cave entrance. The bright light of the moon helped her see Lord Stone issue orders to his servants. *Damn.* He hadn't left them alone as she'd hoped. Alex's blood ran cold, and Charlotte's grip tightened on her arm.

"I need to know what the ladies know and with whom they have shared that information. I don't care how you find out. Timmons, you stand guard while Cantor *persuades* the little ladies to talk."

A sleazy grin crossed Cantor's face as he received his orders.

"I will await your report at my estate. Once you are satisfied you know everything, I do not wish to have any additional problems with them. See to it they never bother me again. It is late, and I do not wish to be disturbed at too early an hour. I shall expect your report directly following breakfast."

"Yes, milord," Cantor answered, eager anticipation evident in his tone.

Charlotte tugged on her arm, so Alex followed her back down the tunnel where they wouldn't be overheard.

"There's no way out; they're too close to the tunnel entrance for us to sneak by them. Maybe we can ambush them as they enter the cave," Charlotte whispered as they both crouched to avoid the low ceiling.

Alex let go of Charlotte to use her arms for balance as she made her way through the cramped tunnel. When her hand slipped into the air, she knew she had reached the cave.

Charlotte whispered, "Go right. I'll go left and maybe we can surprise them before they have the chance to stand up straight." She cursed violently. "If only I had my gun. I think James has it."

Alex suddenly remembered the pieces of warming bricks she had stashed in her reticule. "I weighted down my purse. I can use it as a weapon. I have a few other things up my sleeve as well. Do you have anything on you?"

"No," Charlotte replied. "It probably wouldn't have done any good if I had the gun anyway. I couldn't shoot the broad side of a barn." She laughed quietly, but without humor. "Steven tried to teach me how to shoot, and I just scoffed at him. I said I would never be able to shoot anyone, so why bother. I'll tell you something, I wouldn't hesitate to shoot Lord Stone or that creepy Mr. Timmons."

"Is the gun how you proved to Lord Tyndale you weren't lying about being from the future?" Alex asked curiously.

"The gun, my clothes, my watch, and a few pound

notes I had in my jeans pocket. Sawyer and his cronies were about to strip me down and dress me in period clothing when I regained my senses and made my bid for freedom. I grabbed a gun, but the whole thing backfired, and I ended up causing the cave-in that forced me through the portal. At least I got through with my stuff."

"I wish I hadn't been so gullible. I just went along with everything like a good little puppet and look at me now." Alex could picture how she must look, crouched here in the pitch black. Dirt streaked and grimy, elegant ball gown torn beyond repair, hair a rats' nest of tangles and scattered hairpins.

She reached down and widened a tear in her skirt, straight down to the hem. Her ruined finery caused a small pang in her chest, but she wanted to free up her legs to increase her range of motion.

The shuffling of feet rustled in the tunnel and Alex tensed, all her nerves stretched tight. She gripped her reticule in both hands and held it aloft, prepared to crash it down on whatever body part made it into the cave first. She was done going with the flow.

Whoever came down that tunnel next wouldn't know what hit him.

****

Lord Stone's estate in Hertfordshire was located just south of the caves Alex claimed held a portal to the future. Nicholas and Tyndale agreed not to waste time seeking assistance from Tyndale's home, which bordered Stone's property to the north, and investigated Stone's house first.

Nicholas chafed at the delay. The servants, in various degrees of undress, huddled together in the hall.

His repeated questions returned useless information.

The only servant willing to speak to them had little to say. Yes, he had seen one of the ladies in question, but no, he had no idea where she was at that moment.

The knowledge Charlotte had been there early that morning brought only temporary relief. She had been in perfect health, if her struggles and over loud cursing were any indication, but that she had left early and unwillingly renewed their fears for her safety.

Would their decision to search the estate first cause them to arrive too late to save their women?

They ran to the stables, where a quick jab to the head groom's jaw overrode any objection to their borrowing two of Stone's best hunting horses in place of their own ragged and weary mounts.

The sound of a carriage barreling down the road reached their ears as they were discussing whether to turn off the drive and head over the fields.

"Over there." Tyndale pointed to a row of trees lining the drive to their left and maneuvered his horse behind them. In the dark, it shielded them from sight of the road but provided a decent view of the carriage's approach.

Nicholas had no doubt it belonged to Lord Stone. No one else would approach his manor at such a breakneck pace at this time of night.

The question was whether he had Alex or Charlotte with him. Nicholas kept a tight rein on his fresh, high-strung horse and prayed the carriage made enough noise to mask the restless stamping and neighing of the animal.

A preternatural calm descended upon him as they waited for the carriage to come into view. It was often like this, moments before a battle. He had experienced the sensation frequently during the war. As he'd stood his post among the others, his fears would fade into the background. Time would slow, and he would watch the enemy approach at a crawl until the first cannon fired and set time back in motion.

The carriage careened around the corner, and they got their first good look at the flashy, one-horse cabriolet. Not the type of carriage one would normally drive across country in the middle of the night. It appeared to Nicholas almost as a painting, the image was so clear.

Light from the cabriolet's lantern cast an eerie glow on the dust raised from the horse's hooves. Flecks of spittle at his mouth and lash marks on his sides showed he had been ridden hard that night, and his driver had little care for his welfare.

Nicholas recognized the man holding the reins instantly, and if Lord Stone was driving himself, he must have left his coachman to take care of other business.

"They're not with him," Nicholas said to Tyndale, who nodded in immediate agreement with Nicholas's assessment. "Shall we stop him, before he reaches his estate and has servants to come to his aid?"

"Yes, I believe that would be the wisest course of action," Tyndale responded, his voice as calm and cold as Nicholas's nerves.

Nicholas pressed his heels to his horse's flanks and followed Tyndale to block the coach's path.

Chapter Twenty-Four

The cabriolet's horse came to a screaming stop, fighting the reins that kept him in place, eyes wide in terror at the specter suddenly blocking his path. Nicholas took a moment to admire Tyndale's nerve as the horse bucked and plunged within an inch of his mount.

Nicholas kept a steel grip on his own horse, which looked ready to bolt if not for the calm, firm grip on its head. Nicholas blinked as a gun appeared in Tyndale's hand. He'd never seen its like but had no time to think on it further as he approached the side of the carriage and the cause of all his worries that evening.

That cause seemed much less worrisome face-to-face. Nicholas almost laughed to see the panic so clearly written on Lord Stone's visage. Almost. Then he thought about Alex and what it could mean that Stone was here, without her.

Almost involuntarily, he reached out and grabbed Lord Stone around the neck, dragging him off the carriage and giving free rein to the horse. Tyndale pulled back, and the carriage tore past.

Nicholas let Stone go abruptly and watched as he fell to the ground, sprawled in the mud at the horse's feet. He stood slowly and attempted to wipe the mud from his clothing. As he realized the effort was futile, Nicholas could see Stone's fear change to anger.

"How dare you!" Stone raged. "You will be punished severely for your affront to my person. I demand you turn over your horse to me at once and go fetch my carriage."

Nicholas and Tyndale laughed. Stone's confident demeanor faded slightly as he looked between the two men in the dim light available from the moon and stars overhead. "I fail to see the humor in this situation."

"We simply find it amusing that you demand our horses," Nicholas said, "considering they are yours."

"Mine!" Stone spluttered. "You have stolen my horses! I shall have you hanged for this. I am a Baron, you cannot get away with this atrocity."

"Oh, I believe we can," Lord Tyndale said calmly.

"Tyndale?" Lord Stone asked, his voice suddenly weaker as he recognized his neighbor.

Nicholas watched Stone visibly pull himself together.

"What are you doing on my property, with my horses? I am, of course, always happy to help my neighbors with any trouble they may experience. There is no cause for such tactics."

"I believe there is a very good reason, two as a matter of fact."

Nicholas let Tyndale carry the bulk of the conversation as he dismounted. He then grabbed hold of Stone by his now severely rumpled cravat. He longed to take out his rage on the bastard cowering before him, but they didn't have the time. Who knew what was happening to Alex as they stood there.

"Where. Are. They?" Nicholas asked. Slowly. Deliberately. He pulled Stone closer with each word. Stone's feet just barely reached the ground. His mouth gaped open like a fish out of water, struggling for breath as Nicholas held him up to his own considerably larger height until they were eye to eye.

"You had better tell me they are unharmed, or *I* will hang *you* myself."

****

Alex and Charlotte waited in silence, poised at the entrance to their prison, prepared to fight for their freedom. They had no choice. Talking their way out wasn't an option.

Heavy footsteps thumped down the tunnel. The light of the approaching lantern eased the darkness until they could just make out each other's outline, mirror images in intent as well as form.

Cantor didn't even pause as he entered the cavern, apparently convinced they wouldn't offer any resistance. As his head came into view, Alex swung her reticule as hard as she could, caught him in the jaw and sent his head crashing back into the stone wall. He fell with a soft *thunk* onto the cave floor. Charlotte raced to grab the lantern before it hit the ground.

Alex's chest rose and fell rapidly as she pressed herself against the cave wall and stared down at the unconscious man at her feet. Had she killed him?

His groan made her jump, but his eyes remained closed and he made no attempt to stand. A quick glance up the tunnel reassured her he had entered alone. She rushed across the cave to grab the ropes that had bound her and Charlotte earlier.

She tossed one to Charlotte. "Tie his feet; I'll get his hands."

She wrapped the rope around his wrists and tied them as tightly as she could behind his back. When she was done, she gave them a tug, and satisfied he wouldn't be able to undo them easily, she turned to Charlotte who was doing the same to his legs. "Now what?"

"Let's head back to the surface. Timmons must be around here somewhere, and I'd rather deal with him up there than down here." Charlotte shuddered as she took one more look at Cantor's prone body, before she turned toward the exit.

"Yeah, me too," Alex agreed. She followed Charlotte out of the cave, glad to be leaving the place that would probably be the setting for all her future nightmares.

****

They made their way cautiously up to the surface and paused at the cave entrance. Alex could just make out the first hints of the rising sun lightening the sky. She fought the urge to rush out and get away as quickly as possible. She'd had enough excitement for one night. Charlotte hid the lantern behind her skirts so Timmons wouldn't notice.

He stood at the open door of the carriage Alex had taken to get there earlier. He muttered under his breath as he inspected the inside.

Hah, she thought, with a twinge of satisfaction at the damage she had inflicted so spitefully.

She whispered to Charlotte, "Do you have any idea how to drive that carriage?"

"No, but I could probably figure out how to unhook the horses. Can you ride?"

"No, I never even got near a horse before coming here. I haven't had the time to try to learn to ride one."

She was about to say more when the sound of

horses' hooves reached her ears. Timmons must have heard it, too. He closed the carriage door and turned toward the sound. The knots in her stomach tightened. He didn't seem worried. Help was on its way, but not for her. *Shit.*

Alex searched for an escape route. Bushes off to the side seemed the best option. As long as Timmons didn't turn around, they could make it. It was worth the risk. She did not want to be trapped in the cave. She motioned to Charlotte, and they tiptoed over while the approaching horses distracted Timmons. Crouching behind a large evergreen bush, they peeked out to keep an eye on their guard.

Relief flooded her veins as the horses thundered into view with Nicholas and Lord Tyndale astride. Nicholas pointed a gun at Timmons, and the old man immediately put up his hands in defeat. Catching a glimpse of the murder on Nicholas's face, Alex could hardly blame him.

"James!" Charlotte exclaimed, and she danced out from behind the bush, her face glowing with happiness.

"Charlotte."

He sagged with relief, and Alex wondered why he didn't dismount at once and come to her. Then she noticed the man lying across the saddle in front of him and gasped in surprise. Lord Stone! He looked nothing like the confident, jeering man who had so recently ordered his servants to question and murder her. His clothing was in a sad state, covered in mud and wrinkled beyond recognition. His hair stuck up in places with mud speckled throughout.

James shoved him off the horse. He landed awkwardly, barely maintaining his footing as he clutched the horse's side. Before Lord Stone could move, James pointed a gun at him. A thoroughly modern gun.

"Don't move, Stone." James swung his leg over the horse's side and dismounted. Charlotte immediately rushed into his arms.

Alex stood, her gaze riveted on the rigid set of Nicholas's face. She grimaced at the worry she'd obviously caused him. Shit. When he realized she was out of danger, he was going to be pissed that she'd left him. Again.

His expression softened when he finally caught sight of her. He dismounted and held out his left hand toward her.

The dam broke as she rushed into his arms. The tears she had held back all evening poured down her cheeks.

"Great. All this time I've been steady as a rock. Now it's all over, and I break down like a wreck." She swiped at her cheeks, probably managing little other than spreading dirt over her face.

"Don't worry, darling. I can handle a few tears."

Nicholas's sexy voice rumbled next to her ear, sending pleasant shivers down her neck and shoulders.

A high-pitched whinny startled them both. They swung quickly toward James's mount. It reared on its hind legs, pawing the air. James swung Charlotte out of the way, putting himself between her and the horse. He caught a glancing blow to his shoulder, and the gun flew out of his hand as he toppled to the ground.

While Nicholas ran to calm the horse, Lord Stone sprinted out of the way. He snatched the gun that had fallen practically at his feet and straightened, his legs wide and arms out in front of him.

With horror, Alex realized he was aiming straight at Nicholas. Preoccupied with getting the horse under control, he didn't appear to notice.

She threw herself at Nicholas with a shout. She had no plan on what to do when she got there, but she couldn't stand by and watch him killed.

A white hot flash of pain struck her back, and she collapsed into Nicholas's strong arms. She expected to feel his warmth envelope her as it always did, but her body grew cold instead. She struggled to breathe. She was drowning on dry land, each agonizing breath a desperate bid for life.

Confused shouts and sounds of a scuffle barely reached her ears above the pounding of blood in her ears. She groaned as something hit her side and sent pain searing down her back.

Charlotte screamed, "No, Alex, no!" from a long way off.

She blinked and tried to see her sister's face one last time. She could tell it was Charlotte but couldn't focus.

Her last thought before she lost consciousness was that she was glad Sawyer hadn't told her what would happen. She never would have come.

****

Nicholas clasped Alex's unconscious form. Warmth flooded his hand, and he realized with horror it was her blood. He was losing her. Her life was spilling out of her as she lay within the protection of his arms. Protection. He was supposed to protect her, yet she had given her life for him.

He couldn't allow this to happen. He had to save

her.

Charlotte crouched beside him. He'd barely glanced at her as he'd rushed to pull Alex into his grasp. She ripped a section of her petticoat and pressed it to Alex's wound.

Perhaps... "Charlotte. She's dying. I've seen wounds like this before. She cannot be saved. Here. Does she have a chance of recovery in the future? In your time." He closed his eyes briefly before continuing, "In her time?"

"I thought you didn't believe her," Charlotte said, tears streaming down her face. "Here, apply pressure here." She placed his hand over the wound, and he pressed down gently. "No, you need to be firm. Don't worry about hurting her. She can't feel anything." She grunted as she made more makeshift bandages from her dress.

Tyndale moved around in the background, tying up Lord Stone and his servant. Nicholas focused on Charlotte. He couldn't bear to look on Alex's pale face, to see the blood slowly leaving her. To realize she could die believing he never learned to trust her. She could die, and he had never told her how much he loved her.

"I didn't, but I do now. Trust does not come easy to me. But she deserves my trust, and my love. She doesn't deserve this. Do you know whether she can be saved?"

"Yes, but we have to hurry." Charlotte paused, two fingers pressed to Alex's neck. "You'll have to help me get her to the portal. I can't carry her by myself."

Charlotte tied a bandage tightly to Alex's wound and picked up a lantern. Nicholas cradled Alex in his arms, her head lolling against his shoulder.

"Follow me," Charlotte said. "There are some tight spots. We'll need to work together to get her through them. You won't be able to carry her the entire way."

He walked behind Charlotte, using the light of the lantern to guide him. James followed at the rear, helping Nicholas with Alex when necessary. When the tunnel narrowed, they worked their way through, pushing and pulling Alex as gently and quickly as possible. She remained silent the entire time.

Her silence scared Nicholas deep in his soul.

He should be grateful she remained unconscious. They tried to be careful but couldn't help jolting her as they maneuvered through the tunnels. Had she been awake, the pain would have been considerable.

Yet, a reaction to that pain would have at least been proof she lived. Each time they shifted her, he expected some kind of response—a groan, tears, anything. She remained completely still.

At every point where the tunnel opened up enough for him to carry her, Charlotte rushed to his side to double check Alex still breathed. He greeted Charlotte's order to stop with great relief.

"The portal is down at the bottom of this decline." She pointed ahead of them.

The ground dipped steeply downward and was narrow enough he had to give some thought to how to get Alex down.

"We have to figure out how to get her down there." Charlotte echoed his thoughts. "I don't know if I can carry her all that way."

"You're not taking her. I am."

"What!" Charlotte turned to look at him. "You

can't."

"Why not?" he asked.

"They may not exactly welcome us with open arms." Charlotte gave a quick explanation of her escape from the future.

"All the more reason that I attend to it," Nicholas asserted. "I shall convince them of their obligation to cure her. Now, I believe time is of the essence." He started down the path to redemption.

Chapter Twenty-Five

May 29, Current Year

Nicholas fell to his knees. He tightened his grip on Alex as she slipped. He caught her only a moment before she fell to the ground. His eyes closed. Nausea threatened to overwhelm him. His ears rang and his balance was off. He sat back on his heels to keep from toppling over.

"Not another move."

He looked up and stopped dead. Two uniformed men—no, a man and a woman—pointed weapons at him. Weapons he couldn't recognize, though they certainly looked lethal.

The room was as bright as a sunny day. He looked for the source of the light and squinted at long tubes of light, which hung from the ceiling.

The lighting dimmed and changed. Red light flashed about the room. A horrendous noise pierced the air. The flashing lights distorted the room's appearance, but Nicholas could see the space was no longer a natural phenomenon.

The floors and walls were rough stone but carved in such straight lines it had obviously not happened on its own. Huge chunks of rock lay against a far wall. Portions of the ceiling were missing, evidence of the cave-in Charlotte had described.

He had no time to stare in wonder at his surroundings. "Help me!" He yelled to be heard above the ceaseless noise. He glanced down at Alex, her face pale and still.

No one approached, and he looked up to find out why. They stood silently, their gazes alert and focused on his face. They ignored the blaring noise and flashing lights as well as his desperate plea.

The soldiers, for that is what he realized they must be, kept their weapons trained on him, tension evident in their stance as they waited, most likely for reinforcements.

He couldn't wait for them to figure out what to do, damn it! Alex didn't have that much time. He focused on the woman. Surely a woman would be more likely to give aid to someone in need. "Help her. She is gravely injured. You must help her. Please," he begged.

The woman looked uncertainly at her companion, then down at Alex. She straightened marginally. Her lips pursed, and she nodded slightly.

She turned to place her weapons on a table near the door. She pressed a button on a small box mounted to the wall and said something he couldn't hear. She hurried to his side. "Place her on the floor, help will be here in a minute."

Nicholas placed Alex gently on the floor at his feet. He tilted her on her side and continued to apply pressure on the wound. The flow of blood had slowed, but she had lost so much, it was a wonder she had any left.

The soldier ignored her male counterpart, who nervously adjusted his grip on his weapon and yelled at her to not get too close.

"What happened?" She placed her hands over Alex's wound and indicated she would take over.

Nicholas had no chance to answer. The doors banged open, and more soldiers rushed into the room, followed by a portly man who walked with a confidence that showed Nicholas clearly he was the man in charge. With a simple gesture, the noise pounding in his head silenced and the lights ceased flashing.

The man strode right up to them and shot a withering glare at the soldier whose hands were now covered in Alex's blood. "Back to your post, soldier," he ordered.

She flushed and started to remove her hands. Nicholas placed his hand on her shoulder, and she stilled.

He stood, his movements lightning quick, and for the second time that night, his hands closed around another's throat. He took some satisfaction in watching the leader's eyes bulge as he struggled for air.

He held the man close, between himself and the soldiers, whose guns all pointed his way. He could see the indecision in their eyes. Could they shoot him without harming their leader?

He increased pressure slightly as the man attempted to pull away. "The soldier shall stay where she is until you summon a doctor to take her place."

When the man stilled, Nicholas grabbed hold of his arm to hinder any escape he might attempt and eased the pressure slightly off his throat to allow him the possibility of speech.

The stranger somehow managed to maintain his air of authority, even with the undignified position. He breathed as deeply as Nicholas's grip allowed before saying, "You must leave here immediately and take her with you."

"She will not survive in my time. I have been informed there are doctors here that can heal her. You will summon one here immediately." His teeth ground together in frustration, aware that Alex slipped closer and closer to death with each passing moment.

"I can't do that. I'm sorry she's going to die, but there's nothing I can do. We are not permitted to do anything that might change history. Healing a wound that would kill her in your time is not allowed."

Nicholas's grip tightened involuntarily at those words, and the man's eyes widened in alarm. "You can and you will. Or I will see that you regret it."

He let go as he realized exactly how he would convince them to do as he wanted. He schooled his features to show no emotion as the man stumbled. Five guns now aimed directly at him. While many of them were of the unfamiliar larger variety the first two carried, he noticed that one of the soldiers carried a weapon almost exactly like the one he had seen in Tyndale's hand. He realized from where it must have come.

Their leader straightened himself and laughed coldly. "Just how do you think you'll be able to do that?"

Nicholas nodded toward the soldier he had noticed. "I must say I like your weapons. That one there is quite deadly but unheard of in my time." He smiled grimly. "Except of course for the gun that wounded Alex. It will cause quite a commotion back home when people see this weapon of the future and the wound it caused.

I'm certain I can convince some young craftsman to build more of them. Perhaps I will be known as the inventor of this gun your soldiers favor. Wouldn't that be splendid?"

"You're bluffing," he stated, yet his face had paled.

"I have no need. Alex's sister, Lady Charlotte Creswell, brought a few other items from the future as well. My friend, Lord Tyndale, described them as *truly amazing*—items that were quite obviously *beyond the capacity* of our time. Interesting that you would allow her to bring such items with her."

Nicholas laughed, inflecting as much scorn into the sound as possible. "Oh, yes. That's right. She overpowered your men. I see the mark of her passage all around us." Nicholas nodded at the pile of rubble in the corner. Hate practically poured off the man. The same emotion clogged his own thoughts, but he had the upper hand. "We have no further time to delay. You will see to obtaining assistance for Alex. Now."

The man's shoulders slumped slightly in defeat, though he pulled himself back up quickly and resumed his confident manner. "The paramedics are already on their way." He indicated the soldier still at Alex's side. "She put the call out already."

Nicholas relaxed marginally and nodded his thanks to the soldier. He knelt at Alex's side and pulled her cold hand into his. He leaned over and whispered encouraging words into her ear. "You will be fine. Don't give up, Alex. I love you."

****

Nicholas no longer doubted the existence of purgatory. It was a small room with furniture upholstered in strange fabric that stuck to your skin if you sat still for too long. It was crowded with people who paced restlessly or sat listlessly as they waited to discover whether they would be descending further into the abyss or rising above to join their loved ones in heaven. False hope was continuously raised and dashed as men and women in loose trousers and flapping white coats paused at the entrance to select the lucky few who would journey on.

The man in charge, Sawyer, tried to send him back through the portal, but Nicholas refused. He would not leave Alex. They cowered before him and caved to his demand to accompany her. He would make sure her condition improved.

They had bundled him up and brought him to this modern hell called a waiting room. Sawyer instructed him to speak with no one and gave him a strange set of garments to replace his own soiled eveningwear in an attempt to make him less noticeable.

A soldier sat casually in a chair near the door, just another family member waiting for news, but Nicholas was well aware he was under guard.

He ignored him. They could set all the guards they desired, provided they made no attempt to keep him from Alex's side the moment she returned from surgery.

He did not completely understand why he was unable to attend her during her surgery. He assured them he was no stranger to bloodshed. He had seen horrendous injuries during the war and held the hand of many a fellow crewmember as they suffered amputation or had wounds cauterized. He would not faint or any such nonsense.

They had stared at him in horror, and Sawyer had

ushered him out, leaving the female soldier behind to speak with the doctors.

Sawyer had explained their theory of germs, and that his presence during the surgery could cause fatal harm to Alex, besides which she would be unconscious during the entire surgery and would not be aware of his presence. He had reluctantly left her side and had been waiting ever since.

He brought to mind an image of Alex as she had looked descending the stairs before the ball. How lovely she had looked, her face glowing with health and youthful vivacity. He concentrated on this image whenever he thought of her still and blood soaked body rushed away on a wheeled bed by a large contingent of doctors.

That image could not be his last.

Another doctor paused at the entrance to the waiting room. Nicholas stood as the doctor headed in his direction. Sawyer followed a few steps behind. "Are you Nicholas Somerville? I believe you are a relation of some sort to Alexandra Turner, the young lady with the gunshot wound?"

"Yes. Lady Alexandra is my fiancée." Nicholas kept his voice calm and impassive.

"She's out of surgery and doing well. She's not out of the woods yet, but she appears to be a fighter."

The doctor smiled kindly, and Nicholas allowed himself to smile back in relief.

"Do you know what blood type you are? You might like to give blood while you're waiting for her to be transferred to a recovery room."

"I am not ill. Bloodletting is unnecessary." He frowned. "Save your concern for Lady Alexandra."

The doctor gave him an odd look and opened his mouth to speak, but Sawyer interrupted. "Thank you, doctor. Perhaps we'll donate later."

At this obvious dismissal, the doctor shrugged and left the room.

"I wished to speak more to that doctor regarding Alex's condition. You will call him back to explain his comments," Nicholas demanded.

"She's doing okay. You wouldn't understand anything the doctor could tell you, and I'd prefer you have as little interaction with people here as possible. Your ignorance of common facts will make people suspicious, and that won't help Alex."

Nicholas bristled at the insult, but Sawyer continued in a low voice, glancing around to make sure they weren't overheard, "Simple, everyday items will seem extraordinary to you, and your reaction will cause people to notice you. That's the last thing we need right now."

Still seething, but recognizing Sawyer's point, Nicholas nodded. "When will I be allowed to see Alex for myself?"

"Soon. You'll just have to wait here a bit longer."

Nicholas sighed and sat once again, still in hell but with that glimmer of hope that he might ascend shortly.

****

A woman burst into the small hospital room. Nicholas rose to block her before she could reach the bed where Alex lay still, covered in a starched white sheet with tubes and wires draped under her nose, attached to her arm and affixed to her chest. Small boxes on pedestals near the bed beeped and flashed, while under the window, the large box that kept the air a pleasant temperature added a constant whirring noise to the background.

She skidded to a stop, almost bumping into his chest. She was a tiny thing, her short blond head came only to his chest. Much smaller than his Alex. Her mouth gaped open as she lifted her head to stare up at him.

"Oh!" she exclaimed, a trifle breathless. "Hi. I'm Jessica Faraday. Alex's friend."

He lifted a finger to his lips and gestured to Alex. He kept his voice low so as not to disturb her. "It is a pleasure to make your acquaintance." He inclined his head. "I am Nicholas Somerville, Marquess of Oakleigh. I am Alex's betrothed."

Miss Faraday's jaw dropped and her eyes widened. "Betrothed? Does that mean what I think it means?"

"We are engaged to be married," he confirmed. His heart ached at the knowledge this was a lie. She had never agreed to their engagement.

Her gaze raked over him from head to toe. If he weren't so damn tired, he'd be amused at her temerity. Yes, she was an appropriate friend for his Alex. He recalled Alex mentioning her once. She had, perforce, left out many salient details.

"That's kind of sudden, isn't it? I mean, she never mentioned you and she's been, well, out of the area for the past..." Her voice trailed off and she cleared her throat. "So, ahem, do you know where she's been?"

He regarded her with renewed interest. "Alex confided her plans to you?"

"Yes, we're very good friends. I came as soon as Sawyer," She sneered as she said the name. "told me she'd returned. I came directly from Heathrow the minute I got in. I've been extremely worried about her." She nodded to the bed and frowned. "With good reason apparently. Please, tell me what happened."

Nicholas ran a hand along his jaw. His whiskers scratched along his palm. He refused to leave Alex any longer than necessary and this showed in his appearance. His nose wrinkled at the nauseating smell of his hands. The doctors insisted he bathe them frequently with a liquid that irritated his skin and the smell wouldn't go away.

He indicated two chairs in the corner of the room. He smoothed out the sheet where he'd clasped Alex's hand throughout the long night and placed a light kiss on her knuckles before following Miss Faraday. Once she had taken her seat, he lowered himself with a stifled groan and told her a tale he barely believed himself.

****

Nicholas convinced Miss Faraday to check into a hotel and get some rest, but only after she spoke with the doctors and was reassured Alex was not in any immediate danger.

She seemed like a pleasant woman, but he was happy when she left. Her presence reaffirmed Alex didn't belong with him, and he needed time to think.

He studied Alex's still face. Her color was much improved, and the doctors were confident she would make a full recovery. She needed rest, relaxation, and frequent follow-up visits to make sure her recovery remained on target.

What she didn't need was to suffer the excruciating pain of the time portal, crawl her way up a dark narrow tunnel only to walk several miles across rough terrain to come to the nearest habitation. Travel, even in this century, was to be limited, and from what little he had seen, they traveled in extreme comfort compared to the rigors of travel in his time.

How could he put her through all that? Yet he could not remain. This century was not for him even if he could manage to convince Sawyer to allow it.

He was on borrowed time. A soldier stood guard outside the room at this moment. He had not left Nicholas's side since they arrived. Sooner or later, Sawyer would insist on their return to the past. Alex might not survive it.

He leaned over the bed and kissed Alex gently. Her lips were warm, and it gave him the courage he needed. He could not allow any more harm to come to her. He would do what was necessary, but it was killing him.

He opened the door and motioned to the guard. "I need to speak with Sawyer."

The guard nodded, and Nicholas returned to Alex's side.

A deep sigh came from the bed. Her eyelids fluttered open, and she gazed around the room, blinking rapidly. "Nicholas?" Her voice was scratchy from disuse and barely audible.

"Alex. I'm here. You're home now. You're going to be all right." Nicholas grabbed hold of the hand that trembled as she tried to lift it toward him. He brought it to his lips and kissed gently. "I love you." A smile stole briefly across her face then faded as she drifted back to sleep.

She would be all right. He would see to it. He would convince Sawyer to allow her to stay here, where she would be safe. His life would be over, but hers would go on.

****

Alex drifted in and out of consciousness. She struggled out of the fog that enveloped her head and opened her eyes to look around the modern hospital room in confusion.

"Nicholas?" She could have sworn Nicholas was with her but didn't see him. Had she imagined him?

A petite figure dozed in a chair near the window, a book hanging loosely from her hand. "Jessie?" she whispered. No response. She cleared her throat and spoke a little louder, "Jessie?"

Jessie's head popped up. Her smile turned radiant when she saw Alex's open eyes. "Alex! You're awake. Let me get the doctor."

Before Alex could say anything, Jessie was out the door calling for help. Within moments, the room swarmed with doctors and nurses. After poking and prodding her for a quarter of an hour, they pronounced she was doing well and advised her to get some rest. Jessie came back in as they exited.

She fluttered around the room a moment then settled back down on the edge of the bed. "I was so worried about you."

"How did I get here? How did you find me? I don't really think I was expected to come back."

Jessie's smile had a hint of wickedness that made Alex grin in response. It was so good to see her once again. "Well, I haven't *exactly* made things easy on that Sawyer man since you left."

"Oh?"

"Of course I've been worried about you ever since you told me what you were going to do, and then one day I was watering your plants, as I said I would, when you got a call from Steven Evans."

Alex attempted to sit but pain shot up her side, and she immediately sank back down.

Jessie darted forward at her gasp, a worried frown back on her face. "Here let me fix this for you." She pushed a button on the bed's side rail, and the bed slowly lifted until Alex was sitting in a more comfortable upright position.

"Thanks," Alex got out between breaths, clutching at her chest as she labored to breathe, and the pain slowly receded. "Go on, tell me about Steven."

"He's been frantic about his sister and was calling to see if you had learned anything more. When he mentioned she's a doctor, I realized Sawyer must have lied to you. Steven and I have been hounding Sawyer ever since. We've both called the police, but they're not really following through. I wouldn't doubt that money has exchanged hands." Her disgust was evident in the way she fairly spit out the words. Then the mischievous grin came back. "Of course, that didn't work with the reporters."

A laugh exploded out of Alex before she could suppress it. When it didn't cause an upsurge of pain, she let loose some of the mirth inside. Breathing heavily once again, tears leaking out of the corners of her eyes; she gradually quieted down and admired Jessie. "Oh, I wish I could have seen it. That Sawyer's so used to everyone doing exactly what he wants—when he wants it—it must have thrown him for a loop when a reporter showed up."

"Yeah, well, he wasn't too pleased that I knew where you had gone. The man can curse like a sailor."

"What did you tell the reporter? I'd think they'd

ignore anyone with such a crazy tale."

"I knew better than to mention the time travel aspect. I just told him you had disappeared shortly after meeting with Sawyer, and the same had happened to your sister in England. The guy started looking into Sawyer and found a number of other disappearances that could be tied to him, though loosely. He had no real evidence, but Sawyer apparently tried to order the reporter around and just managed to piss him off instead, so the guy refused to drop it. So when you turned up, Sawyer called me in so I could see for myself that you're alive." She frowned. "I've been giving him hell over your condition. Care to tell me what happened?"

"It's a long story."

"Take your time, I'm not going anywhere."

****

Little by little, and over the course of several days since Jessie and the doctors kept insisting she get her rest, Alex told Jessie all about her time spent with Nicholas. She tried to brush off her feelings for him as nothing more than a passing affair, but she wasn't fooling anyone. Jessie's gaze bore through her, attempting to penetrate straight to her heart.

Jessie wasn't her only visitor. She also received frequent visits from Charlotte's brother, who couldn't hide his worry even though Alex reassured him at every visit that Charlotte was fine.

Steven was very handsome, in a boyish way, that endeared him to Alex straightaway. Though he was actually a few years older, she began to see him as her younger brother. She had the strongest feeling she needed to watch over him, strange as the thought was

333

considering she was the one lying in a hospital bed recovering from a near fatal wound.

His dark hair seemed perpetually messy, and she resisted the urge to suggest he get a haircut. His smile was infectious, and he often joked he must surely have at least one vampire ancestor who passed on his sharp canines and preference for rare steak.

Though she knew he struggled with worry, Alex cherished the time spent with him as he regaled her with tale after tale of Charlotte's wild childhood. She had apparently been quite a handful in her younger days. He had obviously doted on her when they were kids, and they had remained close as adults.

Jessie and Steven kept her so busy and entertained during visiting hours that the time flew by. Alex worked with a physical therapist who praised her progress and determination to recover quickly.

Alex left only reluctantly at the end of each session when a nurse came to escort her back to her room.

Even frequent visits from Sawyer, who pushed for detailed reports of her trip—which she refused to give—were welcome. Adrenaline would course through her body as she fought her disgust for the contemptuous little man who had so deceived her and who knew how many other innocent people who had the misfortune of straying across his path. His visits gave her something to focus her energy on and kept her from wallowing in the pit of misery she sank into each moment she was left alone.

Her thoughts would return to Nicholas in those moments. Deep in the night when everyone slept and even the night nurses spoke in whispers, Alex would lie awake, her heart aching and silent tears wetting her pillow. After the tears dried on her face, she would fall into a fitful slumber, where dreams of Nicholas always ended with him drifting farther and farther away.

****

Though it felt like forever, Alex recovered swiftly, and soon it was time for her to leave the hospital. As she awaited her official discharge, Jessie bustled about the room keeping up a steady stream of light-hearted chatter and packing the few items Alex would be taking home.

Jessie's voice trailed off, and Alex looked up to see Sawyer standing in the doorway. He nodded stiffly to Jessie, a disapproving frown on his face.

She smiled brightly in return. "So, heard anything from Jim at the Times lately?" she asked, not even bothering to keep her tone civil. She had not been pleased when Alex had refused to press charges against Sawyer for kidnapping. They had argued for over an hour before Jessie gave in and acknowledged it wasn't an option given the extraordinary circumstances. Alex would end up painted as a head case.

"The man calls me at least once a week," he grumbled. "I need to speak with Miss Turner, please excuse us."

"It's okay, Jessie," Alex reassured her friend, before she could respond. Sawyer had been careful to visit Alex only when Jessie was unlikely to be around, so they had only come across each other once or twice since Alex's return. That they could barely tolerate each other was plain to see. "I'll be fine."

"I'll wait in the lobby. Steven's bringing his car around." Alex and Jessie planned to stay at Steven's flat for a few days before they took the long flight home.

Jessie cast one more suspicious glance at Sawyer and left, leaving the door open wide behind her.

"Interfering little…" Sawyer's sentence was lost as he turned to close the door, but Alex felt the heat rush to her face in anger over his treatment of her dear friend.

"You can just keep your vicious little thoughts to yourself," Alex said. "She's a wonderful woman who was simply concerned for my safety. The only reason you don't like her is because she's smarter than you and didn't cower in fear when you tried to control her."

"She never would have known anything about me if you hadn't told her. Against orders, I might add."

"You can't order me about you know, I don't work for you. I wasn't under any obligation to—" She held up her hand to stop his response. "You know what? We've been over this enough already. What do you want now?"

"I want to assure you that should you change your mind about returning to your rightful place in time, you have only to call me, and I will arrange for your passage through the portal. I see now that it was a mistake to trick you, but the fact remains, you don't belong here."

"I told you. I'm not going back." Alex shivered, though the air was quite warm in the small, cramped room. An image of a dark cave and shimmering portal assailed her senses. She shook her head to clear it of the vision and looked into Sawyer's eyes.

"I don't belong there either, that has been made perfectly clear."

****

Dinner that night was Chinese take-out at Steven's

place. Alex tried to keep up her end of the conversation, but her thoughts wandered. She was staring out the window when she suddenly realized Jessie and Steven had fallen silent and were watching her. "I'm sorry. Did you ask me something?"

They cast meaningful glances at each other, and Steven nodded his head to Jessie. She took a deep breath and reached out to hold Alex's hand. "We're worried about you, honey."

"I'm fine! They never would have let me leave the hospital if I wasn't." She attempted a smile but knew it didn't reach her eyes.

"I'm not talking about your health, and you know it. You're miserable. You're trying to hide it, but it's obvious. Do you love him?"

Alex's head jerked up, and she stared at Jessie. She had listened to all of Alex's descriptions of her adventures but had never once asked her directly about Nicholas. Now that Alex thought of it, Jessie had pretty much avoided the subject.

"It's plain to see she does," Steven responded.

Wait a minute. She hadn't even mentioned Nicholas to Steven. What did he know about him?

He smiled at her. "Jessie and I have been talking." He reached over and grabbed her other hand. "We wanted to wait until you were better before we discussed this with you."

"Yes." Jessie squeezed Alex's hand gently. "We can't stand to see you so melancholy. I met you when you were at a low point in your life, and even then you were never this unhappy. So…" She took a deep breath. "…we've been talking and decided you should return to him."

"What!" Alex exclaimed. "I almost died, and you want me to go back?"

"From what you've described, it sounds like that particular danger has passed. You're miserable here. So what's to prevent you from returning and being with the man you love?" Jessie asked.

"He sounds like a nice guy. He rushed to your rescue and all that; I thought girls loved stuff like that."

Steven's grin was contagious, and Alex found herself responding.

"Yeah, well. He does have a certain heroic charm." Alex's grin was swift and quickly faded. She pulled her bottom lip between her teeth as she thought about the night she was shot. She relived the terror of seeing Lord Stone aim the gun at Nicholas, the pain that tore through her along with the bullet, and the anguished look on Nicholas's face as he caught her.

"Unless you're scared?" Jessie's quiet voice asked.

"Humph! I've traveled through time, served as a sailor on a nineteenth century cargo ship, survived a knife fight, been tied up in a pitch-black cave with my presumed dead twin sister, been shot—What's left?"

"That he might not love you as you love him?"

"Oh, that," she replied weakly. "Yes, there's always that."

Chapter Twenty-Six

September 18, 1818

Nicholas ignored the noise of a carriage stopping on the street before his front door. His mother and sister likely returning from whatever entertainment they had attended that evening, though it seemed a touch early. He would learn all the details of the evening, whether he wanted to or not, at some point the following day. He was in no rush.

They continuously plagued him with all the invitations that flooded the house, including the one for this evening, though he couldn't recall where they had gone. Even though it was the mini-season and London was much quieter at this time of year, there appeared to be no end to the social whirl. Each night the same, just another display of silly young girls hoping to snare a rich and titled husband. He had no interest and had yet to consider attending even one of the myriad events that consumed fashionable society.

Had his mood been any less morose, he would have considered it amusing. Those same lords and ladies who were so eager to have him present at their next ball would run from him in fear if they hadn't been blinded by his new title and wealth. They would even offer up their lovely daughters on a platter to gain a match with a Marquess. He couldn't help compare them to Alex who hadn't minded his scars and could care less for his title or fortune.

But none of it was able to gain more than a flicker of interest. Four months had passed since he said goodbye to Alex in that hospital room, and his thoughts were still consumed with her. His life was empty without her at his side. He thought constantly of how she would have reacted to each and every event that forced its way into his notice.

He'd briefly considered returning to *The Reliant* until he recognized there would be no relief from that quarter. His ship, and especially his cabin, would be full of memories of her.

At least here, in his home, there were no memories, only crushed dreams. He had pictured her gracing his home, sharing his life, bearing his children. Now she was gone. He had made the choice, better to lose her to another time than lose her to death. It was a small consolation.

A murmur of voices followed the opening of the front door. Not family then, his mother and sister could never manage such a quiet entrance. Silence was a foreign concept to the two of them, he thought fondly. They'd spent too many mute years living under his brother's thumb, to waste any time restraining their voices now they were free.

He wished he could put Alex behind him, if only for their sakes. He loved them and should have cherished his homecoming. He'd been denied it for so long. Instead, he could only notice that Alex wasn't with him, and without her, this house could never be a home.

He swirled the brandy around the snifter, watching

the amber liquid clinging to the sides of the glass, reflecting light from the small fire in the hearth. An image of Alex leaning over him, laughing as they spent delightful hours in his bed aboard *The Reliant*, came to mind.

Stupid, besotted fool. Her eyes were green, not brown. Why does everything bring forth memories of her? The glass slammed into the fireplace. He stumbled back as the flames blazed high, consuming the liquor. The fire reached for him but quickly died back.

He looked at the hand that had so recently held the heavy, crystal glass. He had thrown it without thinking, cursing the alcohol's inability to erase the ache deep in his soul.

Damn. Mother won't be pleased.

The door creaked. "Damn it, I told you I have no wish to be disturbed!" He didn't bother to turn around. Visitors held no interest for him.

"Should I come back later, then?"

Nicholas's eyes closed tight. It couldn't be. It had to be his imagination. She couldn't be here.

Steps approached from behind, and the feather light touch on his shoulder sent a tremor through his body. He turned around slowly, scarcely daring to breathe.

****

Alex fought to keep her voice calm, yet it sounded wobbly and unsure. "Should I come back later, then?" She approached his rigid back; her hand rose of its own accord and rested lightly on his shoulder. Did those vibrations originate with her or him? The cloth covering his shoulder was cool, but she could feel his warmth reaching out to her, tempting her to lay her head on his back and fold her arms around him. Never let go.

He turned slowly, agonizingly so. Her rapid breathing was in direct opposition to his. For a moment, she wondered if he breathed at all. Time crawled in that moment their eyes met for the first time in four months.

He looked worn out. Dark shadows framed his eyes, his cheeks sunken and covered with stubble. The time apart had been no easier on him. He had missed her. He must love her. Her doubts faded, and she took the two steps that separated them and flung her arms around his waist.

He still didn't respond, and she started to pull back, when his arms suddenly surrounded her and he lifted her off the floor in his embrace.

She laughed with the sheer joy of being in his arms again and held on for dear life as he spun her around.

After several dizzying seconds, she was on the ground once again and held out at arm's length. Nicholas's eyes were suspiciously bright. The tenderness in his gaze would have brought tears to her eyes, if they weren't already dripping steadily down her cheeks.

He brushed his thumb gently over her cheek, wiping away the tears. "Don't cry, my love."

"I've missed you."

"And I you."

Alex studied his precious face as his gaze dropped to her mouth, and he slowly bent forward to touch his lips ever so lightly to hers, like a butterfly resting briefly on a flower petal before fluttering away, only to return once more to consume the flower's essence.

The kiss deepened, and his tongue delved into her mouth. Alex heard a low groan, whether it was his or hers, she couldn't tell, didn't care. How long they remained, locked in that heated embrace, was anyone's guess. They eventually broke apart and moved as one to the settee, neither willing to let go for even a moment so soon after they'd found each other again.

For a while they sat quietly together, staring into the fire, Alex's head resting comfortably on Nicholas's chest, his arm across her shoulders. He idly twirled her hair in his fingers. "Your hair is longer."

"I figured the cat was out of the bag, no need to look like a boy anymore, so I let it grow." She patted her hair a little self-consciously. "What do you think?"

"It's perfect. Just like you." He moved away from her, and Alex shivered as cold air replaced the warmth of his side.

She cast him an enquiring gaze.

"I have been pondering the question of where I went wrong in recent events." He grinned. "My mother might disagree with the word pondering. I believe she referred to it as brooding."

"Brooding, huh?" Her brow furrowed as she thought back on their time together, trying to figure out what exactly he was talking about. "Wrong? What do you mean?"

"My proposal of marriage was a dismal failure. I could not understand why, at first. It never occurred to me your answer could be anything other than yes. I believe that to be my first mistake. My second, and the most egregious, was that I never told you *why* I wished to marry you."

"Oh," Alex whispered, eagerly awaiting his answer.

"Alexandra, darling." To her amazement, he sank

to one knee before her. "My heart belongs to you. I have realized my life is empty without you. I love you. Will you marry me?"

Tears of joy sprang to her eyes as she stared at Nicholas. Her lips formed the words, but she couldn't get past the lump in her throat. She threw her arms around his neck instead and leaned in to kiss him. Pulling back moments later, she finally gasped out the answer she had been longing to give, "Yes. I will marry you. I love you."

It would be a long time before any other words were spoken.

A word about the author...

Emma Kaye is married to her high school sweetheart and has two beautiful kids that she spends an insane amount of time driving around central New Jersey.

Before ballet classes and soccer entered her life, she decided to try writing one of those romances she loved to read and discovered a new passion. She has been writing ever since.

Add in a playful puppy and an extremely patient cat and she's living her own happily ever after while making her characters work hard to reach theirs.

Thank you for purchasing
this publication of The Wild Rose Press, Inc.
For other wonderful stories of romance,
please visit our on-line bookstore at
www.thewildrosepress.com.

For questions or more information
contact us at
info@thewildrosepress.com.

The Wild Rose Press, Inc.
www.thewildrosepress.com

To visit with authors of
The Wild Rose Press, Inc.
join our yahoo loop at
http://groups.yahoo.com/group/thewildrosepress/